TEEN SHA
07/17/25

Shaw, Tucker

Right beside you

Right Beside You

PRAISE FOR
when you call my name

A CBC Young Adult, Teacher, and Librarian Favorites Ninth–Twelfth Grade Selection

A Rainbow Book List Top Ten Title for Teen Readers

A *School Library Journal* Best Books of 2022 Selection

A Buzzfeed New LGBTQA+ YA Novels You Need This Spring Selection

"Poignant and uplifting . . . The novel explores the tenacity and strength of queer friendship during the toughest of times, while paying homage to a city that faced significant loss."

— *GAY TIMES*

★ "This is a brilliant affirmation of the power of love on so many levels, with a wide range of appeal."

— *Booklist*, starred review

★ "This book is historical fiction . . . but the frank, personable writing style circumvents many of the challenges the genre often has in generating teen appeal . . . an invaluable addition to a genre that has largely excluded this piece of history."

— *School Library Journal*, starred review

"In 1990 Manhattan the paths of two young men intertwine . . . but the story is not just about their connection; it's about the history of New York and the people who fought and coped, loved and lost, died and survived during the years when an HIV diagnosis was a death sentence. The novel is a love letter to this time and place and to the people of Manhattan. It masterfully pulls at the heartstrings . . . a touching and beautiful story."

— *Kirkus Reviews*

"Copious period-specific pop culture references pepper the novel, whose assured pacing and intimate tone balances elements of promise, possibility, and reality. In Adam and Ben, Shaw effectively captures the era's feeling of pain, uncertainty, and liberation for the gay community."

— *Publishers Weekly*

Right Beside You

TUCKER SHAW

HENRY HOLT AND COMPANY
New York

HENRY HOLT AND COMPANY, *Publishers since 1866*
Henry Holt® is a registered trademark of Macmillan Publishing Group, LLC
120 Broadway, New York, NY 10271 • fiercereads.com

Copyright © 2025 by Tucker Shaw. All rights reserved.

Photo of Washington Square Arch, Library of Congress, Prints & Photographs Division, Anthony Angel Collection, [LC-DIG-ppmsca-69726]

Photo of Fulton Fish Market, Library of Congress, Prints & Photographs Division, FSA/OWI Collection, [LC-DIG-fsa-8d28507]

Photo of Little Italy, Library of Congress, Prints & Photographs Division, Anthony Angel Collection, [LC-DIG-ppmsca-70011]

Photo of Rivington St. and Bowery, Library of Congress, Prints & Photographs Division, Anthony Angel Collection, [LC-DIG-ppmsca-69616]

Photo of the Chrysler Building, Library of Congress, Prints & Photographs Division, Highsmith (Carol M.) Archive, [LC-DIG-highsm-18355]

Our books may be purchased in bulk for promotional, educational, or business use. Please contact your local bookseller or the Macmillan Corporate and Premium Sales Department at (800) 221-7945 ext. 5442 or by email at MacmillanSpecialMarkets@macmillan.com.

Library of Congress Cataloging-in-Publication Data is available.

First edition, 2025
Book design by Julia Bianchi
Printed in the United States of America

ISBN 978-1-250-32710-9
1 3 5 7 9 10 8 6 4 2

For G.

Well, we all shine on.

—John Lennon

It's arresting, isn't it? The way the boy's eyes stare back. As if he is really here. As if this isn't just another image printed on paper, just another photograph in your hand. As if the glint grazing his irises is more than a simple reflection, an accidental trick of the light. Look at the way his eyes narrow, focus, soften. Are they alive? *Let me find you*, they say.

PART ONE

ONE

Have you ever been sitting around, minding your business, maybe finishing lunch or tying your shoe, when something happens—a knock on a door, a ringing telephone—that changes your life forever?

That's what's about to happen to Eddie this very second. Do you see him? Eddie? He's right there, crouched down on the kitchen floor trying to unknot his sneaker, the left one, the one with the fraying lace that he's tied too tightly. He's muttering something under his breath. Something about how much he hates these old shoes. Or maybe something about how much he hates his useless job, how much he hates this useless town. Or how much he hates his best friend for the way she's betrayed him . . .

. . . and there it is. The telephone.

It's a sharp, piercing noise and Donna shrieks. She stares blankly at Eddie and he stares back, like two stunned deer on the roadside, because this kitchen phone *never* rings. The only reason they even still have it is so Donna can make extra money on the weekends selling newspaper subscriptions for the *Mesa Springs Gazette*, and the *Gazette* says she has to use a landline for some unspecified reason. At least they pay for it.

This bears explaining: Donna is Eddie's mother. But he doesn't call her mom or mother or ma. He calls her Donna. He just started doing it one day and it stuck. And it works. Now that he's graduated high school they live more like roommates than mother and son anyway. Like peers. She goes to work in the morning, he goes to work in the morning, and then they come home and eat supper together. Unless she has a date or something.

Another ring. "Should I *answer* that?" Donna asks.

Eddie tugs at the neck of his gray sweatshirt, a size too small with a grease-splatter stain on the cuff. "I wouldn't," he says. "It's probably just someone selling newspaper subscriptions."

"A comedian," Donna says, reaching for the handset.

Eddie looks back at the knot in his shoelace, which he's somehow made tighter. If only he was limber enough to use his teeth.

Donna presses Speaker. "Hello?"

"Oh! You're alive," a voice says. "Where the hell have you been?"

The voice—curt, acerbic, and hassled—belongs to someone named Albert in New York City. He has news about Eddie's great-great-aunt Cookie. Apparently, she's been in the hospital with some sort of infection.

"I've been trying to reach you for two days," Albert says. "Don't you have answering machines out there?"

Donna ignores his question. "Is Cookie all right?"

"Two whole days," Albert says. "Anything could have happened in that time. And you, her only relative, two thousand miles away and unreachable. Do you even care about her?"

"Is she all right?" Donna asks again, and Eddie can hear honest worry in her voice.

Albert sputters and sighs. "Yes. It's minor. But they're sending her home on Saturday and she asked for Andy to come and stay with her while she recuperates."

"Andy? Who's Andy?"

"Your son? Andy?" Albert scoffs. "Surely you've heard of him."

Eddie looks up from his shoe, brow furrowed in confusion, but Donna doesn't look back. Her eyes are fixed on a spot of chipped beige paint on the ceiling.

"I don't have a son named Andy," she says. "His name is Eddie."

"Fine," Albert says. "Eddie, then. He needs to come to New York."

"I don't understand," Donna says.

"What don't you understand? Your aunt is ninety-nine years old and she needs help."

"Great-aunt," Donna is saying, correcting Albert. Her sharp tone pierces Eddie's daydream. He shakes his eyes open to find he's still in the kitchen, still in the world of frayed laces and treacherous ex–best friends. "She's my great-aunt."

"Look, Donna," Albert says. "That's your name, right? Donna?"

Donna doesn't respond. She's still staring at the chipped paint.

Albert continues. "I don't care if she's your great-grand-aunt thrice removed. Someone needs to stay with her and it can't be me. No way. I already come up to her apartment every day to keep the place clean and set her hair. I can't do any more than that. I happen to have my own life, you know. Not to mention sciatica, and high blood pressure, and—"

"I can't stay with her, either, Albert. I have work."

"She didn't ask for you. She asked for Andy."

"Eddie."

"Whatever!"

"Not whatever. His name is Eddie. And he's eighteen. You know that, right?" Donna almost sounds like she's enjoying this. She always lights up in an argument. "What exactly does Cookie expect him to do?"

"*Eddie*, then," Albert says, his voice resigned. "And how the hell should I know? Cookie wants *Eddie*. She said to send *Eddie* to New York. What else can I tell you?"

Albert's words vault into his ears. *Send Eddie to New York.* They tumble and cartwheel through his brain. *Send Eddie to New York.* They spin into colors, shapes, swirls. *Send Eddie to New York.* Eddie closes his eyes and, in a split of a split of a second, he can see it all: He's standing in Times Square, the center of everything, arms extended, head back, a sprawling smile, basking in the light of the flashing marquees shouting about Broadway shows, absorbing every note of the thousand taxi horns blaring at once, drawing the vibrations of the only place Eddie's ever wanted to be deep into his lungs. The exhilaration! It draws him up, up, off his feet and into the air. Crowds cheer as he rises over the skyscrapers like Superman, his body a spiral of music and motion and bravery and belonging. He alights on the balcony of his downtown apartment, scratches his waggle-tailed puppy on the head, and falls into the arms of his movie-star handsome boyfriend. It's a powerful, fantastical, physical vision, and he feels it all the way down his spine. *Send Eddie to New York.* The most exciting words he's ever heard.

He opens his eyes just as Donna exhales, the kind of exasperated exhale that she usually reserves for opening another overdue electricity bill. She reaches toward the chipped paint on the ceiling as if to peel it off, but she can't quite reach it. "Thank you. *Alan.*"

"Albert."

"My mistake. Albert. I appreciate your call. I'll take it from here. Goodbye."

Donna hangs up the phone. She steps up onto a chair and grips the chip of paint between her fingers. As she tugs at it, more paint is released, until she's peeling a swath of beige from the surface like rind from an orange, like skin from a body. In the space left behind Eddie can see that the ceiling underneath is blue, like the sky.

TWO

"I didn't plan for this," Donna says, twisting the pull-tab on her Diet Coke. She tips her head back and combs her fingers through her blond streaks, dislodging tiny beads of hardened hairspray that sparkle as they fall to the drab linoleum floor. "What to do, what to do?"

Eddie watches them fall while he waits for the microwave to do its work, reheating the leftovers he's doggie-bagged home from the kitchen at Sunset Ridge Assisted Living where he works as a prep cook: poached chicken with mashed potatoes (made from dried flakes) and "vegetable medley." What a ridiculous name, vegetable medley. He closes his eyes and imagines a chorus of carrots and peas singing *you say tomato / I say tomahto*, a frozen-foods variety show. Green beans with jazz hands and pearl onions with top hats.

The microwave dings, ending Eddie's silly vision. He slides a plate in front of Donna and sits down at the little dinette table across from her.

"Thanks, kid," she says, sinking a fork into the mound of mashed potatoes.

"Wait," Eddie says. "Salt." He pushes the shaker across the table. Sunset Ridge leftovers always need salt. The cooks there are practically forbidden to use it. Something about excess salt contributing to chronic high blood pressure among the residents.

"And butter," Donna says.

Eddie unwraps a pat of Sunset Ridge butter and pushes it with his forefinger into Donna's potatoes. "I washed my hands," he says preemptively, watching it melt into a little pool. He unwraps another and pushes it in, too.

"Thanks," she says. She takes a bite. "Your hair's getting long."

"Is it?"

"This Albert character is nuts," Donna says. "You taking care of an old lady? In New York City? Ridiculous."

In a flash, Eddie's New York fantasy returns. He's inside his imagined apartment now, sitting across the table having supper. But not with Donna, with his handsome boyfriend, who reaches a thick-wristed hand toward Eddie, taking him by the forearm and smiling broadly. Behind him, the giant canvases he's been working on, sprawling abstract expressionist paintings that, after dinner, they'll sit on the floor in front of and gaze at while they talk about nothing, with Eddie's head in his boyfriend's lap, and his boyfriend's hands in Eddie's unruly hair. He closes his eyes to imagine those hands. Strong, warm, gentle—

—suddenly Eddie's breath is gone. In his reverie he's forgotten he's eating. He's choking on a bite of mashed potato. He drops his fork and throws his hands up to his throat. His eyes start to water, turning quickly to red.

Donna springs up and claps him on the back as he struggles for air, gripping the edge of the table. After a few strong whacks, the potato dislodges onto the floor. Eddie inhales greedily.

"Easy," she says, handing him his glass of water. "Breathe."

He takes it and sips, catching his breath. He coughs again.

Donna holds her hand between his shoulder blades for another moment until he regains his rhythm. He puts a hand up to signal he's all right, and takes another sip. She sits back down. "Don't worry," she says, laughing to comfort him. "No need to choke yourself. You don't have to go. I won't make you."

But she is misunderstanding. He *wants* to go. He *is* going. He is definitely, one hundred percent going. It's so clear to him—the opportunity, the vision, the reality. It's like kismet, fate, already written. He has to go. He gulps some water, then gulps some more.

"She asked for me."

"She's probably delirious from whatever drugs they gave her in the hospital. She has no idea what she's asking."

"What if she does? She's our family."

Donna's fork stalls in the air. She squints her eyes at him, studying his expression, then smiles, bemused. "Oh, you're a good kid. Generous. But, no. I can't force that on you. We'll find another way."

Eddie puts his own fork down. "I think I should go."

Donna laughs. "Eddie, you're young! The last place you should be is stuck in a stuffy old apartment taking care of a hundred-year-old lady. And you don't even know her."

Eddie's mind is racing now. He needs a real argument. While he thinks, he stalls. "She's only ninety-nine."

She rolls her eyes. "Your point?"

Eddie keeps going. "And I do know her. We went to visit once. Remember?"

Donna waves her fork in the air. "You were six. Or were you five? What could you possibly remember?"

"I remember her laugh. I remember the lipstick mark she left on your cheek. I remember she had yellow flowers in her hair and a long skirt with bright green polka dots. I remember she had a pink purse with two stuffed bunnies poking their heads out of the top. And I remember the giant necklace she wore, with the clacking gold beads and that gigantic emerald in the middle. She said it was the biggest one in the world, given to her by a prince, or was it a king?"

As he talks, he wonders if this is really recall, or just a fantasy he once had about her.

Donna tilts her head, studying his eyes. "I can't believe you remember that so well."

"She liked me," he says, certain now that his memory is accurate. "She called me Lollipop."

Donna reaches over and takes his chin in her hand, studying his eyes. "Yes, she did," she says. "And I'm sure she still likes you. What's not to like?"

He wipes his stained cuff across his nose. "Shut up."

"But you can't go to New York. It's too much for you. She needs someone who understands how to take care of her. Someone who understands all the details."

"Who says I don't? I'm around old people all the time at Sunset Ridge. I know how they are, how they think, what they need. I probably know more ninety-nine-year-olds than anyone."

"But they have nurses at Sunset Ridge. Assistants. Administrators. Doctors on call. You wouldn't have any of that with Cookie. You'd be all alone. What if she falls and breaks a hip?"

"Don't they have 911 in New York?"

"What if she needs help going to the bathroom?"

"I can figure it out." His confidence is flowing now, words spilling quickly. "I can help her get dressed. I can help her have a bath. I can make three meals. I'll make sure she takes her pills, whatever they are. I know how to do all those things. I'll fix cups of tea. I'll play cards. I'll run errands."

He blinks and another vision sweeps in: He's on a New York City street, greeting neighbors who know his name as he makes his way from the corner shop to the pharmacy to the stationery store and back again. Everything is sunny and shiny and colorful and melodic and scrubbed so, so clean, like a happy New York movie.

"Eddie?"

He shakes his head to clear the vision and return to Donna. "I can do this," he says. "And besides, can't Albert help if I need it?"

"Yeah, he strikes me as a real team player." Donna pushes her plate away. "Besides, you're only eighteen."

"No shit," he says.

She raises a wry eyebrow. "You kiss your mother with that mouth?"

"Sure do, Donna," he says. "And besides, eighteen is an adult. I can vote, join the military—"

"Not that old cliché." She leans back and lights a cigarette. "Eighteen is a baby and you can't tell me otherwise. Besides, you need more young people in your life, not more old people. You get enough of those at Sunset Ridge."

"What's wrong with old people?" he asks, feeling defensive. He likes spending time with old people. They are so much less annoying than his peers. They don't care what he wears or what songs he likes. They don't spend their lives staring at phones. They don't sit around chasing the latest shiny object on the internet. They tell stories. They play games. They laugh at his jokes, and he laughs at theirs. Sometimes they're mean, but young people are meaner. And old people talk about things that matter, like living, like dying. They even listen when he tries to explain his elaborate fantasies, the ones that crop out of nowhere when he is, for example, microwaving dinner. Maybe Cookie would, too.

"Nothing," she sighs, sounding exasperated now, like a mother.

He plays the card he's been holding. "Donna, how old were you when you moved to Mesa Springs?" He already knows the answer, of course. She was nineteen, only a year older than he is now.

"That was different."

"Was it?" It's not a real question, because he already knows the answer. Things had been very bad back then. She was so desperate to get away from New York, to get away from Eddie's father. She never told him exactly why, but it wasn't hard to guess. "I never asked you how you had the money to move to Colorado in the first place. You were really on your own, weren't you? Did you have anyone to turn to?"

She takes a deep drag. "I had Cookie," she says quietly.

"Was she rich?"

"No," Donna says. "None of us were rich. We never have been. But she helped. Just enough. It's not cheap to fly across the country, you know."

Eddie's mind flashes to the four hundred and twenty dollars stashed in his dresser drawer, saved carefully over the last year of paychecks from Sunset Ridge. "I have one hundred and twenty bucks," he says, keeping the extra three hundred to himself for now.

"You can't make it to New York on a buck twenty. They'll push you out of the plane over Missouri."

"I'll take the bus," he says quickly. "Mesa Springs is on the cross-country route. It stops practically across the street. It has to be cheaper than the plane."

Donna waves her hand through the swirling smoke from her cigarette. He can see her expression beginning to soften. Is he breaking through?

"I was never able to pay her back," she says, looking at the ceiling where she'd peeled away the paint. "I was ashamed about that. All these years, I was ashamed. I suppose that's why we lost touch. She was busy. I was busy."

"Maybe this is the way," he says.

Donna turns her gaze back to his eyes. She squints, focusing. His instinct is to look away, but he fights it, holding her gaze.

"She is pretty great," Donna says. "She ran that bookshop in

Greenwich Village for sixty years. The Contrarian. That was its name. The Contrarian. It really fit her. She always had balls. I guess that's how she made it to ninety-nine. Balls."

Eddie smiles. "You kiss your kid with that mouth?"

"Oh, Eddie. I wish I'd done things differently."

"There's still time," he says.

She tips the rest of her Diet Coke into her mouth, then drops her cigarette, only halfway smoked, into the can. He hears it fizzle in the dregs. She zips up her sweatshirt, a light gray Champion. It used to be Eddie's sweatshirt until he outgrew it a year or two ago. A hand-me-up. It's too big for her, but she says she likes it that way. She gets up and stands by the window, looking out toward the mesa.

"It's not so bad, here, is it? It's not New York City, but it's not so bad." Her voice is melancholy, regretful.

"Do you ever miss the city?" he asks.

"There's no place like it," she says, eyes fixed on the mesa.

Eddie gets up and stands next to her at the window. The sunset is thickening now, saturating the sky a menacing ruby red. Wildfires had been burning across the Western Slope for weeks now.

"What do you want, Eddie?"

He shrugs.

"Do you want to go to New York?"

He shrugs again.

"I would if I were you," she says.

He tips his head to the side and lays it on her shoulder, still watching the sky. She curls her arm up around his chin to his hair.

"I'll trim this tonight," she says, gathering strands in her fingers.

"Okay," he says.

They stand quietly for a minute or two or ten, watching the red sky transform into purple, oxblood. It glows.

"Things haven't been easy for you," she says.

"Or you," he says.

She drops her arm and nudges his head off her shoulder. "You're nuts, you know."

"You always say that."

"And I'm always right." She leans her own head onto his shoulder now, and standing together, they watch the sun finally sink below the mesa. It's dusk now, and Eddie feels like everything is about to change.

Oh, Eddie. Didn't you know by then that everything already had?

THREE

Eddie's head thumps against the window as the Greyhound bus rolls over another pothole, jolting him from whatever this current state of non-wakefulness is. It's certainly not real sleep, not like you get in a bed or a hammock or an interminable algebra class. This is more like a vague semiconsciousness, a hazy, one-eye-open situation that's interrupted every few minutes when your head tips off to the side and onto the shoulder of the wispy-bearded man next to you, causing him to snarl like a badger and fill the air between you with an acrid cloud of toxic breath.

He yawns at the green cornfields sweeping past and wonders exactly where they are. After descending the Rockies, they passed through Denver, then crossed Kansas, Missouri, and Illinois, where a violent June thunderstorm forced them to pull off the road for an hour. They must be in Indiana by now. Or maybe Ohio. He would check his phone, but he's got no signal out here.

This journey is really starting to drag. His legs are cramped, his neck is sore, and he could really use a shower. He would read, but his copy of *Howl's Moving Castle* is up on the overhead rack, stuffed into his duffel bag with a bunch of haphazardly grabbed sweatshirts and socks and toothpaste and stuff. To get it he'd have to ask the snarling badger to move out of the way. Not worth it. He pulls the hood of his sweatshirt up over his head and pretends he's somewhere else. He pretends he's in New York.

Look! Here he is in the doorway of Cookie's building, a giant beaux arts behemoth in a fancy tree-lined neighborhood. She's beckoning him into the gleaming elevator, where she tells the epauletted operator to take them to the very top floor. She helps Eddie into an antique paisley smoking jacket and guides him into the salon, where they recline on plush brocade easy chairs and gaze out across the New York skyline while nibbling on tiny little pancakes piled with caviar. (Not that he's ever had caviar before, but it's what he pictures.)

The bus bumps again and the vision clicks into another, like a television changing channels: Eddie's in an artists' loft now, as big as an ice rink, wearing a paint-splattered work shirt and talking to an impossibly handsome artist about the sprawling abstract expressionist mural that covers the entire wall. Eddie tells him he loves it. The man smiles, then reaches for Eddie, as if to kiss him.

Another bump, another click. Now he's on top of a downtown town house, sitting in a rooftop garden with a circle of witty gay boys in patterned party shirts, chatting among a bounty of cutting flowers—roses, zinnias, cosmos, peonies. They tell racy jokes and sing old-time showtunes Eddie's never heard before but somehow knows all the words to.

Click. He's walking up and down the New York City avenues, through sidewalks thronged with harried, hurried people, jumping away from puddles as city buses roll by, splashing his shoes. Click. He's standing at the edge of Central Park, buying a paper cone filled with fragrant roasting chestnuts from a man with a cart, who points at the penthouses soaring above them and shares gossip about the movie stars and socialites who live up there. Click. He's walking along the river, jostled by roller skaters singing along to disco-blasting boomboxes. Click. A happy young couple asks him to take their picture in front of the Stonewall Inn. Click. He's riding the ferry to Staten Island and back. Click. He's crossing the Brooklyn Bridge on foot. Click, click, click. The visions keep coming—detailed, specific, romantic, full of color. He's very good at this.

His head bumps against the glass again, and Eddie's mind returns, unwillingly, to the bus. He digs into his pocket for his phone to see if he's got a signal now. Look at that, two bars. By habit, he taps into Instagram.

Oh, Eddie. Why? You know better than this. These posts are nonsense. All these photos of your supposed "friends"—that's what the algorithm wants to call them—pretending to have fun. Look at them, hiking, biking, shopping, swimming, arriving at airports, posing on beaches, dancing like fools to silly sped-up songs. All the things that they believe they deserve to be admired for, to be "liked" for. None of it is any more real than his fantasies about eating caviar in penthouses or kissing abstract expressionists in Soho lofts, except that they have pictures. Proof.

He's about to tap out when he spies a photo of *them*. The betraying best friend and her dickhead new boyfriend. He's wearing his basketball tank; she's riding on his shoulders like a toddler. They're both grinning broadly with perfect teeth, like this is some kind of wedding announcement. The caption says "Hard launch" and it makes Eddie want to retch. He thinks back to his fight with her.

But he called me a fag, he said.

It's just a word, she said. It's just how bros talk. Don't be so sensitive all the time. No one cares that you're gay. Seriously, it's the twenty twenties. You got gay marriage. Rainbow flags everywhere. Drag queens all over television. What else do you want?

But they're banning books—

It doesn't mean anything.

But they're passing laws against—

Whatever, those laws are stupid. They don't mean anything.

But the violence is increasing—

Oh my god please stop. This is literally the most boring subject. No one's beat you up, have they? You say what you want. You came out and we celebrated! Being gay is irrelevant now. Okay? Literally no one cares.

Do you care?

No, Eddie. I don't. Just drop it.

Irrelevant, she'd said. As if that's a good thing.

That was the last time he saw her. So much for a best friend.

Eddie is tempted to leave a snarky comment, but instead he unfollows her. It feels good. He unfollows her closest girlfriend, who he's sure would take her side. Energy flowing, he keeps going, systematically unfollowing "friend" after "friend," one by one, feeling a rush of dopamine each time he taps the button. Goodbye, ex-friends. Goodbye, ex-classmates. Have a nice life. Or have a shit one! Eddie doesn't care. He's dropping it. With every mile, Mesa Springs fades farther and farther away, and New York City grows closer and closer. Soon he's down to zero follows. For a grand finale, he deletes the app.

He turns off his phone and smiles silently under his hoodie, feeling strong. Let's go, bus. Let's get to New York Fucking City. Let's do this.

FOUR

It's dark outside now, the second night of this endless odyssey, and Eddie's having another vision. He's sitting with Cookie, next to the bed where she lies quiet and still. The light around them is soft like twilight, and Eddie can hear that her breathing is labored, uneven. He knows she's close to death, and all he can do is stare. Why is he so fascinated by this? He recognizes the stage she's in. She's past the moment, the one he's seen many times before, when a Sunset Ridge resident's eyes change after their treatments have stopped working. He has noticed the way the shape of their mouths sharpens, the way their skin thins to vellum. He's listened to their strange mumblings, watched their childlike expressions, felt them shift from resistant to resigned. He's breathed the air in the spaces left behind when they go.

Where do they go? he wonders. Not the bodies, he knows what happens to those. But everything else. The spirit, the soul, whatever you call it. The life. What becomes of it? Does it just fade into vapor? Is it simply erased? In his vision, Eddie leans closer to Cookie, listening. Maybe she knows.

FIVE

And then, suddenly, he's there! Well, here. New York City. Standing in the Port Authority Bus Terminal staring out onto Eighth Avenue, Eddie smells day-old garbage, not roasting chestnuts. He sees gritty sidewalks, not flowery rooftops. Signs for vape deals, not Broadway shows. People shouting, not singing. He swallows hard as he takes in all the action in front of him—the speeding cars, flashing lights, rumbling trucks, darting jaywalkers, blaring music, people moving in every direction. Some are walking briskly, like they are running late (they are). Some are pacing, like they are anticipating bad news (they are). Some are just standing, looking around, like they are waiting for something (they are). There are old people, young people, people in the middle. Smiling people, scowling people. Chic people, slobby people, harried people, calm people. Tall people. Short people. Fat, thin, loud, quiet, big hair, small hair, every color. There are probably more people on just this block than in the entire town of Mesa Springs. They whoosh past like waves of weather. So many people. So, so many people. They overwhelm him, and the familiar flavor of anxiety bubbles up in Eddie's throat.

He retreats, just for a moment, just to feel some gravity. Tap into your imagination, Eddie. Make up some stories. What about that long-haired man carrying the purple guitar case? Maybe he's catching a bus to Philadelphia for a gig at a big, multigenerational wedding. And that old lady methodically transferring her cigarettes from one box to the other. Could she be waiting for her son to arrive home, finally free from the penitentiary upstate? Tell me about the grizzled man with the anchor tattoo. Is he reminiscing about his tour of duty, forty years ago, when he was crammed with a dozen other young sailors into a bunkroom on a Navy submarine? Eddie lingers a bit on this last vision, picturing all kinds of explicit fantasies.

He exhales. The stories calm him. He takes out his phone and opens his contact list.

"I made it," he says when Donna answers. "I'm at Port Authority."

"Port Authority? Jesus. Get out of that cesspool before you get mugged."

"Mugged?" Eddie hasn't considered *that* version of New York yet.

"Forget I said that," Donna says. "How will you get to Cookie's?"

"I don't know," he says. "Subway?"

"No. The subway is worse than the bus station. Take a taxi. Lemme know when you get there."

"A taxi?"

"Just look for a line of yellow cabs on the street and get in one. I gotta go. Boss is staring at me." She hangs up.

A taxi? Okay. He can do that. He squares his shoulders, hoists his duffel, and conjures confidence. He steps out onto the street and sees a row of cabs idling at the curb. He approaches the first taxi he comes to and opens the door.

"What the hell are you doing?" snaps a woman in the back seat, pushing him away with her foot. "You a moron? This is my cab."

Eddie croaks an apology and the woman yanks the door shut. The taxi speeds off.

The next taxi pulls up, and this one's empty. The driver, who's wearing an NY Mets T-shirt with grease drips down the front, beckons Eddie inside. "Where to?" he barks as Eddie ducks in.

"119 Bedford Street," Eddie says, double-checking the address in his notes app. "Yes, 119."

"Cross street?"

"I—"

"Sixth? Seventh? Carmine? What?"

"I don't know?" Eddie says, answering the cabbie's question with a question.

The driver adjusts his rearview mirror, centering it on Eddie. "Look, kid, maybe you're new to New York, but we don't do numbered addresses here, okay? You gimme the street and the cross street, and then we go. That's how it works. Get it? Let's try again. From the top. Where to?"

"Bedford, um, Bedford and—"

Suddenly, an image emerges in the video screen on the back of the driver's seat, stealing Eddie's attention. It's a photograph of a face, a beautiful face of a young man with pitch-dark hair and luminous, deep-set eyes. Eddie has no idea who it is, but the face teases a bone of recognition in him, like he knows this face, or should. Is this a movie star? Someone from television? The eyes seem to focus in on Eddie, like they're alive. They seem to soften, like they're smiling. Eddie feels his stomach flip, suddenly self-conscious, as if the young man were really here.

Maybe he is here, Eddie. This is New York, remember?

"Kid?"

Eddie, jostled out of the fantasy, opens the map app on his phone to find the cross street. But in this clumsy moment, he fumbles it onto the floor of the cab. "One second," he says. "Sorry."

"Meter's running, kid. You wanna sit here all day? S'okay with me."

Eddie grabs at his phone, but it slips out of his hands again, deeper under the seat in front of him. He sweeps his hand back and forth, hoping his fingers will reach it.

Just as he closes his fingers around it, a shout from outside. "Eddie! Eddie!"

Eddie, startled, looks up. He sees a man with one foot up on the curb, and one foot in the gutter, just feet away from the taxi, shouting. But he isn't shouting at Eddie. Not our Eddie, anyway. He's shouting at a different Eddie, somewhere across the street.

The cabbie is staring at him, or more precisely glaring at him.

"I don't know the cross street," Eddie says, flustered. He starts tapping at his phone.

"Kee-rist." The driver pulls away from the curb with a jerk. "Forget the map. Lucky for you Bedford is only a few blocks long. We'll find it."

"Sorry," Eddie says again.

"Relax, kid, I'm just bustin' yer balls." The driver laughs, then shouts out the window at a cyclist swerving out of the bike lane. "Move yer ass! We got bike lanes for a reason!"

It takes just ten minutes to careen downtown to Bedford Street, and Eddie grips the edge of the seat the whole way. The cab weaves through black town cars, shiny city buses, mosquito-like scooters, jerky jaywalkers. He catches fleeting glints of the New York he'd imagined—skyscrapers, yellow taxis, even a cart selling roasting nuts. But he never imagined it this dense, this thick, this loud, this heavy. How can anyone get anywhere they need to go, with so much in the way? How can they think, plan, feel, with all this weight towering above them? Maybe New York isn't his destiny after all. Maybe he is just too small for this. Maybe this is too much. Maybe he's not enough.

"Look out!" Eddie shouts as a graffitied delivery truck stops abruptly just in front of the cab. Eddie tenses his muscles, and for an instant he imagines the EMTs standing over his mangled body and shaking their heads. *So young*, they are saying as they lick ice cream cones from a Mister Softee truck. *Such a shame.* Eddie finds a split second of comfort in the vision, because it's his, and he knows he can control it. He wills it away just as the driver swerves, missing the truck with inches to spare. Eddie yelps.

The driver smiles back at him in the rearview mirror. "Don't sweat, kid. I've been driving this taxi in this town for a hundred years and I ain't had a single passenger die. Not yet anyway."

"A hundred years?"

"Just about!" the cabbie shouts as he slams the brakes and spins the wheel to dodge another truck. "Welcome to New York!"

SIX

Eddie stands in front of 119 Bedford Street, staring up at the drab brick building, completely devoid of adornment and badly in need of a makeover, especially a paint job. This is nothing like what he imagined on the bus. There's no grand building, no welcoming lobby, no uniformed doorman. Expectation versus reality and all that, again. He re-checks the address.

Yes, Eddie. This is it.

Maybe it's different inside, he thinks.

He shifts his duffel bag to his other shoulder, then climbs the three brusque stairs to the front door, flanked on one side by a panel of buzzers, and on the other side by a sign reading, NO SOLICITATIONS. It's not a very effective note, judging by the number of takeout menus littering the top step. He raises his finger to buzzer 2A. He holds it there for a moment and then presses.

Nothing happens, so he presses again.

Still nothing.

Eddie blinks, and in the tiny moment when his eyes are closed, a new vision sweeps through him. He's alone in New York City, locked out of Cookie's apartment and forced to make his own way. He spends a few weeks on the streets, sleeping on park benches and stoop steps, his clothes progressively rattier, his pockets endlessly emptier. He scrounges the gutters for change. It's a bleak image.

Turn it around, Eddie. You know you can.

Eddie re-directs the vision to the city tennis courts where he finds three cast-off tennis balls and takes them to the subway, where he juggles for cash until he's discovered by a Broadway producer who casts him as an extra in a revival of *Pippin*.

That's more like it. A little optimism goes a long way in this town.

He buzzes again, but there's still no answer. Maybe she's sleeping? Maybe this isn't the right building? Or maybe she's dead, just as he'd pictured on the bus. He pinches his finger to stop the vision before it takes shape. It's an old trick he taught himself when he was young. To help him keep control.

Just open the door.

He turns the knob and the door unlatches. It's been open all along. He looks around. No one else is in sight. Tentative, worried that someone may appear to ask what he's doing here, he steps into the building, then up the stairs to the second floor.

The hallway up here is just as dull as the building's exterior. Patchy flooring, peeling paint, a flickering Exit sign at one end that appears to be nowhere near an exit. He walks the length of the hall, finally arriving at apartment 2A, a dull brown door at the very end with two key slots and a peephole. He kicks away a dust bunny at his feet, and then raises his hand to rap on the door. He knocks twice, softly, and then once again, more emphatically. Nothing happens.

You know what to do. Turn the knob.

Suddenly, a flood of color and life washes over him like a wave, so dazzling and riotous that his breath catches and his heart spikes and his ears begin to thrum. Opening the dull door has unleashed a fantastical new vision that spins like a kaleidoscope, a swirling blur of light in a million hues and textures, shapes and objects vibrating so quickly that he feels his sense of balance dissolve beneath him. Overwhelmed, he grabs the doorjamb to steady himself. He blinks twice to try to clear the vision. But it doesn't clear. It only spins faster. He shakes his head, but it only spins faster. He rubs his eyes, pinches his finger, tells himself to stop it, just stop it right now, but the vision only spins faster, until finally, in a breath of relief, it stops. The colors remain, the shapes and objects and textures, but the motion calms. Eddie regains his breath.

He steps over the threshold and lowers his duffel bag to the floor. He draws the door shut behind him, and as the latch clicks into place, it sounds like a signal: You're someplace else now, Eddie. A whole new world. And it's beautiful. Come inside.

As the room comes into sharper focus, Eddie starts to take stock. Opposite the doorway is a wall of bookshelves, rising from floor to ceiling, filled with hardbacks and paperbacks and photographs and ceramic figurines and rows of paper flowers. An art deco settee upholstered in marigold velvet with amber trim sits just in front of it, next to an emerald-green quilted ottoman trimmed with black fringe just long enough to tickle the brown-and-orange-patterned carpet on the floor. Along one wall is an ancient television console, a bulbous screen fitted into an expanse of woodgrain and brass, its surface crowded with tiki cups and blown-glass bottles in every imaginable shade of green. A pair of spinning barstools covered in pony-print vinyl stands over three pairs of cartoonish old Dutch wooden shoes. He sees a headless dressmaker's mannequin draped with a beaded cape. A glass-front hutch is filled with dozens of snow globes, this one depicting Paris, that one London, another one Honolulu. An elaborate chandelier with pink crystals hangs from the center of the scarlet-lacquered ceiling, casting its translucent shadows over a steel-and-glass coffee table, itself covered in knick-knacks and trinkets and stacks of travel magazines.

Are the walls also lacquered red? It's hard to tell because every square centimeter of wall space is covered by portraits—photographs, drawings, etchings, paintings, prints. There must be a hundred faces staring out from the walls, maybe a thousand. A few he recognizes (Queen Elizabeth in regal regalia, Marilyn Monroe in a white dress), but most he does not. He sees a woman holding a golf club over her head. A man in a silk scarf so long it reaches his feet. A pair of people in beekeeper's bodysuits. A child at a microphone, arms spread joyfully. Two women with exaggerated eyelashes, standing cheek to cheek. A man in matador trousers. A woman with a camellia brooch on her shoulder. Faces everywhere. Gazes and gestures and poses. Some are smiling, some are sorrowful, and some seem to be staring straight at Eddie, assessing him, deciding something, judging. His knees begin to buckle again.

Just then, just before he loses his balance again, a voice cuts through the air, high-pitched and singsong and a little bit raspy. It's coming from the corridor to his right. "Yoo-hoo! Is that you, Lollipop?"

He follows it to a door that's been left slightly ajar. A warm, pinkish light seeps through the crack, beckoning him as a song grows louder.

In old-en days a glimpse of stocking | Was looked on as something shocking . . .

Ah, yes. You know this song, Eddie. Remember? It's "Anything Goes" by Cole Porter, the song that your seventh-grade band teacher insisted you learn to play. Except, you didn't, did you? You quit band instead. Not because of Cole Porter, but because you didn't think you were talented enough to make the music sound good.

"Are you going to stand out there forever? Don't be shy! Come on in!"

Eddie nudges the door open, just enough to crane his head through the opening. And there she is. Cookie. And she looks about as far from death as anything he's ever seen.

She's sitting up at the head of a massive four-poster bed, draped in a resplendent leopard-print dressing gown over a blue satin pajama top, colorful patterned bedclothes gathered all around. Her face is open, broad, with glistening scarlet lips and deep lines crinkled around her eyes and across her forehead. She's wearing a fuchsia beret cocked to one side, with a shocking-orange spit curl snaking out just at her temple. She's beautiful, isn't she? Our Cookie.

She waves a bamboo back scratcher in the air like a conductor's baton, her expression one of intense concentration like a child overseriously playacting as a bandleader. She shimmies her pointed shoulders in time with the music: *And good's bad today | And black's white today* . . .

Eddie's mouth tenses as he watches this alien creature who looks like she sprung from the walls of this apartment, even more colorful and fantastical and bizarre than the rooms around her. He's never seen anyone like her. Is she nuts? Is she unbalanced? Her smile is joyful but her movements are jerky and arhythmic, like she could suddenly hurl that back scratcher at him, inadvertently or by design, and take out an eye. He stands stick-still in the doorway, cautious, ready to duck.

The song is nearing its big finish, and when it reaches the final notes, Cookie throws both hands into the air in a thrust of exuberance and celebration, jangling the stacks of bangles on her wrists.

"*Anything goooooeeesss!*" she belts triumphantly, holding the note long after the music fades out. She thrusts the back scratcher at the ceiling, punctuating the moment like a virtual double exclamation point, before bowing her head twice, once to the left, and once to the right, as if acknowledging an audience, a standing room–only crowd of fans.

After another moment she raises her giant eyes. She is beaming. "How's that for an opening number?" she asks, expectant. "Did you love it? Did you just love it?"

Eddie opens his mouth to answer but no sound comes out. He just stares, agape, stunned and fascinated and frozen in place by this newest vision. This brilliant, baffling, bewildering vision. What on earth has he signed himself up for?

SEVEN

"And now, I am ready to receive your ovation," Cookie says.

"I'm sorry?" Eddie says, perplexed.

She sighs, smoothing the fur-trimmed coverlet over her legs. "Perhaps this isn't true out in the hinterlands," she says, "but here in New York City, after a showstopping rendition of a Cole Porter classic such as 'Anything Goes,' it's customary to applaud in appreciation."

"I—" Eddie utters, not sure what she's just said.

"Clap!"

It's a command, delivered emphatically like a child might after performing a cartwheel, and Eddie obeys, raising his hands and clapping. For emphasis, and to be polite, he whistles.

Cookie responds by clasping her hands under her chin and fluttering her eyelashes. "Well, how about that! A standing ovation! I feel like Judy Garland at Carnegie Hall."

Judy Garland? Does that name ring a bell? Eddie will look it up later. He claps a few more times.

"Oh, it's nice to have an audience. I chose that number especially for you, Lollipop. Because anything does go in this joint. And I do mean anything."

Eddie smiles uneasily, not sure what to do next. Should he approach? Shake her hand? He can't believe she's nearly a hundred years old. He's met his share of centenarians at Sunset Ridge, but none of them were anywhere near this youthful or energetic.

"Don't be shy," she says, and it's the first of many times that Eddie will wonder if she is reading his mind. She reaches over to switch off the old-fashioned turntable on the powder-pink nightstand. "Your Cookie is a little eccentric, that's all. They used to call me strange, or crazy, or even mad, but now that I've lived so long they call me eccentric. Sounds important, don't you think? Like an artist, or a fashion designer, or"—she flutters her eyelashes—"a movie star?"

Eddie can see that she's fantasizing like he does. Common ground, and to see it puts him at ease.

"But whatever it is, eccentricity or madness, it keeps me young."

She raises a red-lacquered fingernail—so shiny that Eddie wonders if it's still wet—to fiddle with her spit curl. "Now then. About my outfit. Do you like it?"

"It's very nice," Eddie says.

"Nice?" Cookie clutches at the layers of beads draped around her neck. "Nice? Try again."

Eddie searches for another word, a bigger one. "Beautiful?"

"Keep going." She raises an eyebrow.

"Stunning?"

"More!" Her eyes are sparkling, broadcasting delight.

"Gorgeous?" He's beginning to melt.

"Keep going!" she exclaims, jubilant hands in the air.

"Splendid? Captivating?" Eddie offers, playing along. The words are flowing now. The banter feels good. "Awe-inspiring! Devastating!"

Cookie beams. "Oh, you are a handsome one. Like a young Randolph Scott. With a little bit of Billy Haines."

More names he's never heard. Eddie shifts from one foot to the other, uncertain how to respond.

"Just say thank you," she suggests, reading his mind again, and then, without waiting for him to comply, she says, "And what's your first impression of your Cookie? Besides stunning, gorgeous, splendid, captivating, and so forth."

"I, uh, I think you are—"

She interrupts. "Be careful. I'm warning you, if you say *feisty* or *sharp as a tack* or anything followed by *for your age*, I'll send you back where you came from faster than you can spit."

"Never," Eddie says. He's learned about these phrases at Sunset Ridge. They're right up there with *ninety-nine years young* and *spry*. Insulting.

He thinks for another moment, searching for words until he finds one that fits. "Lovely," he says, confident. "I think you are lovely."

She considers, taps her chin, and then nods. "All right. That will suffice for a first impression. You may stay. Go and put your things in the closet, where you'll sleep."

He cocks his head at her.

"Oh, it's not really a closet. But it's not really a bedroom, either. A den maybe, or I don't know. A boudoir. But we call it the closet, because it's filled with secrets." She widens her eyes exaggeratedly and holds a finger to her lips. "But don't worry. It's plenty big enough for you. You'll sleep on the fainting couch, of course."

"The what?"

"The fainting couch." She widens her eyes even more and scans him, head to foot and back again, all five feet eight-and-a-half inches. "Yes, you'll fit just fine. And you'll love the fainting couch. It's upholstered in zebra. Zebra print, of course. Not real zebra. I'm not Elsie de Wolfe."

All these names. All these words. Elsie de Wolfe. Randolph Scott. Boudoir. Fainting couch. He shrugs in hapless confusion.

"Don't worry. We'll discuss Elsie later," she says. "Now, be sure to keep your bag tucked out of the way so Albert can vacuum in there. Do you know Albert?"

Eddie thinks. Isn't that the man who called a few days ago? "No, I've never met—"

Cookie interrupts. "He comes every day to help with the big things. Change the sheets, take out the laundry, do my makeup. And vacuuming. He's big on vacuuming. Just adores it. He can be a little prickly, but he only barks, never bites, unless of course you mention his hair, of which he has none. Bald as a bat! And very touchy about it. But he's family. We were married once, you know. Imagine, a husband twenty-five years my junior!"

"I never knew you were married," he says. Or that bats were bald, but he doesn't say that part.

She reaches under her coverlet and draws out a hand mirror, crusted with rhinestones. "I'm full of surprises. Ninety-nine years' worth. Now, go put your things away and wash off that Wyoming residue. It's depressing."

"Colorado," he says. "I'm from Colorado."

"Yes, yes. All those rectangles out west. Who can keep them straight?"

For a split second Eddie considers defending his home state but Cookie's eyes are sparkling, and he is charmed. "I'll go put my things away," he says.

"Right across the hall," she says. "The chamber of secrets. Maybe you'll add your own."

He turns to go.

"Wait!" she chirps. She taps the side of her face. "You haven't even kissed me hello."

Eddie, relieved to have more direction to follow, approaches the bed and leans down to kiss her cheek. Her skin, powdered and blushed, feels so delicate against his lips, so thin, like it could slip right off. Up close, he really sees her ninety-nine years, and a twinge of tenderness sweeps through him.

"There, that's lovely," she says. "Just like me. And one for the other cheek, please. For luck."

She turns her head and Eddie complies.

"Perfect. Oh, it's good to have you back."

"Back? But I've never been—"

"I said," she interrupts. "It's good to have you back. Home."

EIGHT

After his shower, Eddie takes a seat in the chair next to Cookie's bed. A lazy record is playing a soft song and she's humming along as she draws her finger across the pages of the book in her lap, across the photographs, line drawings, text. *The Face of the World*, says the title on the spine. *By Cecil Beaton*. Eddie wonders who that is (add it to the list) but before he can ask, she closes the book and points to a cuckoo clock on the wall.

"It's four o'clock," she declares. "Sherry hour. Time for an afternoon tipple. It's been a tradition in this apartment since the day I moved in. June sixth, 1941. I was nearly eighteen. Everyone was shocked, appalled even, at the idea of such a young woman living alone. But I was a bohemian, and I knew who I was."

"June sixth," Eddie repeats. "Today is June sixth."

"That's right, Lollipop. So let's celebrate. You'll find the sherry on the bar cart in the salon. And as Greta Garbo said, don't be stingy, baby."

"What's Greta Garbo?" Eddie asks.

"Bite your tongue. Garbo's not a what. She's a who." She points to a photograph on the wall, a black-and-white picture of a beautiful woman in profile, looking up and off to one side with heavy eyes and an impossibly long, smooth neck. "Greta Garbo, the most famous actress in the world. And the most beautiful woman of all time. Are you sure you don't know her?"

"I don't," Eddie says apologetically.

"Oh, dear. We do have work to do. Lots of work. We'll start tonight. But first, sherry. Just two glasses today. No one else is coming. That's the worst part about being stuck in bed, you know. You can't have people over for sherry hour. I've tried, of course, but this bedroom just isn't right for entertaining. But never mind. Once I get my legs back underneath me I'll introduce you to everyone. Oh, that will be a wonderful party. How we will dance!"

"Yes," Eddie says, and a vision speeds through his mind. Cookie is not in bed but in a nightclub, dancing energetically in the center of a crowd, kicking up heels and swirling her skirt through the air, a massive smile on her face as a jazz quartet behind her bounds through a lively ragtime tune. She exudes frenetic joy as her curls bounce against her forehead. He blinks, and returns to the moment, where Cookie is still in bed.

"Sherry!" she reminds him. "And after we finish, you can go fetch supper at Grand Sichuan, which we will eat on trays while watching *Anna Christie* on my video tape machine."

⁓

The end credits of *Anna Christie* starring Greta Garbo are flickering on the tiny bedroom television set, just as Cookie slurps the last of her soup straight from the bowl and Eddie inhales the last of his noodles straight from the container. The noodles are spicy, numbing his lips and the tip of his tongue, and he's still hungry after he finishes. He could easily eat another order.

"So," Cookie says as she dabs the corners of her mouth. "What did you think?"

Honestly, Eddie was perplexed by the movie. The picture seemed fuzzy and the sound seemed muffled and he couldn't understand most of what the characters were saying or doing. It's like they were standing around in rooms being sad and talking. Not a lot of action.

But all he says is, "It was interesting."

"Interesting?" Cookie repeats, a tinge of scorn in her voice that stiffens Eddie's spine. "That's faint praise if I ever heard it."

"I thought Greta Garbo was pretty," Eddie says quickly, trying to recover a positive mood. "She seems interesting, too."

"Interesting, interesting," she mutters. "I think you need to learn more about Garbo. Why don't you look her up on your little googler doodad?"

"My little what?"

"You know, that phone-a-ma-jig thing you kids all carry around and look things up on. I'd tell you about her now, but it's time for my beauty sleep. You may take these dishes away. If I need you, I'll ring." She points at a little decorative bell on her nightstand, a pink thing shaped like a flamingo. "It's louder than it looks."

"All right," he says, gathering the dishes.

"Good night, then." She pulls an emerald-green satin sleep mask over her eyes, exhales dramatically, and draws the covers up to her chin.

"Good night, Cookie."

"Ahem?" She taps her cheek.

He leans down to kiss it, and then, for luck, he kisses the other one.

"Now, away," she says, and waves him off.

In the kitchen, Eddie taps *Greta Garbo* into his notes app to remind himself to look her up later. He's too tired now. He washes and dries the dishes then moves into his bedroom. Er, the closet.

To get to the fainting couch, he steps around a side table with carved cat's-paw feet, threads himself between two standing Tiffany lamps, skirts a dresser painted with an elaborate circus scene featuring monkeys in silly hats riding elephants, and nearly trips over a ceramic bulldog sitting in the middle of the floor, wearing a porkpie hat and a monocle. He spots an old gilded-plaster Cupid clock on the wall. It says 9:15, but it's 11:11. He makes a wish.

He changes into his sweatpants and an old *How's Your Aspen?* T-shirt and looks at himself in the mirror hanging behind the door. Dark circles under his eyes. Messy hair. A blossoming pimple on his chin.

As he turns from the mirror his eye is caught by a moody black-and-white portrait of a young man, a boy, not much older than Eddie, with dark hair and long black eyelashes posing against a gray background. He's wearing a white shirt with a crisp, creased, old-fashioned collar and looking off to the side with a sluggish, world-weary expression. He's beautiful, in that way that makes him seem almost familiar. But it's an old photograph.

Eddie lies back onto the fainting couch, plush and, as promised, zebra-printed. It has an armrest only on one side, letting him stretch out. Even if his feet hang off the end, it's better than being scrunched. And much better than a bus seat.

He wedges a check-marked accent pillow under his neck and reaches up to switch off the Tiffany lamp next to the couch. That's when he notices, for the first time, the mirrored disco ball hanging from the ceiling. It spins, slowly, reflecting the lights from the city outside the window, faint flashes casting lazily around the room. As they sweep across the boy in the portrait they seem to animate him, transforming his face into something like life. His jawline sharpens and so does his gaze. His eyes flash, as if he's just noticed something. Something surprising.

But Eddie knows it's just a picture, a moment captured a long time ago, and imprinted on photographic paper. Anything else is just an illusion. But it's amazing, isn't it? You'd almost believe it.

Eddie watches the portrait, transfixed by the young man's beauty, as his heavy eyelids fall. It's been such a long journey. But he's here, now, and he'll sleep, now, under this spinning disco ball in the middle of New York City, two thousand miles from home.

NINE

Eddie's deep in a dream, walking with the dark-haired, sharp-jawed boy from the portrait across the room. They amble through a dark, foggy alleyway down near the docks of a city Eddie doesn't know. It rained a few minutes ago, so the asphalt underfoot reflects misty light up against the boy's chin, creating a shadow just below his lower lip. Eddie, brave here in his dream, reaches up to touch it with the tip of his thumb, gently pressing in, feeling it give. They move closer, bodies pressing slowly but urgently together as they kiss.

And they kiss again.

And again.

Once more. And another.

"What do you want, Eddie?" the boy asks, and Eddie wonders what he means.

As he searches for an answer, a distant trill of laughter distracts him. He pulls back from the boy and cranes his neck to discern who it is, but sees no one.

"Let's go back inside," the boy says, tugging on Eddie's hips. "One more time."

Before Eddie can say yes, the sky above them splits, as if it's not a sky at all but a giant piece of paper tearing itself into two to reveal a blinding light, so harsh and cold that it stirs Eddie from the dream. He's back in Cookie's den, back on the fainting couch, alone again.

But the laughter is still there. Soft, muffled. Is it coming from outside the window? Eddie gets up and pulls his sweatshirt over his head, stubbing his toe on the side table. He swallows a yelp and catches himself on a standing lamp, nearly pulling it over. He freezes, hoping he hasn't disturbed Cookie's sleep.

He peers out the window onto the sidewalk below. No one is there.

Another laugh, this time from behind him, from the direction of Cookie's room. Is someone in there with her? He pads silently out into the hallway, then stands outside Cookie's door, listening. The laughter has stopped, but he does hear voices—no, only one voice, Cookie's voice, speaking quietly and pausing intermittently as if she's on the telephone. But the telephone is in the kitchen. Is she talking in her sleep? Is she all right?

He remembers the flamingo bell. She'd ring it if she wanted him, and the voice doesn't sound loud or angry or panicked. She must just be talking in her sleep or something. Eddie exhales and slinks back into the den. He curls onto the fainting couch and closes his eyes, hoping to get back to the docks, back to the boy, back to the question: *What do you want?*

The sound is shocking, the way it slashes through Eddie's sleep, waking him much too early. It's not an alarm clock, or the traffic outdoors, or even Cookie's flamingo bell. The sound—the searing, deafening sound—is a sigh. A ferocious, violent sigh, the kind that fills the room with a palpable and aggressive air of disgust. It jars Eddie from post-dream early morning sleep (the deepest kind) into disoriented wakefulness. Where is he again? Oh yes, New York City.

The thought sends a wave of excitement through him, but then another sound douses it.

"Hells bells. Look at all this crap."

Eddie relaxes his eyelids just enough to allow in a tiny sliver of light. Through the slit he sees the source of the sounds. It's a man, bald (as a bat), wearing a pale gray tunic over a pair of knee-length shorts, his ankle socks tucked awkwardly into a pair of plastic flip-flops. He's got rings on at least four fingers and one thumb, and a long silver chain around his neck with a gold sun pendant that, if the chain were a few inches shorter, would dangle just at his solar plexus but instead rests on his round belly, creating slack in the chain. The bald (as a bat) man sighs again and curses: "This goddamn room is a goddamn mess."

Eddie, frozen, doesn't move. He holds his breath, reaching for inconspicuousness, but inconspicuousness is a lot harder to pull off when you're the only other person in the room. Maybe he should say hello. Or not. This person seems like they might not appreciate it.

This person, of course, is Albert, just as bald and irritable as Cookie warned. He's huffing and groaning around the den, jerking furniture an inch to the left or to the right and kicking Eddie's shoes out of the way. "Honestly," he mutters as he flips the switch on the vacuum cleaner, which roars to life.

Albert wields the vacuum like a weapon, a jousting lance, stabbing it into the corner just beyond Eddie's head, then whipping it around and attacking the floor underneath the fainting couch, banging into the legs and knocking into Eddie's feet, still hanging off the end.

Eddie doesn't move, and soon Albert is vacuuming his way into the hallway in a cloud of curses, rounding the corner and out of sight. A lingering scent of sandalwood cologne stays behind.

Eddie exhales in relief. But the respite is fleeting: He has to pee, and that means he will have to get up and, unless he's extremely stealthy, cross paths with Albert. He tries to wait, but soon it's unbearable. He rolls himself off the couch, hoping to slip unnoticed into the bathroom. But of course, Albert is vacuuming in there now, so Eddie has to pace the hallway, dancing a toddler's gotta-pee dance, taking care not to trip over the vacuum's power cord, which is growing more and more taut as Albert drives deeper into the bathroom and farther from the wall outlet.

And then, suddenly, the roar cuts off as the plug abruptly dislodges from the wall. The cord goes slack, a flaccid orange twist on the floor.

"God bless America!" Albert barks, stomping out of the bathroom. He glares at Eddie with mismatched eyes—one dark, one light, just like David Bowie. "Why did you unplug me?" he snaps.

"I didn't," Eddie says quickly. "I think you pulled too hard—"

"So I unplugged me? It's my fault?" Albert jerks the cord up off the floor.

"I'm sorry," Eddie says, pitching his voice upward, trying to sound harmless, friendly, small.

"What the hell are you apologizing for?" Albert hisses. "I thought you didn't do it."

Eddie doesn't know what to say, so he defaults to an introduction. "I'm Eddie."

"Good for you."

"You must be Albert." Eddie holds out a hand to shake. "It's a pleasure to meet you."

"Yes, it is a pleasure to meet me," Albert says. "Lucky you." He waves away Eddie's hand and, with a swoosh and another sigh, disappears into the kitchen.

Eddie locks the bathroom door behind him. He has a hot shower and brushes his teeth. He even flosses, a rarity for Eddie, but he's in no rush to emerge. When he finally does, Albert is gone.

Eddie looks around the den for a place to stash his stuff so it won't be in Albert's way next time. He tucks his duffel carefully in the corner, under a side table where it's almost invisible, and nestles his sneakers neatly next to it. He'll put his phone on top of the table.

Except, where is his phone? It was tucked under his pillow. But now the pillow is fluffed and repositioned, and his phone is not there. Maybe Albert stuck it on a shelf?

He looks. Nope.

In a drawer?

He looks. Nope.

Atop a stack of books?

He looks under every piece of furniture, behind every row of books on the shelves, in every nook and cranny in the room. Nope. He checks the kitchen, the living room, even the bathroom. Nope, nope, and nope. His phone is gone.

And he feels the panic, that acrid bile, gathering in his throat. He swallows it back, straightening himself. Don't fall in, Eddie. Don't panic. It's here somewhere. It has to be.

To soothe himself, he pictures walking through New York as if he were born here, knowing every street and every address and which shops are better than the others. He pictures taking lefts and rights and shortcuts through the narrow alleyways, recognizing everyone he sees, never getting lost. He feels free in this vision, unencumbered, powerful, like he knows his way. It holds him just long enough to regain his breath.

TEN

"Oh, don't worry about Albert," Cookie says, her bangles clanking loudly as she checks her eye makeup in her hand mirror. "He'll warm up once he gets used to you. Or, maybe he won't. Anyway, who cares? I'm the boss here. Hand me that wrap, will you? I'm cold."

Eddie takes the paisley-printed blanket from the foot of the bed and drapes it over her shoulders.

"And do you see that stack of cards there? I'm a day behind on opening all these get-well cards." She hands him a letter opener. "Start opening."

"I feel bad," Eddie says, sliding the dull blade into the first envelope. "I think I made Albert mad."

"Don't waste your regret. That's just Albert. He's harmless, except for that awful sandalwood cologne he's been wearing lately."

"I don't want to be in his way," Eddie says, though what he really means is *why does that jerk have to vacuum so early in the morning in the first place?*

"Then don't be in his way," she says. There's a faint annoyance in her voice that makes Eddie tense up. He can't get on her bad side, not yet, not on his first full day here. She holds out her hand for the card.

"I'm sorry," Eddie says, hoping it will smooth out her irritation as he struggles to get the card out of the envelope.

"Why are you apologizing?" she snaps. "Did you do anything wrong?"

Eddie swallows. "Sorry," he says again, still tugging clumsily at the card. "I mean, no, I didn't. I don't think so."

She sighs and shakes her head. "Oh, for pity's sake. Give me that."

The card finally comes free from the envelope. It's an image of a sunrise on the front and the words, *While You Rest, Remember . . . You're the Best.*

She starts laughing. "Is this the most ridiculous card you've ever seen? Oh, I love bad cards."

Eddie picks up another card and starts slicing through the envelope.

Cookie shrugs the blanket off her shoulders. "Too hot," she says.

"Sorry," Eddie says. "I thought you were cold—"

"I was. But I'm not now. And by the way, don't worry. Albert's not angry at you, not specifically. He's angry at *everything*. Just the other day he talked my ear off about how Times Square used to be lawless and exciting but now it's just full of tourists and people dressed up like Spider-Man. He complained about how no one knows how to be a good pedestrian anymore because they're all looking at their little google-ma-jigs. Their little phone-a-ma-bobs. He's mad about how expensive it is to go to the movies, he's mad about how the neighborhood is nothing but banks and fancy boutiques, he's mad about how the piers used to be dangerous and sexy but now the whole riverside is spotless and manicured with grass and trees. And he's mad that he's getting older, although he has no idea what old even means yet. He's mad that the past is gone, replaced by the present. And he's mad that the present will soon be replaced by the future. He hates that time exists."

"Why does he hate grass and trees?" Eddie asks. "I like trees."

Cookie lowers her voice to a conspiratorial whisper, like a friend. "Me too. But don't you dare tell Albert I said so. If you do, I'll deny it."

Eddie smiles. "Deal." He hands her the next card. This one has a cat on the front, hanging from a curtain. *Hang in there* . . .

"Oh, dear," Cookie says, smirking at the card. "Wouldja look at this one? Keep 'em coming."

He hands her another card, with an image of a little boy engaged in a tug-of-war with a puppy. *Pulling for you* . . .

"Oh, they get worse!" She laughs and holds out her hand for another one. "At least they know not to have flowers delivered. I am very picky about flowers, and god knows what they'd have sent over. Birds of paradise, or worse, carnations. It's alstroemerias or nothing, for me."

"Alstro-whats?"

"Alstroemerias," she repeats. "But let's not talk about flowers. I want to know what's wrong. And don't say nothing, because I can see it in your eyes. Something's wrong."

"No, I'm just tired."

Cookie's expression hardens. "Important rule in this apartment," she says. "No lying to Cookie. I've lived long enough to know a lie when I hear it, and you won't get away with it. Understand?"

He swallows and nods.

"So?" she says. "What is it?"

Eddie spins through his mind, searching for a way to bring up the strange one-sided conversation happening in her room last night. He doesn't want to sound like he was eavesdropping.

"Hello?" she says, waving her hand impatiently, bangles clanking. "Sing, Lollipop."

"Well, I—" He clears his throat. "I woke up in the night and heard some noises."

"And?"

"And I got up to find out where they were coming from. They were coming from your room."

"Were you listening at my door?"

"No!" he says.

"What did I just say about lying?"

"I mean, not on purpose. I just wanted to make sure you were okay. It sounded like you were talking to someone on the telephone."

She stares at him, eyes so steady. "So what if I was?"

"But it was the middle of the night. And the phone is in the kitchen. I was confused."

She leans back into her pillow, a sly smile pushing through the annoyance on her face. "You're an astute one, I see. Well. You're right. I wasn't on the telephone."

"Who were you talking to?"

"Is that any of your business?"

She's right, it's not. The things he does in his room with the door closed aren't anyone else's business, so why should Cookie be any different? "You're right," he says. "It's not. It's just—"

"You were worried."

"I'm sorry."

She looks at her nails. "If you must know, I was talking to Dottie."

"Oh," he says. "I didn't know you had a visitor. I didn't hear anyone come in."

"She lives here," Cookie says, matter-of-factly. She moves a pillow off her lap to reveal a framed photograph underneath it. It's a dark-haired woman looking over an old-fashioned typewriter with an intense, perturbed expression, as if she is irritated with whoever is taking the picture. "Here she is. This is Dottie."

Eddie feels his stomach seize. It's a picture, not a person. What is Cookie talking about?

He looks at the photo, and then at Cookie, then back at the photo. "Dottie," he repeats slowly.

"I know what you're thinking," she says, smiling slyly. "You're thinking that I am completely off my rocker."

"No," he says quickly. "I—I don't."

"No?" she challenges.

"I talk to myself all the time," he says, even though it's not exactly true. Sometimes he mumbles to himself, like *where are my shoes*, or *I'm so late*, but he doesn't usually talk to himself. His fantasies are all inside. He works hard to keep them there.

"I didn't say I was talking to myself," Cookie says. "I said I was talking to Dottie."

Eddie looks back at the photograph. He squints his eyes and tries to release his own disbelief, to imagine what the woman, Dottie, would look like in motion, what she'd sound like if she spoke. But it is only a photograph, an inanimate object. It can't carry on a conversation. It can't talk back.

"And Dottie talks back," Cookie says, reading Eddie's mind again.

Eddie searches Cookie's face for a spark of mischief, a sign that she's kidding. But all he sees in Cookie is sincerity.

"You might as well know, Dottie is not the only one here," Cookie says. She points at the wall. "There's also Monty, and Rudy, and Mae, and Judy, and Sal. As you can see, it's crowded."

"I see," Eddie says, trying to add some lightness to his voice, trying to keep his growing sense of worry at bay. Should he be concerned about what she's saying? Is this just Cookie's way? Part of her, what did she call it, eccentric nature? Or is this something more? He thinks back to Sunset Ridge, remembering some of the strange behavior of the oldest patients. They'd sometimes forget where they were, or even who their own relatives were. Sometimes those moments signified dementia, a scary thing to see. But Cookie is thinking clearly. The idea of conversing with a photograph is strange, but she knows it's strange. And she knows exactly where she is, and who Eddie is. And besides, Eddie, is it that hard to understand? Aren't you the boy who spends way too much time in his own imagination? The boy who passes the time picturing the intricate, intimate lives of strangers? The boy who hallucinates in taxicabs, on fainting couches? The boy who—

"Do you believe me?" she asks, insistently interrupting his thoughts.

He doesn't answer.

She tilts her head in defiance, daring him. "Well? Do you?"

He knows there is only one answer she'll accept. "I do," he says finally, and the flash of dissatisfaction in her eyes quickly fades.

She flips the picture over and tucks it under a pillow, signaling the end of this topic. He's relieved.

"Another card!" she chirps, the singsong lilt back in her voice.

He reaches for another envelope. "You have a lot of friends."

"Thousands. And that's not even counting the imaginary ones I talk to at night!"

He drops the letter opener. It lands with a soft thud on the carpet beneath.

She winks. "Let's save the cards for later. You must be excited to get out of this apartment. New York awaits! And I have a few errands for you to run."

Eddie retrieves the opener and collects the cards into a pile. She's right, New York awaits!

"What do you need?" he asks.

She points to a pad and pencil on her nightstand. "You better write these down," she says. "I'm very particular."

She dictates her list, and he writes it down. She checks his work to be sure, then reaches into the pocket of her dressing gown and pulls out a couple of bills.

"Forty dollars should cover it. And take a tote bag from behind the door there. I have at least a thousand hanging from that hook."

Eddie takes down a tote, a blue canvas bag with long straps and the words *New York Film Festival, 1971*.

"Oh, that was a great year at the festival," Cookie says. "Everyone was scandalized by *Murmur of the Heart*. Have you seen it?"

"No," Eddie says. He hasn't even heard of it.

"Never mind. We'll get to it. Now, I would also like you to bring me a photograph of each place you go visit on your errands. I want to know what's going on out there in the city."

"I wish I could," Eddie says. "But I can't find my phone."

Cookie scoffs. "You and your phone. No, I want pictures I can hold in my hand."

"I don't have a camera," he says.

She points her back scratcher at the dresser across the room. "Open the top drawer. You'll find a camera in there."

Eddie opens the drawer, which is stuffed with handkerchiefs, eyeglasses, lipsticks, brooches, and berets in every color and pattern. "I don't see it," he says.

"Look under the switches."

"Switches?"

"Hairpieces."

Eddie moves aside a pile of braids and ponytails but only finds a small, rectangular boxlike thing, brown vinyl and silver metal. "It's not in here," he says. "All I see is this." He holds up the little box.

"That's it," she says. "That's the Polaroid."

Polaroid? Eddie's confused. He's seen instant cameras before, at school, and online, but he's never seen one like this. The ones he's seen are like gimmicks, like plastic toys. But this feels solid in his hand, heavy, substantial. And it looks nothing like a camera. Where is the lens? The viewfinder?

"Here. Let me show you." Cookie takes the box and presses a button on the side. It pops open, accordion-like, revealing a lens, a flash, a viewfinder, and a few more buttons. She holds it up to her eye. "Say cheese!" she commands.

He grins obediently, and she presses the button. The camera whirrs and clicks in her hands.

"Now what?" he says.

"Now we wait." She pats the bed next to her and Eddie sits down. Soon a little white plastic card, about three inches by four inches, emerges from a slot in the camera like a tongue emerging from a mouth. Cookie reaches for it and together they stare as the image slowly, slowly begins to emerge. Just smudges of light at first, and then the outline of a figure. It's Eddie, standing awkwardly with a strained smile. She stares, wide-eyed at the picture, and then begins to giggle.

"What's so funny?" he asks, embarrassed.

"You forgot to zip your fly!" she exclaims, pointing at his jeans and laughing even harder.

ELEVEN

Item 1. One bunch alstroemeria. Do not buy these from the corner deli. They must be purchased from Val's Bloomers on Twenty-Eighth Street. And do not substitute any other flower.

Eddie is standing on the sidewalk at West Third Street and Sixth Avenue with his Film Festival tote bag over one shoulder and no phone. He's studying a crinkled street map of Manhattan, trying to figure out how to get to the first location on Cookie's errand list, Val's Bloomers, as the din of the city ricochets around him. He looks up the avenue toward Midtown, where skyscrapers gleam in the sun. Val's is that way. Who needs a phone?

He passes a ragtag crowd at the public basketball courts, cheering and heckling a four-on-four basketball game. He passes a cabbie shouting a streak of elaborate curses at a jaywalker darting through traffic. He nearly trips over two dogs lunging at each other, tangling their leashes as their owners dance and tug to keep them apart. Clouds of fragrant smoke puff up from a kebab truck as an old man with a staticky bullhorn shouts about the end of days and a woman in a colorful headwrap hawking sunglasses from a folding table shakes her head in bemusement. Three teenage boys twirling Frisbees on their fingertips wait at the crosswalk next to a woman in a black abaya with gold stitching on the sleeves. A man in U.S. Navy whites dives into a cab, narrowly missing a pair of women in gray tank tops arguing about where to have lunch.

The people keep coming. They wear business suits and school uniforms and maxi dresses and Canadian tuxedos and hijabs and Mets caps and nuns' habits and pajama tops and camo leggings and printed kurtas. They walk in sneakers, pumps, sandals, brogues, loafers, flip-flops, stilettos. They race uptown, saunter downtown, jog crosstown, change course on a speck. They spin, twist, step, and leap. Some shuffle, some sprint, some just stand. But they never seem to crash. It's like they know one another, see one another, *are* one another, like everyone in New York is a single being. Everyone except Eddie, who hugs the edges of the buildings to stay out of the way. He wonders if he'll ever learn the dance.

Give it time, Eddie.

Val's Bloomers is easy to find with his crinkled map. The city's grid up here makes much more sense than the cockeyed jumble of streets in Cookie's neighborhood.

Before he enters, he takes a Polaroid of the storefront for Cookie, being sure to center the Val's sign so she'll know he really was there. Inside at the counter, he smiles at a woman in a daisy-print jumpsuit and points at the word *alstroemeria* on his list. "I need a bunch of these."

"For Cookie?"

Eddie's eyes widen. "How did you know?"

"Albert told me someone new would be picking these up," she says. "You must be someone new."

"I guess so," Eddie says. "I'm Eddie."

"Nice to meet you, Eddie, and before you ask, no. I'm not Val. Val died in the eighties. I never met her. Wait here."

She ducks into the back. While she's gone, Eddie scans the store and wonders about Val. He imagines her as a beautiful dark-skinned woman in a different daisy-print outfit, maybe a full, 1950s-style skirt and collared oxford. He pictures the day she assumed the lease on this shop, a slender storefront wedged between two much larger flower sellers. Her business is modest, but her customers are loyal, so she does well enough to make a little living. He sees her in a small workroom above the shop, a room that she's converted into a little studio apartment, with flower-printed wallpaper, upholstery, carpet, bed linens, even towels. Every surface—table, counter—is crowded with vases filled with the fresh flowers that didn't sell that day. She breathes air that's always dense with the scents of roses and lilacs. A sportscaster on the crackly old radio calls a New York Yankees game as she eats raspberries from a bowl. He doesn't see anyone else there, but she doesn't seem lonely. She has friends, flowers. The image makes him feel contented, like a swaddle.

Snap back, Eddie. The jumpsuit woman is holding out a colorful bunch of blooms for you to take. "Last of the alstros today," she is saying.

"Thank you."

"I saved them for you. Well, I saved them for Cookie, but you know what I mean. Tell her to get better soon, would ya?"

Eddie smiles, pays eleven dollars and eighty cents, and leaves.

He hates the idea of carrying a bunch of flowers around the city—the way the bright blooms peek out the top of his tote bag feels conspicuous—but he soon sees that no one here is looking at him or his flowers at all. No one cares. Perfect. Next item.

Item 2. A two-pack of Viva paper towels from CVS on Fourteenth Street, on sale for ninety-nine cents.

This one's easy. He retraces his steps back downtown to CVS, where he takes a photo of the doorway and buys the last two-pack of paper towels they have. Lucky again, even if they won't fit in his tote.

Back on the sidewalk, he sees a pair of goth girls in thick makeup standing next to a fire hydrant, smoking. The hydrant is covered in neon graffiti, made even brighter by the girls' black skirts and combat boots. It's a great picture, he thinks. He decides to capture it for Cookie. He tucks the paper towels under his arm, then pops open the Polaroid and snaps, just as the two girls look over at him and wave. The camera whirrs and spits. Eddie retrieves the little plastic card, then looks back at the girls, who are flipping him off now. Embarrassed, he turns quickly and walks on.

Down the block, some distance from the girls, he looks down at the picture, and gasps.

The girls aren't in the image at all. Instead, the photograph is centered on a boy about Eddie's age, or a year or two older, standing in front of the fire hydrant. His jacket is boxy and cropped, his stovepipe trousers tapered to the ankles. His clothes are frayed, like they've been worn awhile, and his hair falls messily over his forehead to the bridge of his nose. He holds a hat in one hand, an old-fashioned porkpie that reminds Eddie of the hat on Cookie's ceramic bulldog. But it's his stare that takes Eddie's breath. He's looking straight at the camera with a half smile, a knowing expression, eyes piercing through the photograph and into Eddie's own. Shining eyes, impossibly bright even in the sunshine, as if they are lit from within. Eddie's never seen eyes like these, never felt eyes trained on him like this.

Except, *you have seen these eyes before. Remember?*

Eddie thinks back to the taxi at Port Authority. He thinks back to the photograph across from the fainting couch. Those were the same eyes. And now they are here, in this photograph.

But they can't be. Can they? No.

He spins back toward the fire hydrant. The goth girls are still there, looking the other direction now. But the boy in the suit? Nowhere. Not at the hydrant, not up the block, not down the block. Nowhere.

Just then, a roar from underground, and a whoosh of air from the subway grate at his feet. The sudden wind catches the photograph and blows it into the traffic. Eddie watches it dance from car to car to car, until it flutters over a construction barrier and into an open manhole.

Eddie collects his breath. Maybe he imagined the boy in the photo, he thinks. Maybe it was just another imaginary moment. Nothing new.

Item 3. Two pieces of opera cake from Patisserie Gaston on Cornelia Street. DO NOT DELAY, they close at two p.m. If they have no opera cake left, get two eclairs. If no eclairs, two apricot tarts. If no apricot tarts, a package of Fig Newtons from the tobacco shop on Christopher.

Eddie instinctively reaches for his phone in his back pocket to check the time—is it two o'clock yet?—but of course his phone isn't there. He looks around to see if he can spot a clock in a window or ask someone with a watch, but all he sees is a bit of graffiti, a message scrawled on the mailbox at the curb: *It's Later Than You Think.*

Hurry up, Eddie. Hurry up.

TWELVE

Eddie rounds the corner onto Cornelia Street—which is nowhere near as easy to find as Val's or CVS, because it's down here in the mishmash streets of the Village—and spots Patisserie Gaston just as a young man wearing a flour-dusted apron grasps the OPEN sign hanging in the window and turns it around to CLOSED.

Eddie's shoulders sink. It's two o'clock.

How is he going to explain to Cookie that he missed the opera cake window? He imagines just picking up the Fig Newtons (Cookie's plan D) and telling her that the opera cakes were all sold out. And the eclairs and the apricot tarts. But then he remembers what she said about lying. She'll know.

He draws a deep breath and approaches the door and taps on the glass.

The flour-dusted young man looks to be about Eddie's age, so maybe we should call him a boy. He is a half-head taller and probably forty pounds heavier, with the kind of messy curls that look honestly earned after a long shift at work, not carefully cultivated in a mirror. The dark circles under his eyes suggest a sleeplessness Eddie, still recovering from the bus trip, can relate to. He shakes his head and points at the CLOSED sign.

Eddie shouts through the glass. "Opera cake?"

The boy cups his ear, dusting it with flour, too, but it looks to Eddie like the gesture, punctuated by a scowl, is only for show. He's not really listening. Eddie tucks the paper towels under his arm again and struggles to make a little prayer sign with his hands. He crinkles his forehead, hoping he looks something like desperate. "Please?" he mouths.

The boy sighs and unbolts the door. He opens it, just a crack. "What?"

"I just need two pieces of opera cake," Eddie says, conjuring his most pleading expression.

The boy crosses his arms over his apron. "We close at two."

"I know, but—" Eddie drops the paper towels and stoops to pick them up. When he stands, he sees that the boy is smirking. But not in a snarky way. Look at the way the skin around his eyes is crinkling. Like he's suppressing a smile. Eddie knows you can't fake that. He smiles in return, as guilelessly as he can. "I need them for someone. And"—he points at the clock on the wall behind the baker, a digital readout that says 2:01—"Please?" he says again.

The boy looks back into the shop, considers a moment, then opens the door, tripping a little bell that tinkles when Eddie steps through. An angry male voice from somewhere in the back shouts, "Theo! What did I tell you about closing time? When we're closed, we're closed!" The voice has a vaguely European accent, adding to its urgency.

"Oui, monsieur!" The boy puts a finger up against his mouth, warning Eddie to be quiet. He speaks softly, his voice tinged with a rasp that matches his tired eyes. "Opera cake, you said?"

Eddie holds up two fingers.

"You're lucky," says the boy, who Eddie now knows is named Theo, thanks to the angry voice in the back. Theo crouches down behind the counter and pulls out a tray with two pieces of multi-layered cake. "These are the last."

Eddie has never seen opera cakes before. Each rectangle has nine layers, stacked carefully atop one another. A half-inch base of pale yellow cake, then a slightly thinner layer of buttercream, then chocolate, then another layer of cake, then buttercream, and so on to the shiny chocolate ganache top. Eddie is amazed by how perfect and clean the layers are. The sides and corners are perfectly sharp and flush, making each piece look like a miniature building, like architecture. "Wow," he whispers.

A quiet smile speeds across Theo's face, a look of pride as he swiftly folds together a cardboard bakery box, tucking the tabs into the slots and securing them with a snap. Eddie notices a small songbird tattoo on the inside of each flour-flecked forearm, and as Theo carefully places the cakes in the box, the birds flutter like they're in flight. Theo works quickly, confidently, securing the box with red-and-white twine. His movements are so much more delicate and nimble than his thick, heavy hands would suggest. Eddie watches them closely, his stomach stirring.

"Opera cake is such a huge pain to make," Theo is saying, still quietly, almost conspiratorially. "I keep thinking one day Gaston will take it off the menu, but he refuses to let it go. Something about the bakery he grew up in back in France or something. I don't know. He's attached to it and doesn't really care how much work it is because he's not the one who has to come in and do it. I am. Me. The underpaid apprentice. Gaston comes up with the ideas, then sleeps in while I'm up making the sponge, the buttercream, the syrup, the ganache. It takes all night."

"All night?"

"Yep." Theo snaps the twine with a quick jerking motion, then ties it into a delicate, perfect bow. He taps the top of the box with two fingers. "I started this cake at two. And then I had to make the eclairs, the tarts, the petit-fours, all of it. If I don't get going by two or three, I'd never have stuff ready for the morning rush. And those rich cats in their shiny shoes and designer clothes need their brioche hot and fresh first thing in the morning or else we hear about it. You should have seen them when we raised the price of a croissant by fifty cents last month. They lost their minds. As if they can't afford an extra fifty cents. They have no idea what it takes to make this stuff, let alone spend an hour each way on the subway just to get here. 'Why don't you live closer to work?' they ask. I mean, do they even know how much they pay in rent to live in this neighborhood? Are they so loaded they don't even pay attention?"

Eddie hears Theo talking, but his mind has begun to wander. With those tattoos and that scowling expression, Theo looks like he should be in a punk band, not a bakery. He should be on a stage, belting out angsty hardcore lyrics over a mosh pit of frantic fans. He should be peeling off his shirt mid-set, tossing it into the crowd. Eddie envisions the first glimpse of Theo's body as he pulls the shirt up over his stomach. Eddie presses his hands onto the counter to balance himself.

"You wanna know the worst part?" Theo is asking.

But Eddie doesn't hear him. He's stuck on Theo's slick skin, pulsing veins, sharp breath as he comes off the stage at the end of the song. Theo's grateful, exhausted, exhilarated smile as he sees Eddie there waiting for him. The feel of Theo's sweat against Eddie's neck as Theo embraces him, and whispers something dirty in his ear. Eddie pictures himself whispering something dirty back. Imagine! The image sparks a rush of blood through him. All the way through.

"Hello?"

Eddie snaps back, remembering where he is. "Sorry," he says.

Theo shrugs. "The worst part is, I've never even been to the opera. Not once. I make opera cakes all night and couldn't even tell you the name of a single opera. Can you believe it?"

"Wow," Eddie says, still shaking off the mist of his punk-rock reverie. "Well. Thank you for opening the door for me. My great-aunt Cookie will be so—"

Theo holds up his hand. "Wait a second. Did you say Cookie? You mean Cookie over on Bedford Street?"

Eddie, suddenly wary, doesn't answer. He remembers this is New York City, not Mesa Springs. He doesn't know this Theo. Maybe Theo hates Cookie. He shouldn't have said her name.

Theo pushes the box across the counter. "Don't worry," he says, reading Eddie's discomfort. "Everyone knows Cookie around here. And she's one of our most loyal customers. I've never met her because she always sends that mean guy to pick up her orders. What's his name? Alfred or something? Anyway I wasn't even sure she was real until last winter when she sent Christmas cards to me and Gaston. There was twenty bucks folded into mine. I don't know how she would possibly know my name. But it was really cool. Even Gaston liked getting that card, and he hates everything."

"Everything?"

"Bakers are supposed to be grouchy," Theo says, raising an eyebrow. "Didn't you know that? It's part of the training."

"That's weird," Eddie says, conjuring the Eddie from his vision a moment ago, the Eddie bold enough to whisper in Theo's rock-star ear. "With all this sugar around, you'd think they'd be sweet."

Theo freezes, and for a moment, a tiny but eternal moment, stares blankly at Eddie.

Ugh, Eddie. Was that flirting? Oh no. Cringe.

But Theo smiles. Really smiles, like he means it, and a new vision sweeps across Eddie's brain, a vision of them together, living in a little apartment a few blocks over from the bakery, waking up late on Theo's day off to read the paper and drink coffee and spend the whole morning in bed before going out to stroll lazily through the Village, holding hands, making silly plans, living happy forever after. New Yorkers in love.

"Well," Theo says, breaking the spell. "I'm glad to meet a relative of Cookie's. She's the best, so you must be okay, too. Carry the box carefully so the cakes don't smush."

A shout slices the moment in two. "Theo!" It's the angry voice from the back of the bakery again.

Theo's face collapses back into a scowl. The change is swift, like a filter removed, and Eddie feels an icy burst of air. Theo punches at the register. "Nine dollars," he says, the exhausted rasp back in his voice. Whatever they just shared, or whatever Eddie imagines they just shared, has passed.

Eddie hands over one of Cookie's twenty-dollar bills and accepts his change. "Thank you again," he says on his way out the door.

"Okay," Theo says dully. He locks up behind Eddie and turns back in to the shop.

Eddie, laden now with a tote bag of flowers, a two-pack of paper towels, and a box of opera cakes, heads toward Bedford Street. He walks slowly, careful to keep the precious cakes balanced, but his mind is already back at Theo's punk-rock show.

THIRTEEN

"Nice try," Cookie is saying. "But I think you're missing the point."
She's talking about the pictures Eddie took, which clearly aren't what she wanted. For starters, there are only two, Val's and CVS. No Patisserie Gaston (in Eddie's defense, Theo and those tattoos—who could blame him for forgetting?). But the real problem isn't the quantity, it's the quality, and while Cookie's not chastising him, not exactly—she's being gentle, and it's not like he did anything wrong—Eddie is feeling contrite. He's already let her down, and on his first real day here.

He sets the bunch of alstroemeria, which he's trimmed and put into a vase elaborately decorated with pop-art squiggles and curlicues, onto her side table.

"I've been buying flowers at Val's since 1954," Cookie says. "I don't need a picture of the sign out front. I know what it looks like."

"But I thought you asked for—"

"I did," she interrupts. "But Lollipop, look at me. I'm stuck here in this bed. I can't see anything but these four walls. Obviously, they're not bad walls, if you have to stare at walls, but they're not enough. I miss New York City. It is my inspiration, and these days, my medicine. If I can't be part of what's happening out there, if I can't breathe the air on the streets and go outside to watch the people on the sidewalk, I'll do nothing but wither away up here. I'm a New Yorker. But right now I can't take myself into the city, so I need you to bring the city to me."

"Isn't that what these are?"

She shakes her head. "When I ask you for a picture of Val's, I don't mean *just* Val's. I need to see the life around Val's. I need to see who's walking a dog out in front of Val's, and I need to wonder what that dog is feeling. I need to see what trees are in bloom, and I need to wonder whether those blooms are making people happy or making them sneeze. I need to see what the young people are wearing this season, and I need to wonder whether I should be wearing it, too. I need more than just a picture of a sign. I need a picture of life, a picture that *means* something. Do you understand?"

Eddie lowers himself into the chair. A picture is a picture, isn't it? It's a moment, captured and frozen. Proof that something happened, or that something existed. A picture is a fact. At least, that's what it is before you start putting filters on it and manipulating it to try to alter the facts it contains. That's what Eddie's always thought.

"No," Eddie says finally. "I don't."

She points her back scratcher at the wall. "Look. Do you see that photograph there?"

Eddie's eyes follow the back scratcher to a black-and-white photograph in a silver frame. It depicts a woman in casual pants and a henley-style sweater, walking along a sidewalk that looks like it's in New York City. She's striding self-assuredly, her arms relaxed and her head straight. A giant pair of bug-eye sunglasses covers half her face, hiding any expression. But she's not the only one in the frame. There's also a photographer off to one side, looking disheveled and anxious as he tries to keep up, as if he's trying to get in front of her so he, too, can take her picture.

"Do you know who that is?" Cookie asks.

"No," Eddie says.

"Who do you think it is? If you had to guess."

Eddie studies it a little longer. "Someone important, I guess."

"Why do you say that?"

"Because that photographer looks like he's chasing her. Which means there are at least two photographers, even though you can only see one. And the woman, she hasn't stopped to pose, she's still walking, so it seems like she doesn't want to have her picture taken. They look desperate but she looks confident. So, she must be important. More important than they are, anyway. And it seems like she knows that."

He looks back at Cookie. She is staring at him with clear eyes, hands clasped beneath her chin. Eddie can't read her expression, either.

"What?" he says.

"You got all that just by looking at this photograph?"

"Am I wrong?"

"No," she says, her voice dreamy and soft. "You got everything right. That means it's a good photograph, an interesting photograph. It's more than just a picture. It's a window into something more."

She holds up the pictures he gave her of Val's and CVS. "If all I needed was to be reminded what a storefront looks like, these photos would be fine. But I need a window. I need to wonder what the person walking through the frame is thinking. I need to see an emotion on a face that makes me care about their life. I need to see something that makes me imagine what happened before you took the picture, and what happened after. I need to see magic. That's what I need you to bring me. Magic."

"Magic?"

"Magic."

Eddie thinks back to the man at the fire hydrant. Is that what she means by magic? He almost tells her about him, but since he doesn't have the picture anymore, he doesn't see the point. "How do you make that happen?" he asks.

"Ah," she says. "That's the hard part. You have to find a way to attract it. But you can't try too hard, or it won't ever appear."

Eddie shakes his head. "I don't understand."

"It's not enough to keep your eyes open. You have to keep your mind open, too."

He looks back at the photograph.

"That's Jackie O, by the way," Cookie says. "Or, as you might have learned in history class, Jacqueline Kennedy. The first lady back in the early 1960s."

"Oh," Eddie says. He doesn't remember much from history class.

"Anyway," Cookie says. "Do you need more film? We have tons. My friend Ernie worked for the Polaroid company and part of his pension package was a lifetime supply of film. He never used it and left it all to me when he died. Check the wardrobe in the corridor."

Eddie finds the stash of film (she's right, there's tons), and she shows him how to swap out a spent cartridge for a fresh one.

"Perfect," she says. "Now let's practice." She picks up her hand mirror and freshens her lipstick, rubbing her lips together with a smack. She turns the mirror over on the bed and reaches up to her forehead. "Is my beret on straight?"

"Yes."

She flicks her orange curl. "Spit curl just so?"

"Yep."

"How's my fallalery? Do I have enough?"

"Your what?"

"My jewelry. Maybe I need another necklace or brooch?"

"I think you look fine," he says.

She shakes her head. "Why don't you try that again. How do I look?"

He remembers. "Beautiful, gorgeous, breathtaking. Like a million bucks."

She adjusts the shoulders of her dressing gown. "Just a million?"

"I mean a billion bucks," he says. "With a *B*."

"Oh, you sweet talker. Now you go stand over there and let me find my light." She tilts her head slightly to one side, catching a reflected bit of sunshine from outside her window with her cheek. She tweaks her curl one more time, then turns her head slightly and looks up at him with a coquettish smirk. "Okay, I'm ready for my close-up."

Eddie raises the camera and steps toward her, filling the viewfinder with her face.

"Not that close!"

"I thought you said close-up—"

"It's an expression! Haven't you ever seen *Sunset Boulevard*?"

Eddie has no idea if *Sunset Boulevard* is a movie, or a play, or what, but he apologizes, backs up, and takes a picture. The camera spits out a card. He takes it and steps toward the bed. They watch it develop together.

"You look great," Eddie says, meaning it.

"Hmph," she says. "Take another one."

"But won't it be exactly the same?" he says.

"I said another one."

"Okay." He steps back into place, raises the camera, takes another. They watch this one develop. It looks just like the last one to him.

"Again," she says.

"But won't it be the same again? I don't want to waste film—"

"Again."

He complies, two and three more times.

"Should I change a setting on the camera or something?" he asks.

"That won't matter," she says. "The camera isn't the important part. It's just a machine. Take another one."

He takes another, and then another and another, a whole cartridge of film of Cookie, all in the exact same pose, all with the exact same expression. He lays them all down on the bed in front of her, and together they watch them develop.

"Hmm," she says after the images emerge. She picks up a photo and hands it to him. "Not this one."

"I think you look great."

"Yes, I do. But it is not a good picture. No magic." She picks up another. "This one isn't any good, either. Or this one, or this one, or that one."

One by one, Eddie drops the rejects, each one an objectively good photograph of Cookie, into the wastepaper basket by her bed. Soon there's only one photo remaining on the bed. She examines it for a moment, then takes it in her hands. She holds it very close to her eyes, then a bit more distant, then close again. Something comes over her face, a wash of color, light, relief, happiness. She stares at the photograph, mesmerized.

He steps around to her side to look.

There is nothing specific that you could identify in the picture that is different from any of the others, not the setting, not her position, not the light. But this one is different, beautiful in a different way. Something about the light from the window, the way it drapes over her face, amplifying every one of her hundred years in the lines around her eyes, the grooves across her forehead, the nicks beneath her lips—she looks like she's lived forever, and yet, there's an undeniably youthful glow coming through. And something about the way the light hits her eyes, like she has as many questions as answers. The other pictures were fine, and Cookie looked nice in them. But yes. This one is different. Captivating. He sees a story in it. Would he call it magic? Maybe he should.

Cookie runs her fingernail across the image. "There she is," she says. "There she is."

FOURTEEN

Eddie's been out for a few hours, running errands for Cookie: a box of black licorice from the tobacco shop, a tin of lavender lip salve from Bigelow Pharmacy, and a tub of borscht from Veselka, the Ukrainian restaurant in the East Village. He takes Polaroids at each place. Lots of them. He still doesn't know what he's doing, really. Just aiming aimlessly and snapping. But maybe taking lots of pictures, dozens, will increase his chances of catching it by accident. He changes film cartridges several times.

At each location, Eddie stands across the street from whatever he's shooting to fit more into each frame. Maybe if he captures the shop, and the shops next to it, and the sky, and the trees, and the people on the sidewalk, and of course, their dogs, then maybe something remarkable will sneak into a corner of the image, and when he's back at the apartment for sherry hour, and sits on the edge of her bed to show her the photos, then maybe she will see something, and point it out to him, and then maybe he'll see it, too.

He keeps shooting photographs. Strength in numbers, he figures. The more photos, the better chance he'll bring something that Cookie will like. And he really, really wants to do that. He wants to make her happy. That's really the core of his job here isn't it? Yes, he has to keep an eye on her, make sure she takes her medicines, and run her errands. But none of that is as important as making her happy.

But Eddie loses track of time, and is careless on his walk back to the apartment. He gets tangled up in the Village streets. Not lost, exactly, just distracted. Photo after photo.

It's nearly four thirty when he arrives, a half hour late for sherry hour. And Cookie's not in her bed.

He finds her in the kitchen, standing in bare feet, her dressing gown hanging off one shoulder, the paisley wrap on the floor next to one of her berets. He can hear the crackle of the record player in Cookie's room, the needle scraping across the end of a record that's long since finished playing. The sound gives the air a disturbing, sinister tint. His head swirls into confusion.

"Cookie?" he asks. "Is everything all right?"

She turns to him slowly, first her eyes, then her head. She glares not at his face, but his throat. "Where did you come from?" She spits the words, as if she's disgusted. "What are you doing here? I didn't ask for you."

"I, um—" Eddie holds up the take-out bag from Veselka. "I brought the borscht you wanted," he says, trying to sound cheerful.

She sneers at it. "I hate borscht," she hisses, swatting at his hand. "Get it out of here."

Eddie takes a step back. Steady, he tells himself. You've seen this before, back at Sunset Ridge. Remember? This disorientation, this sharpness. Cookie was probably asleep and woke up a little bit disoriented. She got out of bed, still half asleep, and lost her way. That's all. It's not a big deal. Everyone wakes up cloudy sometimes, even you. Right? The important thing is to stay calm. Don't startle her. You don't want her to fall. Move slowly. Speak clearly but gently. Maybe hum a tune. Project confidence, kindness, refuge, like everything is okay. If she sees you panic, or hears it in your voice, or senses it in your touch, this could get worse. Much worse. Swallow that anxiety, that acid gathering in your throat. Stay calm.

He pulls out one of the chairs at the little kitchen table and reaches for her shoulder to guide her into it. To his relief, she allows him to touch her, and she sits without protest. He picks up the wrap and drapes it across her shoulders.

"I thought you'd be in your room," he says, trying to maintain his cheerfulness. "It's sherry hour."

"No, it's not. Sherry hour is over."

He notices a tiny bruise on her face, just below the temple. "What happened to your cheek?"

She ignores his question. "I was going to make us a cup of tea."

"Oh, thank you, Cookie, but I don't need—"

"Not for you! Tea for Tallulah and me." She points at a portrait of a droopy-eyed woman with a long cigarette holder on the wall above the table. "I had to talk to Tallulah."

"Who is Tallulah?" he asks gently.

"Tallulah Bankhead. Are you daft?" The coldness of her voice cuts straight through him, shocking him. He knows she has a sharp edge, but he hasn't seen it in a while. What triggered it today? Did he do something wrong? He feels his heart begin to race, and his mind. He holds his breath, pinches his finger, swallows the bile, the panic, the fear.

He squares his shoulders and digs deep for the firm-but-warm tone he practiced so often at Sunset Ridge. "I don't think you're supposed be out here in the kitchen. I think you're supposed to be in bed."

She scoffs. "Supposed to be, supposed to be," she says, mocking him. She glares at his chin with bloodshot eyes. "Says who? You're not the boss here. This is *my* home."

"Yes," he says. "I know. It's your home, Cookie. And I'm so glad to be here with you."

"My home," she repeats. "I can do what I want."

"Of course you can. You're the boss. But let's go back to your room anyway. Why not? I'll come with you."

He reaches for her shoulder, but she swats him away. "You can't tell me what to do."

"You're right," he says, putting his hand back on her shoulder. He's pulled another Sunset Ridge crisis card: Acknowledge the frustration, but stay consistent. Get them back to where they're safest. For Cookie, that means her bed. "I can't tell you what to do. And I won't. But why don't we—"

"I want to talk to Tallulah."

"I understand," he says, still on script. But it's a lie. Eddie doesn't understand what's happening in her mind at all. It was easy enough to make peace with the imaginary midnight chats—after all, who is Eddie to judge someone else's extensive and elaborate inner life?—but this, today, is different. This is perplexing. Even scary.

"This is my home," she repeats, wriggling her shoulder away from him.

"Yes."

Eddie reaches for her hand, but she pulls it away. She looks so tired. Like she's been wandering through an endless fog, like she is lost, like hope is lost.

She turns back to the photograph of Tallulah. Her glossy eyes linger there for a moment, then move across the wall, filled with portraits. She scans the faces, some of which she's taught to Eddie already. He follows her eyes as she says the names, slowly.

"Billie Holiday. Anna May Wong. Oscar Wilde. Marlene Dietrich." Her eyes return to Tallulah, and then they close. Her shoulders relax. She exhales. "Tallulah."

This time, when Eddie takes her hand, she lets him. He curls his fingers into hers and she grasps back. The pressure of her touch, weak but present, reassures him.

"I'm cold," she says. She looks at her feet, a puzzled expression. "Where are my slippers?"

"I tell you what," he says. "Let's take Tallulah back to your room. You two can catch up in there while I fix a hot water bottle to tuck underneath, by your feet, to warm them up."

"Is it sherry hour?" she asks, her voice smaller now, almost timid, like a child's.

"It sure is," he lies. He takes the photograph of Tallulah Bankhead off the wall. "Let's have it in your room."

She blinks slowly. "You better move Bette Davis out of the bedroom first. She and Tallulah aren't speaking."

"All right," Eddie says as relief washes through him.

He helps Cookie back into bed. She reaches out to touch a petal of the alstroemeria in the pop-art vase, then closes her eyes and, almost immediately, before he can pour the sherry, she falls into a soft, shallow sleep. He watches her for a while until her breath finds a rhythm. Then he gathers up the open envelopes and greeting cards on the floor next to her and tucks the paisley blanket gently around her feet.

It's begun to rain outside. He closes the window, then goes back to the kitchen to fix her hot water bottle. He will never be late for sherry hour again. Never.

FIFTEEN

Donna answers in a flustered blurt: "Hello?"

Eddie smiles. Already, just hearing her voice, he starts to relax.

"Hi," he says, twirling Cookie's phone cord around his finger.

"Thank God it's you. It says Unrecognized Number so I almost didn't answer. You're not a scammer, are you?"

"Yes, I'm calling to scam you from Cookie's kitchen," he says, playing along.

"Good luck," she says. "If you can talk me out of the 356 dollars in my checking account, it's all yours. How's it going out there? How's Cookie?"

This is the question he called knowing she would ask, but it's also the question he doesn't know how to answer. Eddie doesn't want to mention the scene with Cookie in the kitchen. If he tells Donna, she'll only worry, and if she worries, she'll start to think that Eddie can't handle Cookie, and if Eddie can't handle Cookie, his time in New York will be cut short. Not that she can force him to come home—he's eighteen after all—but if she doesn't support the current arrangement she can upend it. She has veto power.

Maybe, maybe there's part of him that wants her to use it. Maybe this is all too much. New York is so big, and for all its exhilaration, it bewilders him, confuses him, scares him. The energy, the light, the noise, the people. So many people. He misses the open sky over Mesa Springs. The air. The quiet. The mountains, always there, reminding him where he is. Back there, he was in control. And when he felt out of control, he could retreat. Not here. There is no escape. He looks at his feet.

"Eddie?"

No, he thinks. Not yet. He *can* handle this. He's sure he can. All of it. Even when Cookie seems to lose it. Even when Cookie gets mean. He's got enough experience, or believes he does, to deal with things. He just, oh who knows. Maybe he just wants to hear her voice. That's all.

"She's great," he says, just a little too brightly. "Really great. Everything's been great. You should see how many get-well cards she's gotten."

The line is silent for a moment. He pictures her staring at the ceiling again, considering the lie he's just told. Because she's certainly detected it. Oh, he shouldn't have called her. Not today. He should have waited until tomorrow, when Cookie's episode is only a memory. When he will surely be feeling confident again.

"She gave me this cool old camera," he says quickly, hoping the subject change will deflect her doubt. "Whenever I go out to do errands, she asks me to bring her pictures."

"Can't you just show her pictures on your phone?"

The impulse to tell her what happened to his phone comes and goes swiftly. It works fine. "She prefers the Polaroids," he says. "She likes to hold them."

"Pictures of what?"

"Of whatever. She likes to see the city." Of magic.

He hears Donna light a cigarette. He pictures her in the kitchen, staring out the window at the wildfire sky. "You're sure nothing's wrong," she says.

"I'm sure."

"And everything is great."

"Everything," he says. "Honestly."

She doesn't answer right away, but after a breath, says, "All right. I miss you, kid."

"You too," he says. This part is not a lie.

Back in his room, Eddie props the picture of Cookie that he took the other day against one of her miniature Rockettes on the table next to his fainting couch. He lies on his side to study the coy expression on her face. What was she thinking about that day? What is she thinking about now?

Outside, he hears a siren in the distance. He wonders what everyone in Mesa Springs is doing right now. Probably drinking Solo cups of beer in a parking lot, bragging about their summer vacation plans, their trips to Cancún or the Grand Canyon. He wonders what Theo is doing right now. Probably sleeping, his broad chest rising and falling rhythmically in the dark, soon to wake up for another early morning at the bakery.

Eddie feels proud that he didn't panic today. He felt it coming, but he kept moving, stayed focused on Cookie, swallowed it away. Can he claim victory? No, probably not. He probably got a little bit lucky, too. Still, he didn't panic, and it feels good.

He reaches for Cookie's photograph and holds it to his chest. Clutching it close, he lies on his back and watches the disco ball spin slowly above. Oh, Cookie, he thinks. Today wasn't good. But I made it through. We made it through.

Eddie will sleep deeply tonight. He won't wake up once, not even when the bright-eyed boy in the photograph across the room turns to him and smiles.

SIXTEEN

Cookie sets her back scratcher down on the bed and holds the clutch of flowers up to her nose, inhaling deeply. "Oh, alstroemeria. You are the prettiest flowers, but you have no aroma at all."

"I'll put them in water," Eddie says.

"Not yet. Let me hold them a bit longer. They go with my outfit, don't you think?"

"They do," he says, and it's true. The colors of the flowers—yellow, orange, pale scarlet—mirror the stripes of the rayon scarf draped loosely around her neck.

"You lovely boy," she says, sounding sleepy.

Eddie is feeling tender toward Cookie today, protective. Yesterday was hard for him, but he woke up this morning feeling like it was probably even harder for her. So as soon as he heard Albert's keys jangling in the hallway, he jumped up off the couch and, managing to avoid Albert, slipped out to buy a fresh bunch of alstroemeria. He waited outside, watching the door until Albert left, before coming back upstairs.

She is in fresh clothes, sitting up on fresh sheets, her hair washed and set, her makeup perfect, all thanks to Albert. She was so disoriented and disheveled and confused yesterday. And cruel. He tries not to think about the way she snapped at him. Like it wasn't even her. But now, rested and refreshed, it's like she's back to the Cookie he knows. But doesn't want to stray far from her side today. Just in case.

He deflects when she tries to send him out on more errands—a fresh six-pack of celery soda from the Second Avenue Deli, a makeup brush from the beauty supply shop on Mott Street—saying that he'll do them tomorrow.

"Would you like to open some more get-well cards?" he asks. "Albert left a stack of them in the kitchen."

"I don't think so," she says. She holds out a hand, bangles jangling. "Come here."

He sits on the edge of her bed, holding her hand, and nods at a photograph on the wall. It's an image of a very handsome young man with slicked-back hair and a smoldering expression.

"Who's that?" he asks. Not that he cares, really. He just wants keep her company, to connect.

"That's Rudy. Rudolph Valentino. A very famous movie star. Everyone adored him back in the 1920s. Albert swears that he had a torrid affair with Ramón Novarro."

"Who?"

She points at another photograph of an impossibly handsome man, also with slicked-back hair. "Him. Also a movie star." She spins a ring on her right hand, repositioning it to catch the light. "But who knows if it's true? Albert is very susceptible to such gossip. But if it is true, it's a shame they never had a chance. They had to stay in the closet if they wanted to work in Hollywood. Stupid, of course. But that's how the world was."

Still is, Eddie thinks.

"Things are different now, they say," Cookie says. "Maybe that's true. What do you think?"

Eddie's face goes hot. He's not quite ready to talk about sexuality with Cookie, especially not his own. He's not ashamed of it, and he assumes she knows. But still. He's afraid that as soon as he confirms it, it's all she'll want to talk about, and he wants to keep that part of himself to himself for now. So he shrugs. "I don't know."

"Well," she says. "Maybe some closets aren't so bad, at least for a little while. A place to be safe, to figure things out, to dream. To invite someone else into every now and then, if you wanted to?" She raises an eyebrow.

Eddie doesn't answer.

She sighs. "Anyway, Valentino died at thirty-one. My mother said the doctors knew he was going to die because there was no cure for his disease, but they never told him."

"I would want to know if I was going to die," Eddie says.

"Would you?"

He doesn't answer right away. For a flash, he imagines a doctor in a white lab coat telling him that he was going to die in three days. What would his reaction be? Shock? Anger? Sadness? Relief? He pictures himself absorbing the information silently, feeling the world around him begin to soften into mush. He imagines standing up, leaving the doctor's office, and walking down to the street. He looks up the avenue, and then down it, unsure which way to go first, feeling every minute tick underneath his feet. He feels a surge of bravery and begins to walk across the street, not waiting for traffic to pass. He strolls squarely, calmly, unrushed and unbothered, with more confidence than he's ever walked with before. He wonders where he's going, but before he finds out, the image fades.

Cookie is talking. "I would, too. I would want to know, so I had time touch up my lipstick," she says, and begins to laugh quietly.

Eddie tugs at his collar, uncomfortable. He can feel Cookie looking at him, like she's waiting for a response, but he doesn't offer one.

"Did I frighten you yesterday?" she asks abruptly.

Eddie scrunches his shoulders. He's been wondering if she even remembered yesterday. He wasn't going to bring it up in case she was embarrassed, or worse, in case she was angry with him. He's not sure why she would be, but he's seen it happen before.

"No," he says, and it's an honest answer, because fear isn't exactly what he felt. Concern, panic, uncertainty . . . but fear? No.

Oh, come on, Eddie. You were scared out of your wits.

Eddie knows this is true, but before he can say more, Cookie speaks again.

"People tell me that they think I'm fearless, and I never contradict them, but it's not true. Oh, I'm fearless with my outfits, fearless with the way I speak, fearless in how I laugh or cry. But I'm afraid of so many things. You can't help it, you know. It just happens. It just appears. Sometimes it comes at the right time, like if you're at the edge of a cliff. Fear tells you to step back. But sometimes fear is a trick, a trap, like when you fear judgment from someone else. You have to reject that fear. You have to step forward then, into the danger, not back and away. It's hard, but it's the only way to tame it."

Eddie looks at his hands. A thousand fears race through him. None of them are a cliff's edge. All of them are people—perceiving him, assessing him, judging him, shaming him. Each one stings.

"What are you afraid of, Lollipop?" Cookie asks.

"I don't know," Eddie says, and it's not a lie. He's afraid of so many things, but he's ashamed of his fear and he doesn't want Cookie to see that. He wants her to trust him, to believe in him. He wants her to think he's strong.

"They say Dorothy Parker was fearless," she says, pointing at another picture, the dark-haired woman at an old-fashioned typewriter.

"I've heard that name before," Eddie says, a faint English-class memory sweeping through his mind like a wisp of steam. "Was she a writer or something?"

"A poet, an essayist, a critic. The smartest person in New York. All through the 1920s she spent her afternoons in the bar at the Algonquin Hotel with all the important writers and thinkers, all the, you know, what's the word? The intelligentsia. But she was the smartest of all. She ran circles around all those brilliant men." Cookie reaches under her pillow and retrieves a tattered old paperback with the title *Enough Rope*. She hands it to him. "This is for you. You can tell because I've written your name on the title page."

He opens it, and she points. "See? Eddie. Right there. I even spelled it right."

Eddie smiles.

"These are some of Dottie's most famous poems. Maybe reading them will help you know her when you find her."

"When I find her? But isn't she—?"

Cookie leans back on her pillow with a satisfied smile.

"I hope you don't have plans this afternoon. I haven't seen the Algonquin in years. But you'd better hurry, if you want to be back by sherry hour with a picture."

SEVENTEEN

Eddie checks the clock in the kitchen. It's 1:40 p.m. He better hurry, because Patisserie Gaston closes soon, and he's determined to buy opera cakes for Cookie. He knows he'll have to carry them with him up to the Algonquin, and back downtown afterward, but he really wants sherry hour to be perfect today, and that means opera cakes. He grabs the camera and ducks out.

Across the street from Gaston, a sudden swell of anxiety stops Eddie. Stay cool, Eddie. Theo's just a boy. And you don't have time to stand around and talk anyway. Just get the cakes and go.

The little bell over the door tinkles as Eddie steps in at 1:55 p.m. Theo's back is turned. His round shoulders are dusted with flour, his apron tied into a perfectly even knot around his back. How does he do that? How does he get it so straight, so symmetrical? Eddie imagines Theo reaching behind himself, his hands and fingers moving so smoothly and perfectly, carefully creating a perfect bow, like he's done a hundred thousand times before. For a second, Eddie wonders if Theo will remember him. Theo probably sees dozens of customers a day. Maybe hundreds. He could have erased Eddie from his memory as easily as swiping crumbs off a counter.

But instead, when Theo turns around at the tinkle of the bell, his face brightens in recognition. "It's you," he says.

"Hi," Eddie says. He hates the way his voice sounds, tinny and light. He clears his throat, hoping for a different timbre. "Hi, Theo." A little better.

"Hi, um—" Theo laughs. "You never told me your name."

He's been thinking about you, Eddie.

"I didn't?" Eddie says. Foolish. Obviously, you didn't. Why would Theo say so, unless you didn't?

"No. And I've been wondering."

Eddie, inconspicuous Eddie, draws a breath and answers, "I'm Eddie."

Theo's face slides into a smile. "Hi, Eddie," he says, slowly, resonantly, confidently. "Opera cake?"

"Yes please," Eddie says. "Two."

Theo moves slowly, lifting the tray out of the case and carefully placing two cakes in a box. Eddie watches the clock, worried. It will take him a half hour to get uptown, probably, and a half hour to get back, so if he wants to make it to Cookie's by four he needs to get a move on.

"Hold on a minute," Theo says. "Let me make these special." He takes the cakes back out of the box, then ducks into the back.

"Aren't you closing now?" Eddie asks, glancing up at the clock on the wall behind the counter.

"Don't worry," Theo says, emerging with a pastry tube in one hand. "I'm in no rush today. Gaston's gone for a chiropractor appointment. I thought I could personalize these. It'll give me a chance to practice my penmanship. Er, chocolatemanship." He smirks playfully and looks up at Eddie, clearly expecting a laugh.

Eddie just stares at the clock on the wall above them.

"Crickets, huh?" Theo says. "Okay. Well, how do you spell Cookie?"

"Um," Eddie says, getting the joke—obviously a baker knows

how to spell Cookie—but time is ticking past quickly. Oh, he wishes he could stay. But he can't miss the four o'clock deadline again. He needs to get to the Algonquin and back as soon as he can.

"Oookay," Theo says. "I'll start with *C* and see where I get. Do you want a cup of coffee while you wait?"

He shifts from one foot to the other impatiently. "I, I'm sorry," he says, sliding a bill across the table. "But I'm kind of in a rush. How much are the cakes?"

Theo looks up, a quizzical expression. "I thought I could write—"

"I know, I'm sorry," Eddie interrupts. "But I really have to go. Next time?"

Theo puts down the pastry tube and reaches for a box. "Sure," he says, his voice dejected. "Next time."

EIGHTEEN

Eddie is sitting on the subway, heading uptown to the Algonquin. On the seat next to him is a white paper bag with twisted-paper handles and the word GASTON printed on the side, and in his lap is the book of Dorothy Parker poems. He opens it at random, to this couplet:

> *I think that I shall never know*
> *Why I am thus, and I am so.*

He reads it twice. He likes the way it sounds, the way it feels in his mind. He wonders if she was being serious or silly when she wrote it. Maybe both.

He daydreams. A quiet vision takes shape, of the boy, the one from the picture in Eddie's bedroom. He's sitting next to Eddie on the subway and reciting the poem as they ride. He smiles as he speaks, eyes shining. The train stops at Thirty-Fourth Street, and the boy is gone. Some passengers exit, others enter, and the train starts again. A new vision now. It's Theo, his hand upturned on his lap, exposing his wrist. Eddie reaches over to touch the songbird there, but before he makes contact, the train stops again. They are at Forty-Second Street, jolting him out of the vision.

He gets up and steps into the station, then up the stairs and onto the street.

NINETEEN

The clock above the lobby bar at the Algonquin says 2:30 p.m., but it feels later in here. The light is very low and it takes a minute for his eyes to adjust. Soft music plays over the quiet lilt of conversation; groups of two and three and four people sit around small tables or slump in wingback chairs under lamps, with shopping bags from Saks and Bloomingdale's and Apple at their feet. People with money.

Eddie looks down at his worn-out pullover and torn jeans. He doesn't belong here. He's never really been in a hotel like this before. The fanciest hotel he ever stayed in was a roadside motel on the way to Padre Island in Texas, when Donna saved up enough money to drive down for a few days with her friend Louisa. The motel didn't have a bar, but it did have a vending machine with candy bars that only cost a quarter. Eddie had been seven, and they were only there for one night.

He chews on his insecurity, savoring its familiar flavor. He could just snap a quick photograph and leave. He'd be able to come up with something to say to Cookie about it by the time he got back.

But *no lying to Cookie*, remember? So he takes a seat at an empty table in the back of the room. He sets the white paper bag from the patisserie in the chair next to him and the book and camera on the table. He orders a Coke from a gray-haired waiter in a red vest.

Eddie looks around, taking in the old photographs hanging on the wall behind him, many of them taken here at the Algonquin in years past. One, captioned *1926*, shows patrons gathered in small groups near the taps, some standing, some perched on stools. Others are scattered in ones and twos among the tables throughout the room. The men wear wide-leg trousers and mustaches; the women are in drop-waist dresses and T-strap shoes. The room itself has changed, of course—new furniture, new carpeting—but not entirely. The layout is similar. And it's still a quiet, dark, fancy hotel bar that feels like it's been here a long time.

He rests his hand on the camera. He needs to find a way to take a decent photo in here, one that reminds Cookie what the Algonquin looks like, but also has that thing she talked about. The magic. But how to find it? He thinks back to all the photos he took of Cookie in her room, one after the other, reject after reject, before one, inexplicably, stood out. He can't do that here. He can't point and shoot photograph after photograph, firing the flash over and over, just hoping for something to happen. It would be easy on a phone, stealthier. But with this big, flashing, whirring camera, he'll only get one photograph, maybe two at most, before people start staring and getting annoyed.

Might as well do it now. Eddie opens the camera, aims it at the bartender, and snaps. The flash goes off, startling him even though he knew it was coming. Several people at other tables look over. He waves at them sheepishly and lowers the camera. It spits out a photo. Eddie holds it in his hands, waiting.

And then, suddenly, a voice from behind him. "Your martini, sir."

"My what?" Eddie says, looking up. He slips the still-undeveloped photo into his book.

A waiter is standing by Eddie's table, balancing a tray on one palm, with a towel hanging over his forearm. This is not the waiter Eddie ordered his Coke from just a minute ago. This waiter has thick dark hair, pomaded and combed very neatly, and a pristine white dinner jacket. No red vest. His eyes are cast down as he places a small cloth napkin on the table, then carefully sets a cocktail glass on top, centering it just so. It's filled to the rim with a clear liquid, and resting inside is a trio of olives skewered on a metal spear.

"Extra dry," the waiter says. "As requested."

"But I ordered a—"

"A martini," the waiter says. "Excellent choice." He smiles at Eddie, and that's when Eddie sees his eyes.

And he freezes. He knows those eyes.

The eyes are luminous, glowing like beacons, at once sharp and shimmering and a thousand other colors. Eddie remembers an exhibit of beetles at a museum in Denver that he visited on a school trip, where he saw the incredible rainbow stag beetle, with a shell that changed colors depending on where you stood. When Eddie was still, the beetle was deep brown. But when he moved, the colors of the beetle began to flow like liquid across the exoskeleton, like oil on a puddle—green, indigo, violet, scarlet, copper, gold. It mesmerized him, the most beautiful thing he'd ever encountered. Until, maybe, now.

The eyes belong to the boy, of course. The boy from the fire hydrant, from the taxi, from the photograph in his bedroom at Cookie's. Unmistakably him.

"May I bring you anything more, sir?" The waiter continues to smile. Not a typical waiter smile, the kind where he's just being polite, but a real smile, an open smile, a magnetic smile.

Eddie's breath shortens. Sweat pools at the base of his spine. He blinks. He blinks again. He rubs his eyes, grabs the tip of his finger. Relax, he tells himself. This is just a vision. Embrace it. Breathe.

Eddie stares up at the open smile.

"Sir?" the waiter repeats.

Eddie knows he's been asked a question. He knows that the customary thing to do, when asked a question, is to provide an answer. But something is stopping him. His brain, or his mouth. He tries to engage his voice, to push air through his larynx, to say something . . . but nothing comes. Why? This is his own vision! He should be able to say anything, to be anyone. Nothing but confidence in your own imagination, right? Come on, Eddie. Speak.

But he can't speak. He just stares.

The waiter smiles patiently.

Finally, Eddie manages to croak out a sound, something like *no*. He strains to add a *thank you*, but has already lost his breath again.

The waiter leans in, as if sharing a secret. "Remember," he says. "If anyone with a badge comes in, a cop or a soldier or anyone at all in a uniform, that is not gin in your glass. That's water. Prohibition, you know. Liquor is illegal. Officially, at least." His lips are so close, Eddie can feel his breath on his ear, raising goose bumps across his skin.

The waiter straightens again, winks, and turns back toward the bar. Eddie watches him walk, spellbound as the waiter—no, not just the waiter, the beautiful boy with the shining eyes—drifts away across the room, collecting empty glasses and emptying ashtrays as he goes.

Eddie watches him until he disappears through a service door. It swings closed behind him. Eddie watches it until it stills, then looks around warily.

He sees a pair of young women in snug, old-fashioned cloche hats, laughing with a young man in a brown pin-striped waistcoat. They're just across from a group of men in high-waisted trousers and shiny brogues, gesturing extravagantly with their cigarettes and stabbing fingers at a newspaper as they argue across the table. At one end of the room, he sees a middle-aged woman sitting alone and looking wistful as she tugs at the collar of the fur jacket draped over her shoulders. The barkeep, in a trim black tuxedo, polishes glasses while scanning the room from behind wire-rimmed spectacles. It all looks exactly like the picture he'd just seen on the wall. Only, this isn't a picture on the wall. This is . . . real?

Eddie pinches his finger again. He reminds himself to breathe. No, this isn't real. This is only another fantasy. Nothing to be freaked out by. This one is more vivid than usual, that's all. Maybe it's because of New York City. Everything is amplified here, even your imagination. That's all this is, right? Your imagination?

Except—this vision feels different. This vision feels physical, alien. Like it's not something Eddie's built himself, but something he's entered from outside. He can't grasp the controls, can't move the levers. The way the room has transformed around him, it feels real, like life. Not like something he's conjuring, but like something that's happening to him, whether he wants it or not.

Don't panic, Eddie. Just breathe. It's not a bad vision, is it? Why not see where it takes you?

He runs his finger across the outside of his martini glass, tracing a squiggle through the condensation. He doesn't take a sip. He's not thirsty.

He drops his gaze to his lap, and gasps. Whose clothes are these? Whose nubby wool trousers? Whose watch chain? Whose suspenders? Where are his jeans? His sneakers? He puts a hand up to his hair. It's sticky from pomade.

Just to his right, he hears a peal of laughter. He turns to see a large round table with seven men and one woman sitting around it. The men are bookish, buttoned-up, fingers tucked into their watch pockets. But she is different. She is striking. Small, hunched, with a wavy bob parted to one side and tucked messily behind one ear. A strand of pearls falls over the square collar of her staid black dress. With one hand, she fiddles with the pearls, with the other, she waves a cigarette in the air. She is speaking, animated and passionate, while the men stare, rapt.

"But Dorothy—" one of the men says.

She flicks her cigarette at him dismissively. "Bennett, I meant what I said. Heterosexuality is not normal. It's just common."

The men all laugh and she leans back, confident and satisfied, and takes another drag.

As if she feels Eddie watching her, she glances over to meet his gaze. She holds it, eyes boring into his, as she tips her ashes onto the floor next to her and smiles. Eddie stares back, agape, disbelieving. She nods, then turns back to her conversation.

After a moment, the waiter approaches again, bobbing his head to the music from the piano in the corner, where a man wearing a carnation in his lapel plays and sings a tune that Eddie recognizes. It's Cole Porter, of course:

I happen to like New York / I happen to like New York.

As the song reaches its climax, the waiter puts a hand on Eddie's shoulder and sings along. The warm pressure of his fingers sends a shock down Eddie's spine. It feels like desire, and Eddie tumbles inside. What is this place? What is this fantasy?

TWENTY

When the song ends, Eddie reaches for the camera on the table. He raises it, aims it at the piano player, and presses the button. The flash fires again, this time reflecting from the piano man's spectacles and back into Eddie's eye, blacking out his vision. Shocked by the sudden burst of light, he draws a hand over his eyes.

And then: *Crash!*

Someone just dropped a tray of drinks behind the bar, piercing the room with a brittle eruption of sound, rupturing the moment.

Eddie opens his eyes to see that the bar is back to where it was when he got here. He's in his own clothes now, his own jeans and sneakers. The woman at the next table is checking something on her laptop. A pair of men at the bar are arguing about whether to get tickets to *Merrily We Roll Along* or *Kimberly Akimbo*. The bartender is calling over a waitress to help him reboot the electronic payment system. It's the twenty-first century again and Eddie's little hallucination is over. Just a boy in a hotel bar with an un-sipped Coke on his table, his Polaroid, and Cookie's copy of *Enough Rope*.

Dazed, he leaves ten dollars on his table and gets up to go. On the way out, he notices the clock over the bar again. It says 2:31. Only a minute has passed. Strange. It feels like he's been here for longer than that. Even the song itself lasted several minutes. He wonders for a moment whether this place is enchanted, but decides that the missing time is just more evidence that it was all a vivid vision.

∽

On the subway downtown, back in the real world, Eddie remembers what the woman in his vision said: *Heterosexuality is not normal. It's just common.* It's a pretty good line, if he does say so himself. Because he made it up, of course. He made all of it up—every flash of light, every clink of glass, every swirl of cigarette smoke. Even the electrifying touch from the waiter. The only part he didn't create was the Cole Porter song. That he imported from band class. That's what he tells himself. That's what he'll believe.

He steps off the train at the West Fourteenth Street station by accident, a stop too early. But he doesn't worry. He can walk from here. He has time.

As he walks, he constructs another fantasy, to prove he still can. He pictures himself with a group of young men in 1920s waistcoats leaning on a Ford Model A at a corner newsstand. He blinks and makes a new one: a trio of uniformed Navy officers waving pamphlets at passersby, recruiting young men to join up to fight in World War II. And another: a group of 1950s beatniks in stovepipe chinos, smoking outside a coffee shop, swapping tattered paperback poetry books. The visions are clear, vivid, thick with detail. Are the specifics accurate? It doesn't matter. They're his own, and he can change them as he likes, turn them off and on, banish them at will. He breathes deeply and smiles at the sidewalk, balanced again.

He winds through the Village toward Bedford Street with the camera strap over his shoulder and the paper bag with the opera cakes hanging from his fingers. He feels gravity under his sneakers and wonders about the centuries of people who've walked over these same cobblestones. He glances up at the windows of the old apartment buildings and wonders about the generations of tenants who've leaned out of them. He wonders how old the cracks in the sidewalks are, how they came to be. He wonders how Manhattan can hold so many stories. What a sturdy little island. What a rock.

TWENTY-ONE

The realization comes quickly and strong on Carmine Street. Eddie has made a mistake. He's left his copy of *Enough Rope* at the Algonquin. In his confusion, he managed to remember the opera cakes and the Polaroid, but not the book. It's probably still sitting there now. Dammit. It's just after three now. He doesn't have time to go back for it. What's more, he has to pee.

But look, New York is coming to the rescue. There's a used bookshop just ahead. He can buy a replacement, and have Cookie write his name in it again. She'll forgive him.

"Can I help you?" the man behind the counter asks when Eddie steps into the dusty shop. His elaborate mustache curls up at the corners, reminding Eddie of Cookie's spit curl.

"Can you tell me where the restrooms are?"

"Customers only," the man says.

"Okay," Eddie says.

"Are you going to buy something?"

"Well, I'm looking for Dorothy Parker." Oh, if this guy only knew, Eddie thinks.

"Essays or poems?"

"Poems."

"Straight back, next to the restrooms," the man says, fiddling with his mustache.

Eddie heads to the back, pees quickly, then finds the poetry section. The shelves here reach from the floor to the ceiling, rows and rows of them in uneven aisles. They're packed with books, thousands of books or maybe millions, Eddie thinks. They are stacked horizontally, vertically, one on top of the other, some even piled on the floor like stone cairns.

"You okay back there?" the man says, suddenly standing right next to Eddie.

"Um, I'm looking for *Enough Rope*."

"No," the man says. "Sold the last one a few months ago."

"Are you sure?" Eddie asks. How could anyone possibly know what's in this chaos, even someone who looks like he sleeps here? "Is there anywhere else it could be?"

"Are you saying my store is disorganized?" the man snaps.

"No, I just—"

"Look, kid. I know every book in here. And there is no *Enough Rope*. Hasn't been for months." He starts walking back to the front counter, then stops and turns. "Unless a customer mis-shelved it. Happens all the time. Check the reference section."

"Reference?"

"Next to poetry," the man says. "Everyone gets confused."

"Okay," Eddie says. "Would it be under—"

But before he can finish his question, another customer enters and the man turns back to the front of the store.

Eddie scans the poetry shelves one more time, then steps over to reference. He runs his finger across the spines, but there's no Dorothy Parker. But he does see a copy of *Bartlett's Familiar Quotations*, and a memory whooshes over him.

On his tenth birthday, Eddie was given a copy of *Bartlett's* from a man Donna was married to for a couple of years. The inscription inside said, "I bet you'll be in this one day" or something equally impersonal, the kind of thing only an awkward, temporary stepfather would write. He tossed it when that stepfather left. He never really read it anyway. He was too busy with his favorite books: *Kasper in the Glitter*, *Tuck Everlasting*, *Eragon*. Not *Bartlett's*. But still, he reaches for it now.

He sets down the opera cakes and opens the book, letting the pages fan out from under his thumb. He loves that sound. He remembers being very young, napping on the couch with his feet in Donna's lap while she would read one of her science fiction paperbacks, listening intently to the way the paper softly rustled as she turned the pages. He remembers imagining what was in the book she was reading. Was she reading about an adventure in the mountains of Mars, where alien animals roamed freely? Was she reading about a lost spaceship, visiting distant worlds as it tried to find its way home? Was she reading about an evil empire in a distant galaxy planning to invade Earth? He never asked. He always preferred imagining.

Bartlett's is organized by speaker or writer, and in the spirit of today, Eddie turns to the section labeled *Parker, Dorothy*. He finds many quotes: "Hold your pen and spare your voice" and "I've never been a millionaire but I know I'd be just darling at it." The quips make him smile. It's no wonder Cookie likes talking to Dottie. She seems clever, funny, ironic. Like someone who has a lot to say. Er, *had* a lot to say, he reminds himself. *Bartlett's* says she died in 1967.

He's about to close the book when one more Dorothy Parker quotation on the page jumps out at him.

Heterosexuality is not normal. It's just common.

What? Impossible. That's not her line, that's his! He just made it up back at the Algonquin. He must be seeing things. He rubs his eyes and reads it again.

Heterosexuality is not normal. It's just common.

He reads it over and over, disbelieving. How can this be? The words are exactly the same. Almost too exact, actually. But maybe this moment is just a vision, too? Maybe he's just imagining the words on the page. Maybe he's imagining this bookshop. That must be it.

Eddie gingerly closes the book and slides it back onto the shelf, slowly, like it's something breakable that he shouldn't be touching in the first place.

"You find what you need?" the mustache man shouts.

It's time to get back, Eddie. Sherry hour soon. He says "thank you" to the man on the way out the door, and heads toward Bedford Street.

TWENTY-TWO

"Tell me, Lollipop," Cookie says when Eddie enters her room with two glasses of sherry and two pieces of opera cake. "Did she say anything interesting?"

PART TWO

ONE

They say that New York never sleeps, and tonight, neither does Eddie. He can't shake the vision from the Algonquin, can't make sense of how different it is from the fantasies he's created and controlled before, can't understand how it felt so detailed and physical and real. He's always been able to spark and grow and sculpt and buff and tweak his fantasies, then tuck them safely away when he's finished. But not this one. This one he can't contain. It churns through his chest, insistent and relentless and stubborn.

No, sleep is not in the cards for Eddie tonight. Lying there staring at the disco ball, both of them spinning, spinning, trying to make sense of what he saw, or thought he saw—it's unsettling, unbearable. He has to do something to stop the spin. So, he ties on his sneakers and slips out into the night.

Soon he is standing on the empty Cornelia Street sidewalk at four o'clock in the morning, a funny hour in New York. It's less sinister than, say, two thirty, because the earliest of the early morning workers have started to stir. The garbage trucks begin to roll, the delivery vans start to make rounds, the extra-eager go-getters start pulling on their workout clothes for a pre-office visit to the gym. And of course, the bakers have been at it for hours. Dawn is still an hour or more away, but the darkest part of the night has passed.

Theo is standing here, too. He's in the doorway of Patisserie Gaston, his rolling pin at his side. His face is smudged with flour, and his whole body—arms, shoulders, neck, everything—is tense with incomprehension and suspicion. Eddie wonders what he'd do with that rolling pin if Eddie were a threat—a burglar or some other kind of menace. He wonders if Theo would have whacked him. The way he grips the rolling pin suggests he's used it before.

"What are you doing here?" Theo asks in a voice that's half perplexed, half suspicious.

"Sorry," Eddie says, holding out his hands, palms up. "I couldn't sleep, and went out for a walk and then, I don't know. I just ended up here."

"And you pressed your face up against the window and scared the shit out of me at four o'clock in the morning," Theo says. He lowers the rolling pin.

Embarrassment sinks through Eddie. "I'm sorry. I'll go."

"No," Theo says. "I can't allow that. You'll just press your face up against the dry cleaner window at the end of the block, and then the bodega, and before you know it someone calls the cops and you're hauled off to the precinct, and the truth is, I don't make enough money to bail you out."

Eddie lowers his head and turns away.

"Hey, wait," Theo says, and his voice sounds like refuge. "I'm kidding. But why are you wandering around at this hour?"

It's a good question, and Eddie has a hundred answers. But he won't offer any of them. He won't explain to Theo that the reason he can't sleep is because he's been freaking out about a bizarre vision that he had at the Algonquin. He won't tell Theo that the panic didn't truly take hold until long after, when he turned out the lights and tried to close his eyes. He won't say that lying still became impossible. He won't acknowledge that wandering the streets in the dark, in a city he's only just coming to know, is probably reckless. He won't admit that he came to Cornelia Street like a magnet to steel, because despite everything else clogging his brain he hasn't stopped thinking about Theo, about his opera cakes, about his songbird tattoos. He won't mention any of that. He'll just say, "Restless, I guess."

"I get that sometimes, too," Theo says. "But why don't you come in? I just made a fresh pot of coffee."

Eddie offers another sheepish protest, "I shouldn't be bothering you," but Theo insists and soon Eddie is sitting on a stool in the corner of the patisserie's working kitchen, holding his paper cup of coffee in two hands like an actor in a coffee commercial and watching Theo roll, cut, and shape a batch of buttery dough into croissants. The aromas in the air—yeast, butter, baking bread—captivate Eddie, who's only ever smelled anything like it outside a Subway shop, or when reheating dinner rolls at Sunset Ridge. These scents are so much better than those, though. Fresh and warm and luxurious. He fills his lungs, over and over.

"Is it always like this in here?" he asks.

"Like what?"

"It just smells so good."

"Best thing about this job," Theo says. "Gaston tells me I'll tire of it one day, but that day hasn't come yet. The smell of things keeps me awake at this hour. That, and Gaston's list."

"His list?"

"He leaves a note for me every night, telling me what I need to make. Sixty of this and thirty of that and an extra two dozen of these. And croissants. Always croissants."

Theo rolls his wheel-cutter across a sheet of laminated dough to create little triangles, then carefully twists each one into a little crescent shape. He fills a tray with a dozen of these, covers the tray in plastic, then writes the time—*4:15 A.M.*—on a piece of blue tape that he affixes to the plastic. He slides the tray into the steel cabinet on the back wall.

"Proofing cabinet," Theo says. "It's exactly one hundred fifteen degrees in there. They'll rise to twice as big and be ready to bake in ninety minutes."

"We never had one of those at Sunset Ridge. All we ever did with bread was reheat it."

"Sunset Ridge?"

"I used to work in the kitchen at a retirement community. But just prep stuff. Chopping vegetables, finishing plates. Never baking, except chocolate chip cookies."

"Chocolate chip cookies count as baking."

"Yeah, but croissants are different. Yeast and all that."

"All it takes is trying."

Theo spreads another sheet of dough onto the counter and begins cutting and twisting again. Eddie is fascinated by his movements, so steady and deliberate, but so quick.

"You're fast."

"Gaston would kill me if I didn't have croissants done for opening. I'm not exaggerating. He'd actually chop me up into pieces. Little ones." He points at a wall of kitchen knives.

Eddie laughs. "How did you learn to make croissants?"

"From a book. It took about a week to get a feel for the process, but I didn't get good at it for a few months. Croissants are easy to learn, but hard to master. Most things are like that in baking. That's what they tell you in culinary school apparently."

"You didn't go?"

"No. I can't afford that. But I got a used textbook from one of the big schools, and I've studied it so hard I could recite it to you from page one. Honestly, I think that's why Gaston hired me. He hates culinary school. He thinks they coach the creativity out of you. He thinks culinary school teaches rules instead of ideas. But food is not like that, he says. Food is too personal for that. You should taste the soul of the baker who kneaded the bread, he says."

"Do you believe that?"

Theo stops for a moment and taps his rolling pin on the edge of the counter. "I'm not sure," he says. "Maybe. There is something different about something made by a machine and something made from scratch. I don't know if it's the soul of the baker, but it's something. Then again, the same person, the same soul, can make the same thing exactly the same way, over and over, a hundred times, and it won't ever come out exactly the same. Ninety-nine of them will be fine. But one will be different. One will be amazing. And you'll never know exactly why."

"Like photographs," Eddie says quietly.

Theo looks at him. "Huh?"

Eddie shakes his head. "Nothing." He nods at a stack of pastries on the far end of the counter. "What are those?"

"Pastry braids," Theo says. "You hungry?"

"No, but—"

"Cherry or almond?" Theo asks.

Eddie considers. This feels like a test. He doesn't want to fail, so instead of choosing, he asks, "Which do you think?"

Theo picks up one of each. He slides them onto a napkin in front of Eddie, then fills his cup with more coffee.

Eddie bites into the cherry one first, feeling the layers of pastry give under his teeth. The crust melts on his tongue in a rush of butter, followed by a bright, tangy-sweet burst of cherry. The flavor saturates his tongue, and he groans in appreciation.

"Try the almond," Theo says. "Almond is the best."

He's right. It's even better, with a flavor that reminds Eddie of warm caramel.

Eddie watches Theo's wrists as he fills another tray and slips it into the proofing cabinet. "It's so weird to be up when everyone else is asleep."

"Welcome to my world. Sometimes I lose track of what time it is. Like, during the day, when the sun's up, you can kind of tell by the light if it's ten in the morning or four in the afternoon, you know? But at night, you're never really sure. An hour can pass as quickly as a minute, and a minute can feel like eternity. Sometimes I'm like, what even is time? You know?"

"I guess," Eddie says, thinking back to the Algonquin, and how time seemed to fold back on itself in there.

Theo points his rolling pin at Eddie and cracks a half smile. "Wanna try?"

Eddie shakes his head. "That's okay. I'll just screw it up."

"Nah, I won't let you. Because—"

"Because Gaston will kill you and chop you up into little pieces."

"Wrong. He'll kill and chop us both. And we'd never have a chance. Just look at all the knives around this place. Now go wash your hands," Theo points at a sink in the corner. "And then come here."

Eddie gets up off the stool, washes and dries his hands, and stands at the counter. Theo drapes an apron over Eddie's neck, then carefully ties it behind him to secure it, his fingers grazing Eddie's lower back.

"Hold this," Theo says, handing Eddie the rolling pin. He tosses a handful of flour across the counter, then drops a ball of dough in the center. "Now," he says. "Roll this out flat, to about a quarter inch thick."

Eddie looks at Theo, then at the dough, unsure of how to start. "Just, press down?" he asks.

"Yes," Theo says. "Use two hands to keep it even. Put the pin in the middle of the dough and roll outward toward the edge."

Eddie follows Theo's direction, but the pin wobbles unsteadily as he rolls. He overcorrects and pushes too hard on one side, tearing the dough. "Sorry," he says.

Theo stands behind Eddie and reaches around with his much longer arms, placing one hand on each end of the rolling pin, just outside Eddie's grasp. "Gently. Don't hold it too tight. Let the pin roll freely between your fingers."

Eddie relaxes his grip, letting Theo drive. They roll out from the center of the dough in one direction, then the other. Theo turns the dough on the counter, and they roll again, coaxing it into a rectangle. Eddie feels the pin spin lightly against his palms and fingers as they go. Theo's pace increases, and with each spin of the dough little clouds of flour burst into the air like puffs of smoke, showering down onto Eddie's sneakers. Soon the dough is flat and even.

"Look at that," Theo says, his voice a vibration. "You did it." He pats the dough with his hands, songbirds grazing the tops of Eddie's forearms, sending electricity glinting across his skin.

Eddie feels Theo's breath across his neck, Theo's chest against his shoulder blades. He wants to lean back into Theo's body, to push his head back into his neck, to get closer. But he won't move, for fear of upsetting this exquisite balance. He won't do anything to break this moment (minute, hour, eternity).

Theo begins to hum. Not a tune, just a tone, creating a vibration in his chest that rolls into Eddie's back and through his body. Eddie exhales, relaxing his stance almost imperceptibly. Theo's muscles tense around him, strong and gentle and protective. He is so solid, Eddie thinks. So confident in his posture. Feet planted so firmly against Eddie's. Arms wrapped so stably around Eddie's chest. They are so close now. This is so real. Eddie closes his eyes. Time stops.

"Holy shit," Theo says, breaking the spell. "It's almost five. We're opening soon." He steps back and nudges Eddie out of the way, breaking the spell, and turns his attention, mental and physical, back to the dough. He cuts twelve new triangles, swiftly rolls them into identical croissant shapes, and slides them into the proofing cabinet. "Okay, done. They'll be ready to bake soon. Now I've gotta get these opera cakes put together. It never ends."

"Not ever?" Eddie says.

"Nope," Theo says. "Not ever."

It's Eddie's cue to go, and so he twists the magnet away from the steel and leaves.

TWO

Back at Cookie's, Eddie is in a defensive posture, leaning against a different kitchen counter, definitely not Theo's.

"This is your fault," Albert is saying, or more precisely, hissing, as he rubs another blob of antibacterial gel into his palms.

"I didn't do anything," Eddie says quietly.

"*I didn't do anything*," Albert mocks, aping Eddie's voice with an exaggerated whine. "If you weren't out there sucking up germs—and God knows what else—then Cookie wouldn't be sick. This could be pneumonia! Do you know what pneumonia means at her age? She could die, Eddie. It could kill her, and that would be on your head."

Eddie scours inside for the courage to talk back, to stand straight and vigorously defend himself. He doesn't find much.

"Well?" Albert demands.

Keeping his eyes on the floor, Eddie mumbles, "How do you know she didn't catch it from you?"

Albert gasps in disbelief, hand at his own throat as if grasping an invisible strand of pearls. He squares his shoulders and glares.

Eddie shrinks, preparing for more venom.

But it doesn't come. "Just wash your hands," Albert says, slumping away into the other room. "Wash everything. God knows where it's all been."

The doctor arrives a few minutes later. "I never, ever do house calls," she says. "Except for Cookie." She closes the door to Cookie's room behind her, leaving Albert and Eddie in the hallway. They stand in a thick, icy silence, each wishing the other would just dissolve away. They wait no more than ten minutes, but it feels like a thousand.

Eventually, the doctor opens the door and announces that Cookie's temperature is only slightly elevated, and that her lungs sound perfectly clear. She names the affliction: a common cold.

"It will pass soon," the doctor says. "She's as spry and feisty as ever."

"I heard that!" Cookie's voice is scratchy but clear. "Don't call me feisty."

"I rest my case," the doctor says, rolling her eyes.

Eddie and Albert exhale in unison, relieved. It's a fleeting moment of solidarity that dissipates quickly and leaves no warm residue.

The doctor prescribes aspirin, a twice-daily anti-pneumonia pill—a prophylaxis, just a precaution—and rest. "Keep the apartment warm. Keep her cup filled with tea. Soup for lunch and supper, fruit for breakfast. Ginger ale if her stomach gets upset. And no alcohol for six days at least."

"But she has a glass of sherry every day at four," Eddie says.

"No alcohol," the doctor repeats.

"But she's had sherry hour every day forever." Eddie grabs a sherry glass from the counter. "She doesn't have very much. Look how small the glasses are."

"No."

"She'll kill me."

The doctor squints at Eddie. "I think you could take her."

"But—"

The doctor sighs. "Half a glass, no more." She stuffs her stethoscope into her bag and zips up her track jacket. "I'll be back on Thursday."

Albert closes the door behind her, then turns to Eddie. "You're lucky," he says. He shoves a handful of get-well cards into Eddie's chest and sweeps out the door behind the doctor. Gone.

Gone, but not forgotten. Albert's darts found their mark and now Eddie is pacing the apartment with panic acid on his tongue. What if Albert is right? What if Eddie is the cause of Cookie's cold? What if he picked up a bug at the Algonquin, or on the subway, or at the patisserie? He weaves through the crowded furniture, sits down, stands up, opens the blinds, closes them again, straightens a pile of books, reorients the headless mannequin, turns it back again. Starts over. He should have asked the doctor if he was the culprit. He should have said something, had her examine him, too, had her take his blood or swab his nose or whatever you do to figure out if someone is an infectious killer. What if this really is his fault? What if Cookie gets really sick? What if—? She'll be fine, she'll be fine, she'll be fine. And if she isn't? Unthinkable.

Let's stop on that absurd word: *unthinkable*. No one who ever says it really means it. An unthinkable disaster. An unthinkable situation. They actually mean the opposite of unthinkable, because they're already thinking it. What you're thinking is not unthinkable, Eddie. She's almost a hundred years old. No matter how spry or feisty. But stop thinking it anyway.

He straightens a picture on the wall that's gone atilt. He steps back, inspects, and straightens it again. Feels good. And then another picture, and another, and—

The peal from Cookie's flamingo bell shocks him out of his spiral. It's lunchtime.

"How are you feeling?" he asks when he brings a tray with

chicken and rice soup and a few crunchy carrot sticks. The soup is from Albert. He says he made it a week ago and had it in his freezer, but Eddie has his doubts. He thinks it's from a can.

"I'm fine," she says, slurping a bit of soup off her spoon. "But this lunch is terrible. Why can't I have something that tastes like something? A pastrami sandwich maybe?"

"I'll fix it," he says, and takes her bowl back into the kitchen. He cuts open a lime and spritzes juice over the soup—a trick he learned back at Sunset Ridge—then crumbles a few tortilla chips over the top and hits it with a little dash of Tabasco before bringing it back in. "Try it now."

She groans doubtfully and takes a reluctant spoonful, but when the soup hits her tongue her face brightens. She tilts her head, focused now, and has another bite. "Oh, this is much better. This has personality now. Why don't you have some?"

He makes himself a bowl, and they eat together in silence. When she finishes, she sneezes, twice, shaking the bed, then lies back onto her stack of pillows with a contented expression on her face. "Thank you."

"What should we do this afternoon?" he asks, clearing away her tray. "We could open some more get-well cards, or we could watch a movie, or listen to music, or—"

"Don't tell me you're planning to hang around here with a sick old lady," she says. "The sun is shining. And you're young. Go be free. Sit by the river. Take a picnic to the park. Find someone to kiss!"

Eddie scrunches his forehead. A vision of Theo speeds through his head. He shakes his head and looks away, straining to keep his face as blank as he can. "I want to be with you."

"Well, then," Cookie sighs. "How about a cup of tea?"

"I'll fix you one," Eddie says. "There's plenty in the kitchen."

"No. Not the tea in there. I need the fennel tea from Citarella up on Sixth Avenue."

"But that's so far. I don't want to be gone that long. What about at the deli around the cor—"

"Honestly, Lollipop. You are acting like I'm on death's door, which I am not. I said I need fennel tea from Citarella. Capital-C-i-t-a—"

"All right!" he says, putting his hands up in surrender. "You don't have to spell it! I'm going!"

"Sixth Avenue and Tenth," Cookie says. "Right across from the Jefferson Market Courthouse."

"Jefferson Market Courthouse," he repeats, pretending that he knows what she means.

She taps the record player with her back scratcher. "'Ev'ry Time We Say Goodbye,' please."

Eddie drops the needle, and Ella Fitzgerald starts to sing. Cookie sings along. "*Ev'ry time we say goodbye / I die a little . . .*" She really leans in on the word *die*, winking at him. Eddie scowls.

"Just a little joke," she says, and he can't help a small smile.

She taps her cheek with a lazy finger, and he kisses it. Her eyes droop as she presses the kiss into her skin.

"Off you go," she says.

"I'll be back soon," he says. He grabs the camera and slips out the door. He'll get the tea, snap a photo, and be back very soon, before she wakes up.

THREE

Citarella is temporarily closed. Not for long, according to the store manager out front who's telling the crowd of frustrated shoppers, just temporarily. It will reopen just as soon as the fire department leaves. Someone set off the alarm, he says, but there's no fire. No danger. He says it emphatically, a little too much so for some customers, who peel off and reroute to another grocery store up the street. To the prospective customers who remain, including Eddie, who is taking Cookie's strict instructions seriously, the manager hands out complimentary cans of flavored seltzer. Watermelon, peach-raspberry, and lemon. Eddie, who hadn't realized he was thirsty until he saw the beads of condensation clinging to the outsides of the cans, chooses lemon.

While he waits, he crosses the street to investigate a striking old building he sees there, a striped brick thing with a soaring circular clock tower and elaborate windows all around. He's walked past it once or twice already, but never took a closer look. No time like now.

It seems old, like it's from a different time, one of those buildings in New York that stands out not for its shiny steel or gargantuan size, but for its anachronism. It reminds Eddie of a fairy-tale castle, a folly designed and built in isolation before a neighborhood sprung up around it. If it were set on a foggy hillside or on a cliff overlooking the sea, it would surely be inhabited by a brooding monster or a hapless prince or a family of quirky, comic witches. Eddie can picture them cackling over a cauldron of newts' eyes and bat wings.

The sign on the front door reads: JEFFERSON MARKET LIBRARY.

But Cookie said Jefferson Market Courthouse, not Library. What gives?

He scans the stonework. A faded etching reads: THIRD JUDICIAL DISTRICT COURT-HOUSE.

A market? A library? A courthouse? Eddie wonders what the story is. Maybe Cookie knows. He'll take a photo and ask her about it later.

He stands next to the building and aims the camera straight up, framing the spire against the blue sky. The image won't show all the things he knows Cookie will want to see—people on the sidewalk and all that—but it's such a beautiful sky today, endless and open, like the sky in Mesa Springs. He almost, but not quite, misses home for a second, then snaps the photo and gathers the little plastic card when it emerges. Before it develops, he turns and points the camera back to street level, aiming it across to Citarella for another picture. Cookie would enjoy seeing the commotion over there.

Except . . . looking through the viewfinder, he sees that the people and firetrucks gathered outside the store are gone. The store itself is gone. In fact, he can't even see the building across the street where Citarella should be, because there's an elevated train track in the way, massive iron legs holding up a viaduct with a train rolling past. The street itself is dirt, not paved, and it is crowded with cars, mostly old-fashioned and boxy, with dull black finishes and slender-spoked wheels. They send puffs of black smoke into the air as they chug along. Two or three much shinier sedans swerve through, sleek and long and languid in their cruising. He also sees a horse pulling a buggy with the words *Windy's Seltzer* stenciled onto the side, and underneath, *Try it with Fox's Syrup!* A man with a drooping handlebar mustache and the reins draped across his lap sits on a bench atop the buggy. He scowls at Eddie as he and his horse pass.

It's a vibrant vision, and Eddie would linger in it if he could, but he's eager to get the photo of Citarella for Cookie. He lowers the camera and rubs his eyes to clear it.

But when he opens them, the seltzer buggy is still there, plodding along in the shadow of the elevated train, through the black cars, the sedans, and the dust. To his left, a man in a bowler hat, his hands tucked into the pockets of his nubby woolen jacket, walks slowly with a woman whose hair tumbles across a faded gray damask dress just skirting the dirt.

To his right, three girls in pale blue dresses with nautical flap collars and mud-spattered stockings skip in a circle, chanting *Spanish dancer, turn around! Spanish dancer, touch the ground!* A fourth child, younger than the rest, darts around and through them, laughing as she goes. As she dives between two of the girls, one of them snatches her blue sailor's cap and tosses it into the air. It catches a breeze and lands at Eddie's feet.

Eddie reaches down to pick it up and notices his own feet. They aren't laced into sneakers anymore. He's wearing dusty, worn, black boots with leather straps, boots that look like they've walked forever to get to where he's standing now.

The little girl races over, giggling. She smiles up at him, unafraid and self-assured. "Try it on!" she shouts, but before Eddie can obey, she reaches out and snatches the cap out of his hand. "Mine!" she shouts, still laughing. She turns and runs back to the others, who begin their dance again. *Spanish dancer, turn around!*

Eddie looks back at the mysterious boots. Where did they come from? He wiggles his toes and feels stiff leather against them. He takes a step and the boots move with him. They fit perfectly. They are *his* scuffed black boots. And these are *his* woolen trousers, and *his* white shirt and black work jacket. And, he realizes when he reaches up, this is *his* nubby, frayed newsboy cap. Everything feels like it belongs on him. What is happening?

A shout arises from behind him. "She's coming out!"

Eddie spins to see a crowd of young men dressed in old-fashioned clothes like his, only much cleaner—their trousers much less dusty and wrinkled, their shoes much less scuffed—gathered around the steps at the entrance to the Jefferson Market building. They are buzzing, talking over one another, pushing against one another, flipping their floppy hairstyles and trying to get closer to the door, which is no longer glass, but wooden. A burly man in an old police uniform stands in front of it with his arms crossed, blocking the entrance.

"Back up!" the cop booms. "Clear the way!" The crowd ignores him, pushing even closer.

After a moment, a thud signals the unlatching of the door, and the crowd goes silent. The door starts to swing open, slowly, slowly. Every boy in the crowd cranes his neck in anticipation, Eddie, too. The burly policeman steps aside as the door opens fully and a small, bleach-blond woman in a giant fur coat steps out, flanked by two more uniformed guards, one on each arm, epaulets on their shoulders and thick belts around their waists. They wear smug expressions, as if proud to be escorting her, but they scowl as the crowd erupts into cheers. "Miss West! Miss West! We love you!"

The woman beams unabashedly in response. She strikes a seductive pose in the doorway, and then another, winking and smiling to the crowd as she steps, drawing in their energy, sending it back tenfold. Eddie is entranced. She is like a magnet, drawing his eyes and holding them tight. It's as if this is a stage, and a spotlight far above the scene is fixed on her. She knows everyone is staring at her as she vamps—the definition of conspicuous—and revels in it. How confident she must be! How self-assured! She is extraordinary, a star!

"My beautiful boys!" she says, her voice barely detectable amid the whoops and shouts. "My pansies!" She raises her arms over her head and throws her hips to one side, then the other, a kind of dance. Everyone follows the movement, throwing up their own hands and hip-switching with her. She laughs, blows a kiss, and starts stepping down the stairs, clutching the guards seductively.

"This is a travesty!" one young man yells, holding up a newspaper with the headline, *Mae West Arrest! Police Close Show.*

"Anti-American!" another shouts, holding up the headline *Mae West Defies Cops! Indecency Is Charged!*

Soon everyone in the crowd is shouting. "Injustice! Injustice! Free Mae! Free Mae!"

"Where are they taking her?" one boy shouts.

"Welfare Island!" another answers. "They'll force her to wear a muslin slip!"

"No, they won't!" says another. "She'll bring her own unmentionables! Silk and satin!"

"Boys, boys," she says, smirking and vamping as she reaches the bottom of the stairs. "Make way, my lovely garden laddies."

"And ladies!" one boy shouts.

"And ladies," she echoes, winking.

"Stand back!" Her police escorts push the boys aside as the woman shimmies into the scrum. She doesn't rush, soaking in the adoration, even as the cops swat their hands away.

A man who doesn't appear to belong to the core gaggle of boys approaches the woman. He takes a pencil out from behind his ear and taps it on the pad of paper in his hand, ready to write. "I'm a reporter with the *Morning Telegraph*. Do you think this sentence will end your career?"

She pauses, and the crowd goes silent waiting for her answer. She taps her finger to her chin as if she's thinking, then turns flirtatiously to the reporter and says with a lazy wave of her hand, "I expect this will be the making of me."

The crowd erupts in laughter and cheers.

"Goodness, what a beautiful coat!" one boy shouts as she follows the guards through the crowd.

"Goodness?" she says, taking the boy's chin in her hand. "Goodness had nothing to do with it."

The boys cheer again. Eddie cheers, too.

She swings her hips and shoulders in exaggerated circles as she walks, playing to the crowd. Whistles and whoops fill the air as she and her uniformed escorts, who, despite their practiced scowls, appear to enjoy basking in her glow just as much as everyone else, approach a police wagon at the curb.

When she reaches the wagon, she turns to the crowd and raises an arm to wave.

The boys cheer. "We'll wait for you!" they shout, and, "Forever!"

One of her guards opens the door to the wagon. She taps his cheek, like a lover saying good night, and slips inside. The wagon pulls off and away, the crowd of young men chasing after it as it goes, kicking up dust from the unpaved street.

Eddie stands and watches it go, as entranced by her words—*Goodness had nothing to do with it*—as by her presence. Who is she?

The dust clears, and the crowd disperses, and there's only one young man left from the crowd. He's dressed in gray and standing calmly on the curb, looking straight at Eddie and smiling warmly. It's the boy again, and this time Eddie isn't surprised but fascinated, not only by the boy's beauty, but by his familiarity. Almost as if they know each other. Do they know each other?

The spiral of anxiety spins again through Eddie's stomach. Easy, he tells himself. The boy is not real. None of this is real, right? Just another vision. So why can he smell the exhaust from the police wagon? Why is the dust in the air stinging his eyes? Why can't he blink this away? The boy begins walking toward Eddie.

Eddie feels for the Polaroid at his side. He raises and aims it at the boy, who stops short. He squints at Eddie, as if he's trying to figure out what Eddie is doing, what he's holding up.

And then, a flash of recognition. The boy appears to understand. He brushes his hair off his forehead and smiles. A broad, deep-rooted smile that eclipses everything else in sight. It is an extraordinary smile, infectious, and Eddie feels one start to surface on his own face.

Eddie snaps. The camera begins its whirring and spits out a plastic card. Eddie holds it carefully in both hands. The crowd disperses around him, some chasing the police wagon, others breaking off into pairs, arm in arm. The sole cop left at the courthouse door lights a cigarette, looks around, and steps back inside. A train approaches on the elevated track, its rumbling growing louder. Eddie looks back at the picture. It should have developed by now, but all that's emerged is a black square. Nothing. No picture at all. Eddie shakes it. Nothing. He shakes it again. Nothing.

"Hello! Hey!"

It's the boy, shouting over the din of the train, and he's walking toward Eddie again.

But before Eddie can answer, a siren wails from across the street, sharp and abrupt, like a needle piercing the scene. The sound shocks him, searing his ears. He flinches, stumbling backward and nearly losing his balance. He catches himself on a lamppost, then looks over to see if the boy heard it, too.

But the boy is gone.

FOUR

Eddie spins this way, that way, eyes frantic, searching for the boy. He takes a dozen steps uptown, then turns back downtown. But there's no sign of him at all. No sign of anything that he's just seen. Everyone who was here a moment ago—the crowd of boys, the glamorous woman, the scrum of reporters, the elevated train, the police wagon, Eddie's scuffed black boots and frayed cap—all gone. Only the Jefferson Market building remains, surrounded by the same Sixth Avenue that was here before the vision, filled with taxicabs and zigzagging cyclists and harried modern-day pedestrians in maxi skirts and high-tops and ironic T-shirts, tapping on phones and sucking on vape pens. He hears a rap song from a car stereo, watches a delivery driver munch a handful of french fries, sees a flashing Don't Walk signal reflected in a pool of motor oil in the asphalt.

He closes his eyes to try to reconjure the vision, to return to the fantasy. It should be easy enough. He's been woken from dreams before—called on in class, summoned by his boss at Sunset Ridge—but he's always been able to get back when he's wanted to. This time is different, though. This time it doesn't work. He strains, focusing his mind, willing the vision, his vision, to return. But it doesn't. It won't. It stands at a distance, separate from him, unreachable. He concentrates harder. Still nothing.

His stomach churns, a mash of confusion and anxiety. He can't do the one thing he's always been able to do, to find his way back inside, to return to the fantasy world. Where is his power? Where is his imagination? Why isn't it working the way it's supposed to?

Unmoored, he shuffles slowly over to the curb. Uptown, he sees the towers of Midtown, all shiny glass and steel. Downtown, the soaring Freedom Tower, jabbing the sky with its spire. Everything looks so crisp in the sun, so sharp and defined. So real. The vision, the moment, is over. Nothing left but the tower of the Jefferson Market Courthouse. Or, Library. Whatever it is.

He exhales, feeling a stealthy exhaustion creep up from his sneakers. How is he suddenly so tired? He slumps down to the edge of the curb and sits, hanging his head between his knees.

Sit here for a minute, Eddie, to return to yourself. Just for a minute. That's all it will take. A minute, no more.

FIVE

How long is a minute? Just sixty seconds? Why do some minutes feel so much longer? Why do some feel so much shorter? A minute, is it mutable? The way it bends, twists, folds over on itself. Is it a minute or is it an hour? Is it a day, a week, a lifetime? Forward is backward and now is later and present is past and the boy is real and the boy is not real and it doesn't really matter, does it? It's all the same. All you need is to sit here on the edge of this curb, with your sneakers in the gutter and your head between your knees, just for a minute, and everything will fall back into place. There's nothing to fear here, not in this minute. Nothing to worry about. Nothing to long for, nothing to miss. He'll be back, or he won't. It makes no difference. You just need a minute (a day, a week, a lifetime) and everything will make sense again. That's all you need, Eddie. Just a minute. That's all.

SIX

Look up, Eddie. Someone's talking to you.

"Are you okay?"

Eddie, still struggling to reroot himself, hears a voice above him. He squints up to a figure standing in front of him with an outstretched arm, motionless against the city streaming along behind him. He is only a silhouette, backlit by the searing sun, his face in shadow, a hazy halo glow around the edges. Where did he come from? Eddie squints. Does he know you? The figure dips his head to one side, and the sun slices into Eddie's eyes. He squeezes them shut, a protective instinct.

"I'm fine," Eddie mumbles. He waves his hand through the air, as if to shoo the intruder.

"Let me help you up."

Eddie shakes his head. "I said I'm fine," he says, or tries to say, but he can barely hear his own voice.

The shadow takes a step back. "Are you on something?"

"No."

"Come on," the figure says, insisting now. "Grab my hand."

Eddie looks back up, reluctantly, and that's when he sees it, right there on the inside of the outstretched arm. A songbird.

Theo.

Eddie searches for a feeling of relief. This should feel like good luck, to have a friendly hand held out to help him. He should smile sheepishly, take the hand, say thank you. But instead, Eddie hides his face and wishes he would dissolve into nothing.

"How long have you been sitting here, Eddie?" Theo asks, using his name, which only makes this worse.

"How . . . long?" Eddie chokes out, not sure what the answer is. A minute (a day, a week, a lifetime). "I was just, um, I was just fixing my camera." He holds the Polaroid up to Theo, as if it proves something.

"Uh-huh." Theo sounds skeptical. Incredulous. He takes the camera, strings it over his shoulder, and holds out his hand again.

Eddie ignores Theo's hand again and grasps the curb to push himself up. He manages, without falling, because Theo's other hand is steadying his back.

"I've got you," Theo says. Gentle words. When Eddie's back on his feet, Theo takes Eddie's face in his hands. He searches Eddie's eyes, probably to see if they're dilated, or bloodshot. But don't worry, Eddie. They're clear. Confused, maybe, but clear.

Eddie closes them anyway. Oh, what he would give to slide back into the fantasy, back into his dusty work jacket and scuffed black boots. Back into the shadow of the Jefferson County Courthouse. Back beside the elevated train. Back to that other world. *Spanish dancer, turn around! Spanish dancer, touch the ground.*

Theo is talking. "You said you're staying with Cookie, right? On Bedford Street?"

Eddie nods. "Yes," he musters. "But I'm fine." His voice wobbles.

"Why don't I walk you there."

"I don't need—" Eddie starts. "I'm not lost. I know where to go."

Theo doesn't pay attention. He looks down Sixth Avenue. "Come on," he says, hiking Cookie's camera over his shoulder. He begins to walk.

And Eddie, like a child, follows.

~

"You have a key?" Theo says at the front door of Cookie's apartment building. It's the first thing either of them have said since they left the curb.

"Yes," Eddie says, reaching into his pocket.

Theo turns to face the street, away from Eddie. "I don't know what's going on right now," he says, and it almost sounds like he's talking to himself. "Here's a boy who comes into the bakery after closing time. And he's cute, with this kind of mysterious, awkward smile, and it makes me want to open the door for him. He's there to buy opera cakes for the famous Cookie, who everyone knows is the coolest person in the Village, and that makes me think he must be something special, too, because whatever Cookie's got must rub off on a person. And he flirts with me a little, at least I think he does, and I'm watching the door every day wondering when he'll come back, and then he does come back, and I learn his name, and that name is Eddie, and I want to know even more about Eddie, but then, just like that, he's gone again. And then, last night, he shows up out of the blue, looking a little bit lost, but he comes in, and has coffee, and talks, and we make croissants together, and it feels like something, like I'm getting to know someone. And now, today. This. He's on the curb, alone, confused, mussed, looking as strung out as anyone I've ever seen. I don't know what to think."

The words shame Eddie, and he chokes on his own breath. He can't even look at Theo. He can only look down. "I'm not strung out."

"If you say so," Theo says. He hands the camera back to Eddie. He also holds out a white paper bag with twisted-paper handles. Eddie hadn't noticed him carrying it until now.

"What's that?"

"Just take it," Theo says, pushing the bag into Eddie's chest. "For Cookie."

Eddie takes the bag, obediently, and Theo turns away, back toward Sixth Avenue.

Where is he going? To the subway? Uptown, downtown? Eddie doesn't know. In a split second he imagines Theo's life, imagines him riding the subway to a street at a different end of the city. He imagines him climbing stairs, up to a little studio apartment, not much more than a bed and a chest of drawers, a little kitchenette in the corner, a window with bars across it that looks out over a church. A lamp, a stack of books. He imagines Theo sitting on the edge of the bed and taking off his shoes, then lying back, tucking the songbird tattoos behind his neck, cradling his head in his hands to watch the sky through the window until he falls asleep.

Eddie should shout after him, shouldn't he? He should run to him, catch up, say something, acknowledge Theo's kindness, try to explain what happened today, apologize for something, say thanks for the cakes. Say *goodbye, Theo* or *see you around*, but words feel a thousand miles away from his tongue right now. There's no way to explain what's happened, and besides, Theo is already rounding the corner at the end of the block. Gone.

Only then, on the empty street, does Eddie find his voice.

"Thank you," he says, to no one. The words boomerang back, an echo that mocks his sudden, gutting loneliness.

SEVEN

Back upstairs, Eddie realizes he has no fennel tea for Cookie. What's worse, he's got to figure out a way to tell her that she's only getting a half glass of sherry today, like the doctor ordered.

He looks for a smaller glass and finds one, but she'll notice. He considers watering the sherry down, but she'll notice. He considers dropping a big ice cube into her glass along with the drink and saying that's how Dorothy Parker took hers when he "saw" her at the Algonquin. But she'll notice. He has no choice but honesty. He won't disobey the doctor, so a half glass is all she'll get, and that's that. He pours two half glasses.

Cookie taps her glass with a lacquered nail. "Why so stingy?"

Eddie shrugs, hoping she'll read in the gesture that he's doing the best he can.

"That damn doctor," she says, her voice thick with disappointment.

Eddie kisses Cookie on the cheek, hoping the gesture will soften her, and it does.

"You're forgiven this time. But you could have least brought opera cakes."

Opera cakes. The words bring Theo to mind and Eddie closes his eyes. Theo's disappointed expression out on Sixth Avenue. Theo's soliloquy to no one down on Bedford Street. Theo's kindness, consistency, strength. Shame sweeps through Eddie. He'll never be able to face Theo again. He's going to have to find some way to keep her supplied with opera cakes from Patisserie Gaston, without going himself. He can't find another bakery. Maybe Theo has a day or two off each week, Eddie thinks. He could stake out the shop to figure out which days those are. He pictures himself hiding behind a car, watching, waiting to see who unlocks the door at two o'clock in the morning.

Swat. It's Cookie's back scratcher smacking him on the shoulder. She smacks him again, then waves it in the direction of her dresser.

"I said," she says, her voice rising. "You could have at least brought—"

He sees the white bag with the twisted-paper handles on the dresser. "Opera cakes!" he yelps. He jumps up and into the kitchen for plates and forks.

After they sip their sherry and finish their cakes, he hands her the picture he took before his strange vision, the shot of the Jefferson Market Library spire set against the blue sky.

"Oh, the old courthouse," she says brightly. "And the women's house of detention. That's where they held Mae West after her arrest."

"Who?" Eddie asks.

"Mae West. She was such a big star when I was a child. The most famous woman in the world. An actress, a playwright, a movie star, a rebel. They arrested her for obscenity. Or, come to think of it, they officially called it something like public nuisance. All because she wrote a play with homosexuals and hedonists and other so-called deviants. It was too popular, I guess, standing room only, and that's why they had to arrest her. The cops wouldn't have cared if it wasn't a hit. It was such a scandal. I was just a kid but I remember.

She loved it, gave interviews to all the papers. It made her even more popular."

She points at a stack of books on her nightstand. "That's her book. The one on the bottom."

Eddie studies the book cover. There's no title on the front, just a photograph of a glamorous bleach-blond woman reclining luxuriously in a lavishly decorated bedroom, admiring her face in a hand mirror just like Cookie does.

"She had the best one-liners. Like, 'It's not the men in your life that counts, it's the life in your men!' And 'When I'm good, I'm very good. But when I'm bad, I'm better.'" Cookie laughs and taps the book with her back scratcher. "Go ahead, read!"

"Aloud?"

"How the hell am I supposed to hear you if you read silently? And don't start at the beginning. Never start a book at the beginning. Pick a page in the middle."

Eddie opens the book at random, about halfway through, clears his throat, and begins reading: "'The homosexuals I had met were usually boys from the chorus of some of the shows I'd been in. I looked upon them as amusing and having a great sense of humor. They were the first ones to imitate me in my presence.'" He feels his face get hot. He closes the book.

"Cat got your tongue?" Cookie asks.

"No, it's just," Eddie starts, then stops. "I don't feel like reading."

"The fairies and pansies loved her," Cookie says, looking at herself in her hand mirror. "She always put them in her plays and the crowds loved them. They were the toast of the town!"

Fairies? Pansies? Eddie stiffens at the words. They sound like slurs.

"Oh, Lollipop," she says, reading his expression. "I know we don't use those words anymore. They were typical at the time, but no more. Words are always changing. Fairies, pansies, queers, inverts, gays. I'm always hearing a new one. It's not easy for an old lady like me, but I try to keep up. Anyway, the authorities couldn't stand Mae West. But they're always so shortsighted, authorities. Don't you think?"

Eddie looks again at the photograph of the woman on the cover of the book. "Why isn't there any title on this book?" he asks.

"Flip it over," she says, and he does. There, on the back of the book, in bright pink letters, is the title: *Goodness Had Nothing to Do with It.*

He stares, unbelieving. That's exactly what the woman said in his vision. Exactly. Word for word. It's happened again. He waits for the familiar fluid to rise in his throat, the panic, but it doesn't come. Somehow, he's not surprised.

"I'll go wash the dishes," he says.

"Forget the dishes," Cookie says. "Let's listen to some music."

Soon he's sitting at the foot of her bed, fiddling with the Polaroid camera as she swings her back scratcher in the air to keep time with the old blues song playing on her turntable. Eddie is fascinated by the music. Even though the recording is old and scratchy, the instruments and beat are lively and quick, and the singer's voice is like something he's never heard. It sounds far away, scratchy and obscured because the recording is so old, but the tone is so rich and precise and brassy and full. *Red beans and rice*, she sings. *Greasy bacon in the pot.*

"Who is that singer?" Eddie asks.

"That's Gladys Bentley," Cookie says, pointing at a photograph on the wall of a tall black woman in a men's suit—white tails and top hat—posing with her shoulders squared and her head tilted back, smiling confidently. "She was something else. She packed 'em in at the speakeasies. Oh, I wish I'd seen her sing back then. You know, she used to change the lyrics of the songs she sang, depending on where she was performing."

"Why?"

Cookie leans forward. "Because sometimes, she wanted to sing about women, not men. So she changed 'he' to 'she' in her love songs."

"You mean she—"

"Draw your own conclusions," Cookie says. "All I know is that people went wild for it. She was famous for flirting with women in the audience. The newspapers said she even got married to a woman in New Jersey, but I don't see how that could be true. Two women can't get married to each other."

"Yes, they can," Eddie says.

"Oh, that's right," Cookie says, straightening the marabou collar on her polka-dot dressing gown as the music begins to fade. "Two women can get married now, can't they? Or two men. It still seems incredible to an old lady like me. Incredible and beautiful. Flip that record, will you?"

Eddie turns over the record, and the music begins again.

"Now," Cookie says. "How about another errand? In the closet, you'll find a stack of shoeboxes. The second-to-bottom box contains a pair of shoes. Blue ones, with a strap across the front. Fetch them for me."

Eddie stands up and enters Cookie's closet, so overstuffed with a million shades of fabric that it's hard to push through to the stack of shoeboxes. "Is there a light in here?" he shouts.

"Good one," she says. "You think I'm a Rockefeller? Second-to-bottom box. Got 'em?"

"I think so," he says, backing out of the closet and placing the box on her lap. She opens it to reveal a pair of pale blue, stack-heeled

Mary Janes with gold clasps on the buckles and shiny lavender tips. She claps her hands together delightedly.

"Ah, my lovelies. I haven't seen you in years. But you are the perfect shade to wear with my turquoise and gold caftan, which I intend to put on as soon as I get out of this bed, but you need new soles." She turns to Eddie. "I need you to take them to the shoe repair on MacDougal Street. I need them to be ready for me when I am."

"There's a shoe repair shop right around the corner, you know. A lot closer than MacDougal."

"How interesting," Cookie says. "But these shoes need to go to Hangout Shoe Repair over on MacDougal. Got it? Flowers from Val's, shoe repair at Hangout, opera cake from Gaston. That's how it's always been, that's how it will always be."

"I'll do it tomorrow," he says, sinking lower in the chair. He's more tired than he realized.

"Wrong," she says. "You'll do it today."

"But it's already six thirty and—" he begins, but he can see in her face that she's not listening. It doesn't matter if he's still shaken from today. It doesn't matter if the sherry's made him a little drowsy. It doesn't matter that even if he takes the shoes tonight, there's no way anyone will get to them before tomorrow. None of it matters. When Cookie makes up her mind, her mind is made. Eddie has no choice.

"You better hurry if you want to make it there before they close at seven. Oh, and pick up some pizza on your way home, would you? A few slices from Joe's on Carmine Street. It's on the way home from MacDougal. Here's another twenty. Off you go."

"Carmine," Eddie repeats. "MacDougal. I'll go now."

"Wait!" Cookie says, and that's all she needs to say. Eddie leans down to kiss her.

EIGHT

Eddie is standing on MacDougal Street, in a now-familiar posture to him (and us). He's got his feet spaced a couple of feet apart for stability, the camera strap around his neck instead of his shoulder, and the camera itself held up to his face. His expression is strained, squinty as he centers the doorway of Hangout Shoe Repair in the viewfinder and waits for something to happen.

It's an uninteresting little storefront, wedged between a Japanese restaurant and a candy shop, but when two club kids in acid-green bodysuits enter the frame, the image comes alive. They notice him and stick out their tongues just as he snaps the photo. Cookie will love that. The club kids laugh and stroll on. Eddie slips the little plastic card into his pocket and steps into the shop.

It's a tiny space filled with shoes in various states of repair. Eddie counts seven levels of shelves lining every wall. The bottom shelves are filled with boots, then wingtips, then loafers, then stilettos, then pumps, then slippers, then sandals. A glass counter sits near the back, its case filled with shoelaces, shoe polishes, brushes, buckles, and rubber shoe covers for sale. Behind it, Eddie can see a small recess with two workbenches covered in tools, sheets of leather, eyelet fixtures, and rags.

A balding man with a wild comb-over stands at one of the

workbenches, the only other person in here, as far as Eddie can tell. He's wearing a leather apron and banging a hammer against the sole of a brown suede oxford. He doesn't notice Eddie, so after a moment, Eddie taps the counter bell.

"Gimme a minute," the man mumbles, the nail held in his teeth bobbing up and down as he speaks. He takes it out and bangs it into the shoe, then inspects his work. Satisfied, he turns to Eddie. "Whaddya got?"

"Just these," Eddie says, holding out the blue shoes. "They need new soles."

The man takes the shoes and turns them over. He scrutinizes the scuffs, the soles, the heels, then turns them right side up again. His forehead crinkles as he runs his fingers over the seams. "I know these shoes," he says. "These are Cookie's shoes. How did you get them?"

Eddie draws back, shocked by the question. This man must see a thousand shoes a week, but he knows these? "I, um—"

"Answer?"

"She's my great-aunt," Eddie says. "How did you know they were hers?"

"I know my customers," the man says in a dull monotone. He takes out a claim check card and starts filling it out. "They'll be ready in a few days."

"A few days," Eddie repeats.

"Say hello to Cookie from me, wouldja?" the man says, tearing off half the claim ticket and handing it to Eddie. "I'm Paulie."

"I will. How long have you known her?"

Paulie scowls. "Longer than you have," he says. "My great-grandfather opened this place in 1927, after the nightclub closed down. Eve's Hangout. Pop kept the name. Well, part of it. It's been mine since 1986."

"Eve? Who's that?"

Paulie waves away the question. "Look, kid, I'm busy," he says. "Thursday." He disappears into the back, his comb-over bouncing against his skull as he walks.

Eddie looks around. There must be a thousand pairs of shoes in here, some shiny and new-looking, others rough and worn. Some look contemporary, like they've only been bought this year. Others look ancient, like they've been forgotten in the shop and Paulie never called to follow up. He imagines a story for a pair of two-tone vinyl bucks, how they'd belonged to a rockabilly wannabe in the 1980s who never made it. He pictures the owner of the knee-high black boots with the pirate buckle, and how she had a night job taking tickets on Broadway. He wonders about the twin pairs of yellow fleece baby booties, and why they look like they've never been worn.

So much life in this shop. Maybe he'll take a picture in here. It's not the kind of thing Cookie usually asks for, but maybe she'll like it. He stands just next to the entrance, to fit as much of the shop as he can into the frame, and snaps. The camera clicks and whirs, and soon he's holding another plastic card, watching for the image to emerge. But the card stays blank. Must be a dud, he thinks. He raises the camera to try again.

But when Eddie looks through the viewfinder, the shoes are gone. The counter, the workbenches, the footwear accessories, all gone. This isn't an empty shoe shop at all. This is a nightclub, and the door behind him is straining as people push through and into the room, crushing their way in. They seem to enter all at once, just as a loud, jazzy song starts to play. Suddenly, everyone is dancing. Fast, frenetic steps.

Eddie is jostled from all sides by the raucous crowd. They poke and pinch him as they swirl past, mouths wide with laughter as a vocalist warbles a lively song. "*I don't want no man that I got to give my money to,*" she sings. Eddie listens to the voice, rich and syrupy with a distinct growl, almost like the one he'd just heard at Cookie's.

It's happening again but Eddie doesn't feel panic this time. Urgency, sure, and some disorientation. But not panic. Just curiosity. Energy. He squeezes through the dancers to the side of the room and steps up onto an overturned soap box. His head above the crowd now, he takes a deep breath, drawing in the sweaty, humid air. There must be a hundred people in this tiny space, all moving in time, and not one of them is a man. Sure, some are dressed like men, in dark pinstripe suits and slicked-back hair, while others are in gold and violet dresses adorned with fringe. But they are all women, as far as he can tell. They dance in couples, cheek to cheek, laughing and twirling and kicking and singing along. He looks down at his own clothes. He's in pinstripes, too. No jeans, no sneakers.

Eddie cranes to see the singer. She's wearing white tails and a top hat, commanding the room from a small platform where she's surrounded by three musicians on piano, clarinet, and standing bass. Her white tails sway behind her as she smiles and sings in her growly voice.

As the song reaches its crescendo, the crowd cheers with delight, and after her final note the singer looks straight at Eddie. He recognizes her perfectly now. It's Gladys Bentley.

"'Red beans and rice'!" someone shouts, and everyone cheers again.

Just then someone shouts, "Cops!" and Eddie spins to see four policemen at the front door, holding up police batons and shouting, "This is a raid! You're all in violation of the New York City cabaret statute!" Screams of protest and fear fill the air as everyone starts pushing in opposite directions, some toward the cops, some away from the cops, some just in panicked circles. Eddie can see they are trapped. There's nowhere for anyone to go. The lights flicker off, leaving the chaos in total darkness.

Eddie feels a hand on his elbow, tugging at him, pulling him through the crowd. Eddie trips behind as he's yanked through the curtain behind the stage and into an even tinier space. A small gas lamp flickers weakly, and in the dim light, Eddie sees who's grabbed him. It's a boy. It's him. The boy with the eyes.

"It's you," Eddie says, or thinks he says. He can't hear his own voice in here. All this chaos.

The boy probably doesn't hear him, either, because he doesn't answer. He just takes Eddie's shoulders, steadies him, and points to a door leading out the back. "Get out!" he shouts. "Get out before the cops take you!"

"What?" Eddie shouts. "What's happening?"

But the boy still doesn't answer. Instead, he slips a folded piece of paper into Eddie's chest pocket just as the curtain behind them is ripped from its pole, and the melee spills through toward them, dancers falling over one another, and the boy pushes Eddie, violently almost, through the back door, to safety. Eddie tumbles off the two steps and into a small fenced-in courtyard, landing on a pair of overstuffed trash bags. Behind him, the door slams shut with a crash loud enough to scare the pigeons pecking at the garbage.

He lies still for a moment. He's not hurt. He catches his breath, then raises his head.

There's no one out here in the twilight. Just Eddie, in the same jeans and sneakers he wears every day. No noise is coming from inside. Just the sounds of the city. A siren, a car horn, the sound of a storefront grate closing. He opens the latch on the gate leading into the alley and steps out. It's eerily silent. The only person he sees is a short man in tan Dickies and a ribbed tank top, sitting up against a wall and smoking a cigarette. Eddie stares at the man for a minute, maybe two, before the man notices.

"Fuck is wrong with you?" the man says, pointing at his wireless earbuds. "I'm on the fucking phone." He flips Eddie off and turns his back.

Eddie blinks, breathes, and checks his shoulder for the camera strap. It's there. It's just after seven. He closes the gate, then walks through the winding alley and back out onto MacDougal Street, which is just as it was before he entered the shop. Even the club kids in green are still there, walking back down the opposite sidewalk. Nothing's changed. Nothing's happened. Nothing's different at all.

Eddie feels for the piece of paper in his chest pocket. He's certain it won't be there.

But it is. And it's a note. *Let me find you*, it says. That's all. *Let me find you.*

NINE

"It used to be a little nightclub," Cookie is saying as she gnaws on a bit of pizza crust and studies the photo Eddie took of the shoe repair shop before he went in. "Well, sort of a nightclub. It was also like a café. Eve's Hangout, it was called. That was before my time, though. It was shut down when I was still a toddler. The cops said they had no choice because there was alcohol on the premises, and it was Prohibition. But I don't buy that reason. Thousands of places served alcohol back then. I think they shut it down because they didn't like the clientele."

"Why not?"

"Some people say they had a sign on the door that said, *Men are admitted, but not welcome.* See what I mean?" Cookie shakes her head. "I don't know if it's true. Anyway, the cops decided they didn't want it there and so they raided the place. Took everyone to jail, and I don't even want to think about the stories I've heard about Welfare Island."

"Isn't that where Mae West went?"

"Yes, but she was different. She was a star. They treated her well. If you weren't a star, you were treated very poorly. Very poorly."

"That's terrible." Eddie remembers how determined the boy was to get him out of Eve's when the cops showed up. He must have heard those stories about Welfare Island, too. He was trying save me, Eddie thinks.

"It gets worse. They convicted Eve of obscenity, and it would have been bad enough if they'd just kept her in prison here. But Eve was born in Poland, so they deported her back to Poland. After a few years back in Europe, the German Nazis arrested her because she was Jewish. She died in a concentration camp."

Eddie's stomach sinks when he hears this. The club he'd just been in, or imagined, was so joyous, so boisterous, so romantic, so fun. Why did its story have to have such a brutal ending? And what about the boy? Did the cops haul him off to Welfare Island, too?

Cookie notices. "You look like you swallowed glass."

"I'm fine," he says.

It's late now, very late, and Eddie's not sleeping. Cookie's been talking in her room for the last hour or so, to Dottie or Tallulah or Mae, who knows. Her voice is muted and calm. Every now and then she laughs, a muffled giggle from the next room. It's a happy sound, and it makes him feel peaceful after this strangest of all days. It makes him feel secure, safe, calm. At home.

He casts his eyes at the folded piece of wrinkled paper on the table beside him. It shouldn't be there, he thinks. It came from inside a vision, a fantasy, but there it is, sitting there. *Let me find you.*

Or is it? Is Eddie just imagining the note, too? Is it a mirage? Is this whole trip to New York just a giant hallucination? Eddie shuts his eyes tightly. Maybe if he keeps them closed all night, everything will make sense in the morning.

But the note is still there. Pulsing. Alive. Insistent, like a chant.

Let me find you. Let me find you. Eddie takes it back up in his hands. Yes, it's real. Listen to it crinkle as he unfolds it.

He reads it again. *Let me find you. Let me find you. Let me find you.*

What does it mean? Is it telling me to wait, to be patient? Is it telling me to leave a window open? Is it just fucking with me? Did I write this note?

Eddie gets off the sofa anyway, gets a pad and pen out of the drawer, and tries to mimic the handwriting. No luck. It's not his hand. Not even close. But whose?

Who are you? he thinks, staring at the letters. What is your name?

He lies back down and takes the Polaroid camera in his hands. Its vinyl casing is cool under his touch. What is it about this camera? All these visions, these episodes happen when I have this camera in my hands. There's no other explanation, is there?

A shard of light from the disco ball above sweeps across the camera, across the floor, and up the wall opposite, animating the bright-eyed boy in the picture. *Let me find you.*

Here, under the lazy spin of the disco ball, it almost sounds like a dare.

Eddie decides, in his midnight state of mind, that it's a dare he should take. He doesn't have to wait for the boy to find him. He can use the camera. He can find the boy himself. He'll do it first thing in the morning.

Or so he tells himself, for about two minutes. Because Eddie will never sleep now. He has to find out if the camera works, if he can call the boy. He has to know if the boy made it out of the Hangout. He has to know if the boy is okay.

He has to know if any of this is real.

Cookie will be fine without him here. She has Dottie and Tallulah and Mae to keep her company for now. And if he's wrong, if he can't call the boy, maybe New York will distract him from this feeling. Maybe New York will calm his relentless questions.

He ties on his shoes, grabs the camera, and slips out the door, silent as a secret. He doesn't bother leaving a note. He won't be gone long.

TEN

First Eddie tries the sidewalk outside Jefferson Market, dark and quiet at this hour. He snaps a photo of the spire, with the moon peeking out from behind it. Nothing happens. No change in scenery, no bright-eyed boy. He trudges uptown in the dark to the hydrant on Fourteenth Street. Snap. No boy. Nothing. He stands across the street from the Algonquin. Snap. Nothing. He winds back downtown to the shoe repair. Snap. Nothing.

So none of it is real? Not the camera, not the boy? Nothing at all?

This is the question that steers Eddie, whether he knows it or not, to Cornelia Street, to something real, to Theo. From the sidewalk he can see straight through the window of Patisserie Gaston, past the counter and into the back kitchen, where Theo, under a flickering fluorescent light, putters around in the workspace, tying on his apron, taking down mixing bowls and ingredients from the shelves, lining baking sheets with parchment, heating the ovens.

Eddie watches as Theo dips his hand into a steel bowl to retrieve a half-handful of flour, which he tosses across the countertop in a cloud. He watches him push into a ball of dough with his palms, pressing down and across, then turning it, folding it, and pressing into it again, leaning the weight of his body into the motions, head tilted in concentration. Eddie counts four turns, eight, sixteen. Every movement is precise, confident, rhythmic, and it soothes Eddie to watch. Theo is real. His hands, his voice, his body, his breath, the way he presses into the dough, the way he pressed against Eddie as they stood at the counter. Theo is real.

Eddie raises the camera, frames the window perfectly in the viewer, and snaps a photograph. He retrieves the little plastic card and holds it out in front of him, watching, waiting. But it's another dud. No image at all.

He tosses it aside carelessly and walks on.

He won't even remember taking the picture. He won't know that the image that emerges, long after he leaves Cornelia Street, isn't one of Theo working in the bakery, but of a young woman in ballet flats, standing on tiptoe, straightening shelves of books—beat poetry and experimental fiction and political manifestos. Eddie won't ever see this image. It will be swept into a trash bin and sent to the landfill.

But her story will come to him one day, the story of when she was little, five or six or seven years old, packed with her parents and two brothers and a dozen other families into a row house up on Tenth Avenue. Kids were always outside then, growing up, playing, working. You never knew exactly where they lived or who they belonged to. Except for her. She was different. Everyone knew her.

The basement of their building was a nightclub, it's hard to remember the name, Hell's Bells or the Roger Room or something silly. A speakeasy, a dark and dusty bar with a stage at one end and a wind-up Victrola for when the band didn't come. They hosted vaudeville acts at first, then pansy parades and drag shows. You never asked who owned it, but they were kind to her father, when he worked behind the bar. Her mother sewed all the costumes—the corsets, the stoles, the gowns, the hats. Sometimes even the big names would perform: Bert Savoy, Gene Malin, the real queens. They fascinated that little girl. The way they moved, sang, talked. The way they transformed. She would sit in the dressing room, at the end of the wall of mirrors, to watch them get ready. The foundation. The kohl. The rouge. The stained lips. The pinched cheeks and spit curls and Gibson girl hats, which always made her laugh, they were so funny and old-fashioned. The queens were superstitious before their shows, kissing a photograph of Sarah Bernhardt or Libby Holman for good luck on their way to the stage.

She'd watch the stage through a crack in the wall, rapt, mesmerized, marveling at the way they'd swish through the crowd, flirting with patrons and singing those silly old songs we all loved, "I'd Rather Be Spanish than Mannish" and "I've Never Seen a Straight Banana." She'd be asleep by the time they finished their performances, curled up right there on the dressing room divan, and they'd lay a coat over her to keep her warm, and they'd keep their voices low as they cleaned their eyelids with cold cream and shared cigarettes. The last to leave would always carry her upstairs, where her mother was waiting at her sewing table. "Until tomorrow," they'd say to each other. And tomorrow always came.

Of course, all that was before her father and two brothers died in that terrible car accident on that beautiful summer day, coming home from the beach. She and her mother survived, but her mother was never the same after that. Her grief was so great. She rarely came downstairs. But the little girl had more mothers than ever. Even after the Crash, when she and her mother were destitute like everyone and lost the upstairs apartment, she came to the nightclub every night. They fed her supper, trimmed her hair, made sure she had books for school. She was never alone. Not once. Not until the coppers finally came to close the place down. But she was older then. She knew who she was then.

Maybe one day Eddie will know, too.

ELEVEN

"You seem troubled," Cookie says when Eddie comes in to say good morning. She's right, of course, although that only covers part of what he's feeling. He's disoriented, perplexed, overloaded, exhausted. He's seen a lot in the last day (year, century). He's seen Mae West be hauled away to jail. He's heard Gladys Bentley sing. He's been passed a note by a vanishing boy. And he's been up all night, wandering, confused, unsure what's real and what isn't. But he doesn't answer her. He wouldn't even know where to start.

"Lollipop?" She pokes him gently with her back scratcher. "What gives?"

He avoids her eyes. "Nothing," he says softly, struggling even to form that word. "I'm not troubled. I'm not troubled at all."

It's a lie, and Cookie knows it. "Well, you should be," she says. "Every eighteen-year-old should be troubled. If they have half a brain, that is. And you have more than half."

Eddie looks away for an awkward, silent moment.

"Let's have some music," Cookie says, pointing at the record player.

Eddie lowers the needle, and a woman begins to sing. Her voice is smooth, and the way she enunciates her Ts and rolls her Rs makes her sound very glamorous.

This funny thing called love / Just who can solve its mystery?

"Who's singing?" he asks when he comes into her room.

"That's Libby Holman," Cookie says. "Do you know her?"

"Nope."

"She's out in the hallway. Second frame to the left of the kitchen door. Bring her in."

Eddie finds a photograph of a dark-haired woman in a cinched satin dress holding a cigarette. "Is this her?" he asks, handing the photograph to Cookie.

"Oh, look at her," she says, lightly touching the woman's face. "Just look. Have you ever seen such gorgeous lips? A perfect Cupid's bow. You'd never guess how scandalous she was. They say she really got around. Men and women. Tallulah Bankhead, Josephine Baker, Louis Schanker. I remember being no more than ten and seeing her picture in the paper, draped in mourning clothes after the suspicious death of her millionaire husband. They indicted Libby but had to drop the case because there wasn't enough evidence. She swears she didn't do it, but I'm sure she's hiding something. I ask her every chance I get."

"Mysterious," Eddie says, understanding that Cookie talks to Libby, too. Believing it.

Cookie giggles. "She was always a favorite of the boys," she says. "If you know what I mean. I think they loved the drama of her. They called her the 'purple menace.' Probably because of her purple lipstick. She performed at all the balls."

Cookie sings along to the next line in the song. She looks expectantly at Eddie, as if waiting for an answer. What *is* this thing called love?

He only shrugs.

"I think love tells us who we are," Cookie says, answering the question herself. "I don't mean just being loved, I mean giving love. It tells us that we belong in this world. All of us. Even the strange ones, the different ones, the special ones. The ones who talk to pictures—"

Eddie tenses.

"The ones who go wandering at night—"

Us, Eddie thinks. He looks away.

The song ends, and Cookie lifts the needle from the album. "Now," she says. "I need an errand. Albert's birthday is next week, and I always get him a ticket to the opera. The great Metropolitan Opera. Do you know how to get to Lincoln Center?"

"Yes," Eddie says reflexively, quickly. He's eager to get back out in the city, eager for another chance to find the boy. "I mean, no. But I can figure it out."

Cookie raises a skeptical eyebrow. "I thought you lost your little googler."

"I don't need it," Eddie says. "I have the map you gave me."

She grins. "Good. Now. Buy a single ticket in the balcony section. It doesn't matter which show. Except not *La Bohème*. *La Bohème* puts him in a bad mood for a week."

"He's always in a bad mood," Eddie mutters.

"Especially bad, I mean," she says. "Anyway, pick any night in September."

"I thought you said his birthday is next week."

"The opera is dark in the summer, so September is the best we can do." She unzips the makeup pouch on her lap and takes out four twenty-dollar bills. "The tickets are expensive, but Albert is worth it. This should leave you enough for a birthday card from the drugstore. Make it an extra sentimental one. You know, something like a winged angel, or dolphins jumping over a rainbow. Something with a rhyming poem about how the passing years remind us of the beauty of eternity, or something equally ridiculous. Albert hates cards like that."

"But don't you want to get him a card he will like?"

"Would you?" she says, eyes twinkling. "No. Sappy and sentimental is your goal."

"Got it," Eddie says, already tightening the laces on his shoes. "Want me to flip the record first?"

"That would be grrrrand," she says, imitating Libby Holman's accent. She picks up her hand mirror to check her makeup. "Now kiss me, and go."

Soon Eddie is boarding the 1 train, a straight shot up to Lincoln Center. The car is crowded but he finds a seat at the far end, holding the Polaroid camera in his lap. He looks at the floor as he rides, studying the shoes. Fila sneakers, open-toe wedges, combat boots, Uggs. All different. He imagines their stories. That pair of scuffed loafers? She's on her way home from a bank job, where she's just received a long-anticipated promotion, which means she will have to start wearing more expensive shoes. The green Crocs over the polka-dot socks? He's heading to the dog groomer to pick up his Yorkie, Elaine, who he'll tuck into his shoulder bag and carry with him to his DJ gig at a club in Queens. These are familiar visions. Comfortable, controllable. Eddie relaxes into them, letting them roll through his head like lazy waves on a lake.

At the Sixty-Sixth Street stop, Eddie exits the train, finds the box office, buys Albert's opera ticket, then picks out a birthday card at the CVS on the corner, an overly saccharine one with flowers and a silly poem about gratitude and gladiolas, just like Cookie instructed, one that he knows Albert will hate. Eddie hopes Albert really hates it, not love-hates. But as long as Cookie's errand is accomplished, it doesn't really matter. When he's done with his purchases, he's left with only a quarter. Not even enough for a candy bar.

TWELVE

Maybe he should stop trying. Maybe the key is just, like the note suggests, to wait. Wait and let him find you. That's what the note said, didn't it? *Let me find you.* It didn't say *Find me.*

How long is that going to take? And what if he never does?

The last thing Eddie wants to do right now is go home, so he walks over to Central Park. He wanders past the Heckscher Playground and up through Strawberry Fields. He winds past the carousel, the mall, and the Sheep Meadow, passing hot dog vendors, paleta carts, buskers, and ice cream trucks. He threads through cyclists on the West Drive, gets chased by angry swans at Turtle Pond, and nearly trips over a couple making out in the Ramble. Eventually he finds himself on the verdant Great Lawn. There, near the Jackie Kennedy reservoir, he lies down in the grass to think. Or maybe not think.

The grass is so lush, so soft, and Eddie's more tired than he realized. With heavy eyes, he watches the sky above him, electric midsummer blue with lazy white clouds. One cloud snakes through the sky like a feather boa. It reminds him of Cookie's marabou collar. Another looks like one of Cookie's berets. Another forms a ring, almost like one of her jangly bangles. He sees Cookie everywhere in the sky. He aims the Polaroid and shoots, just to see what happens.

But the picture doesn't come out. The sky is too bright,

overexposing the image and leaving just a big, bright, blank space. Oh well. He tucks it into his pocket. He'll throw it out later. He's so tired now. He's had so little sleep lately.

He's not sure if he falls asleep or not, but when he opens his eyes and sits up, there's a boy standing over him, not two feet from Eddie, in jeans, Nike sneakers, and a flat-bill baseball cap that looks like it could have been bought yesterday. And peeking out from under that bill: those eyes, like stars.

"Hello, Eddie," the boy says, his voice clear and confident. "I'm Francis."

PART THREE

ONE

Eddie scrambles to his feet. It's him. It's really him. Not a twin, not a cypher, not a doppelgänger, not a look-alike, not a coincidence. It's the same boy, from the taxi, from the photograph, from Jefferson Market, from the Hangout. He's right here, standing on the grass in the Great Lawn, casual and relaxed and confident, like he's always been right here, like he's always been real, like he belongs.

Hello, Eddie. I'm Francis.

Eddie can't speak. Can't answer. Can't move a single muscle. He just stands, eyes wide, absorbing the boy.

Look at him. Look at his nose, strong, broad, a little crooked, maybe broken once. At his chin, somehow both rounded and square. At his ears, his neck, his jet-black hair, peeking out from his cap. At his lips, deep red, a small cut on the lower lip. His Adam's apple. His shoulders, capped over long arms. His wrists, sinewy and pulsing.

Eddie searches for the boy's hands but he can't see those. They're buried in his pockets.

"I'm Francis," the boy says again. "That's my name."

Eddie understands the meaning of the sounds, knows the words, hears the boy's voice perfectly. But he can't answer. He's struck silent, looking up at the boy's eyes, hypnotized.

The boy's expression morphs from a friendly smile to a look of concern. "Eddie?" he asks.

That's you, Eddie. The boy has said your name. But still, Eddie can't speak. His eyes move up to the bridge of the boy's offset nose, and then to his irises, his impossible rainbow beetles, each a pulsing glow of green and gray and violet and gold and a thousand other colors besides.

Speak, Eddie. Move your mouth. Use your tongue and teeth and breath and speak.

"Francis," he says finally, and that's all he says.

"Yes," Francis says, holding his cap to his chest. "That's me. I mean, that is I. If I remember my grammar lessons correctly. It's been some time since I sat in school."

"Francis," Eddie says again.

"Still me," Francis says, and his smile widens. He excavates a hand from his pocket and holds it toward Eddie to shake. Eddie takes his hand, and the electricity of the contact makes him gasp. His skin is warm, alive, fitting snugly into Eddie's. Francis grips tighter. He doesn't let go, holding on a beat longer than a handshake would require, and then another beat, and another. They stand, just like that, hands clasped in greeting, like a photograph, a frozen moment.

"I'm pleased to meet you, Eddie," Francis says, extracting his hand. He pats Eddie on the shoulder. "Finally."

Finally.

Eddie, still struggling, only manages, "Me too," immediately feeling stupid.

Francis smiles. "Good." He nods toward the east side of the park. "I'm going that way."

Eddie can't tell if it's an invitation or the beginning of a goodbye, so he just says, "Oh."

Francis takes a step. Eddie doesn't follow. Francis turns back and raises an eyebrow. "You should come, too."

It's not a question, it's a statement, and if Eddie were thinking clearly, if he were certain this was real, he would say something like *why?* or *where?* He would be, if not suspicious, at least inquisitive. What does Francis want?

"Wait a second," Eddie asks. "How did you know my name?"

"Lucky guess, I guess."

"Seriously," Eddie says, digging in. "How?"

Francis's face takes on a puzzled look, as if the answer should be obvious to Eddie. "It was in your book," he says.

Eddie's eyes glaze as the memory comes over him. This boy was at the Algonquin, too. He was his waiter. He must have picked up the book after—after whatever happened that day.

"It's probably still in the Lost and Found closet," Francis is saying. "I don't think they ever clean that out. I'll look next time I'm there."

Francis is still speaking when an image of Cookie suddenly floods into Eddie's brain, the vision of her standing, disheveled, in the kitchen. He can't leave her too long. The sun has gone behind the clouds now, and Eddie's not sure what time it is.

"I have to be somewhere," he says.

"Now?"

"By four."

"Oh, don't worry about that," Francis says. "You'll have plenty of time. All you need, actually."

"But—"

Think, Eddie. This is a stranger. This is the first time you've met him. Is he dangerous? Is he a stalker? The Pied Piper? Is Francis even his name? You should ask him some questions, Eddie. Where do you want to take me? Why do you want me to come?

Oh, but look at that confident smile. He's happy to see you. And you wanted to find him, didn't you? You walked around most of the night, searching. And now here he is, this magnet, inviting you, special Eddie, into his world. Are you going to change your mind?

"Don't you want to come?" Francis asks.

Eddie takes a breath and then—curious enough to be brave, or trusting enough to be foolish—he hears himself say, "Yes."

Francis's face dissolves into a smile again. "Good," he says. "Let's go this way. I have so much I want to show you."

TWO

Eddie follows Francis by a tentative half step as he leads him through the park. He starts to notice that everything around them is different, nothing like it was a minute (hour, decade, lifetime) ago. The grass at their feet is brown and desiccated, not green and lush. The sky is gray, not blue, and the buildings around the park barely clear the tops of the trees, save for a small handful of ornate towers to the south.

Francis's clothes have changed, too. His jeans aren't jeans anymore; they're nubby gray trousers, frayed at the hems and held up by suspenders over an old-fashioned white henley with the sleeves pushed up. He wears a tattered newsboy cap and muddy black boots lashed with strips of brown leather. Eddie checks his feet, now clad in scuffed boots of his own. His trousers match Francis's almost exactly, except for a hole at the knee. He wears no suspenders over his itchy muslin shirt. His tote bag is gone now, but the camera still hangs from his shoulder.

What is going on? Eddie's mind races too fast to ask the question out loud. It's all he can do to see everything and to keep up with Francis, whose pace seems to increase with every step.

They walk through a cluster of rickety shacks, simple structures of plywood and canvas that look hastily erected. Men and women gather around them, all dusty faces and ratty clothes. Some sweep listlessly at the ground with their feet, others stand in groups of three and four, talking quietly.

Boys and girls with sunken eyes play lazily with sticks and rocks. A child in a makeshift burlap tunic with faded letters across the chest spelling out *Thrifty Brand Flour* approaches with upturned hands, stopping them. She looks up through her curls and holds out her palms, as if she keeps her hands like this all the time, just in case something falls into them. She strains to smile, but conjures a sparkle in her tired eyes. Eddie smiles back, an instinctive response, then digs into his pocket, relieved to find the quarter left over from the opera tickets and birthday card. Not much at all, he thinks, though when he presses it into her palm she lights up, squeaks in jubilation, and races off, kicking up tiny clouds of dust with her bare feet. He wonders where she'll go, and hopes she'll be safe there.

"They say a depression is coming," Francis says, watching the girl run and duck into a lean-to. "I say it's already here. Look around at this shantytown. Can you believe the government allows people to live this way?"

Eddie hears a rustle of paper to his left. It's coming from a small hand-fashioned tent, really just a couple of rusted poles with a bit of fabric hung over for shade. Inside he sees a pair of men in dirty clothes spooned together on the ground. They are covered by sheets of newspaper, peaceful in sleep. They fit together so perfectly, these two men, and Eddie wonders who they are, how they found each other, how they live.

"Come on," Francis says.

"Where are we going?" Eddie asks, his voice louder and more anxious than he expected it to be. "I really, uh, I don't want to be late."

"Don't worry, you won't be."

"Are you sure?"

Francis stops and smiles. "I promise." He points at a gate leading out of the park. "This way. Fifth Avenue."

Eddie swallows his apprehension as they step onto the avenue and turn downtown. They hug the curb to avoid the traffic—the avenue is thick with it. Ford Model As and Buick LaSalles fight for space with smoke-choking city buses and clomping horse cabs, the crush punctuated every now and then with an extremely fancy sedan. The one up ahead is the biggest car Eddie's ever seen, a convertible coupe that seems to stretch halfway down the block, all yellow and green and polished chrome. It glints in the sun, as if mocking the shantytown behind them. Pedestrians stop to ogle as it rolls to a languid stop at the intersection.

"Nice Duesey!" Francis shouts.

The driver stares disapprovingly at the boys, then revs the engine. It spits out a cloud of black exhaust before disappearing around the corner.

"The fat cats love their Duesenbergs," Francis says, shaking his head. He points up at the soaring apartment buildings above them, behemoths of limestone punctuated with carved gargoyles. "They live up there, in apartments in the sky, way up in the lap of luxury, looking down at the rest of us in the dirt scrounging to get by. But the rich don't care. As long as they get their satin sheets and caviar, there's no depression for them. If the rest of us are poor, it must be our fault. But I would never trade my boots for an automobile. Not even a Duesey. Much easier to get around town on foot. Easier to escape on foot, too." He raises an eyebrow. "You never know when you might have to make a getaway."

"What do you mean?"

Francis doesn't answer. He just steps off again, an even faster pace now, long strides, and Eddie trots to keep up. They continue down Fifth Avenue, past the southern edge of the park, past the newsreel theaters ("It's gotten harder to sneak in since the talkies took over," Francis says), past several automats ("The best place to swipe leftover bread from people's trays"), past haberdashers and bootmakers and opticians and churches and betting parlors. The sidewalks get more and more crowded by the block; soon they are groaning with people. Office workers in gray suits and felt fedoras, shoppers in floral dresses and woven cloches, kids in hair ribbons and scally caps. They dodge pairs of cops swinging batons, a line of nuns in black habits, an old woman on a stoop with a boxy handbag in her lap, a stray terrier begging for scraps, a weary-eyed man in a tattered brown overcoat holding a sign saying THANKS FOR NOTHING HERBERT HOOVER. They hear Spanish, Italian, German, Chinese, Creole, and Russian. They hear English so saturated with Irish tones and trills that Eddie doesn't even know it's English, until Francis answers back.

They walk past the majestic St. Patrick's Cathedral at Fifty-First Street, past the gaping construction zone at the Rockefeller property, all the way down to Forty-Second Street, where the massive New York Public Library and its protective stone lions rise like bulwarks.

Francis points downtown toward a towering structure. It is unfinished, but already it stands much taller than the rest of the buildings in Midtown.

"Can you see the workers up top?" Francis says. Eddie squints but can't see anything. "Here," Francis says, draping one arm around Eddie's neck and pressing his palm into Eddie's chest, sending a shock through Eddie. He points with his other hand to the top of the steel framework. "Follow my finger. See? They look like ants up there, and we look like ants to them. They say no one's ever fallen off, but I don't believe it. They work up there, a hundred stories up, not even a rope."

Eddie forces his focus onto the building and away from Francis's touch.

"They're calling it the Empire State Building," Francis says. "The newspapers say it'll be finished next year, 1931."

"Next year, 1931," Eddie repeats. "So that means this is—"

"—1930," Francis says, nonchalant, casual, as if this is just a little chat about unimportant details, as if identifying what year they're in is as unremarkable as identifying what time of day it is.

"It can't be," Eddie mutters, too quietly for Francis to hear. "It can't be real."

Except Francis does hear, or else he reads Eddie's mind (which wouldn't surprise Eddie; nothing would surprise him at this point). "It can be," he says. His voice is so relaxed, familiar, calming. He pats Eddie's chest again. "And it is. Look around."

Eddie takes in the concrete and steel and dust and businessmen and mailmen and pickpockets and shoppers and streams of office workers, some swinging black lunchboxes, others pale blue handbags. He obeys and takes a listen, to the honking buses and shouting newsboys and rumbling trucks and a lone trumpeter playing valiantly against the din as he busks for change. It's New York City, bustling and alive, almost a hundred years before his own time. I am here, Eddie thinks. It's not possible, it makes no sense. But Francis is right. I am here.

"It's real," Francis whispers. And then, like a breath, he releases Eddie. "They say there'll never be a taller building. They say the laws of physics won't allow it. But they said the same thing about the Chrysler Building, remember?"

Eddie shakes his head.

Francis laughs. "Of course you don't," he says. "But I do. Anyway, I can't wait to go up to the top. I'm afraid of heights, though, so you'll have to come with me and hold my hand. Will you hold my hand?"

Eddie looks up at the building again, growing dizzy as he raises his eyes. He's not sure if it's the height of the building or the idea of holding hands with Francis that makes his knees buckle, but before he falls, Francis is right there, steadying him.

"Sorry," Eddie says, flushing red. He crouches down to pretend to tie his boot. He's still wobbly and loses his balance, tipping to the left. But Francis's leg is there to catch him again.

"Got you," Francis says.

Eddie closes his eyes for a moment to catch his breath. He half expects all of this to disappear while he does it, and that he'll wake up back in Central Park, looking at clouds.

But Francis is tapping him on the shoulder. "Up you get," he says, and then turns west onto Forty-Second Street. Eddie follows close behind as they snake between two young men wearing Macy's sandwich boards, advertising a summer sportswear sale. "How do you do, Clarence," Francis says to the taller one with the black driving cap.

"Francie," the man says. He mock-salutes him.

"What am I, chopped liver?" the shorter one says. He swats Francis on the shoulder.

"Oh, hello, Martin," Francis says. "How do you do, too?"

Francis doesn't wait for an answer. He smiles at Martin—how easily Francis smiles!—and keeps going. Eddie trots to keep up. "Who were they?"

"Oh, just a coupla Macy's boys. That store is full of—" Francis turns to Eddie. "Well, you know."

"I do?"

"Sure you do."

Eddie drops a step, falling behind. How easily Francis had said that. How clear his meaning was. Francis knows that Eddie knows. And that means Francis knows something about Eddie. And for the first time he can remember, it doesn't chafe to feel seen. It feels good. Yes. He is conspicuous to Francis and it feels good.

At the corner of Sixth, Francis stops in front of two carts selling roasted chestnuts. "Hungry?"

Eddie is surprised that anyone's selling roasted chestnuts on a summer day, but they smell so good. He approaches one of the carts, but Francis nudges him to the other one, where a tiny old man with deep forehead wrinkles stands waiting. "Trust me," he whispers. "His are better." And then, to the man, Francis holds up two nickels. "Giacomo! Due!"

"Due," the old man says, handing over two paper cones filled with warm chestnuts dusted with salt and sugar. Eddie pops one in his mouth. The flavors of chestnut and caramel flood his tongue.

"Giacomo has the touch," Francis says. "He makes them taste like candy."

They cross Sixth Avenue, and now they're entering Times Square, a riot of flashing marquees and sparkling billboards and cars and buses and people and people and people!

Francis points to a cluster of young men in white shirts and brown suspenders, three or four of them, laughing together. He raises a knowing eyebrow. And there's another cluster, and another. They're standing, talking, looking around in that secret, coded way that won't give them away except to eyes that know the code. Francis knows that Eddie recognizes the code. That feels good, too.

"Times Square. Where the boys are." Francis puts a hand on Eddie's shoulder. "Of course, what do you expect, with all these theaters around? You can't put on a play without a few homosexuals in the cast, not to mention backstage. It's a law of nature. Of course, the big producers try to pretend we don't make the whole theater business run, but Broadway would collapse without the pansies."

Pansies. Eddie flinches at the word like he did last time he heard it, but Francis—just like Mae West, just like Cookie—says it easily, earnestly, with no hint of cynicism. Only warmth and . . .

"Without us, I mean," Francis says.

. . . and pride.

After a sharp turn up Broadway and then a jag west on Forty-Fourth Street, Francis stops underneath a poster for a Greta Garbo movie, *Susan Lenox: Her Fall and Rise*. It shows the movie star in a passionate embrace with Clark Gable. "I don't know why Greta Garbo is hugging Clark Gable," Francis says. "When everyone knows she's in love with Mercedes de Acosta."

Eddie has never heard the name Mercedes de Acosta, but he does know Greta Garbo, thanks to Cookie. "I like Garbo," he says. "I think she's great."

Francis raises both eyebrows. "You know Garbo?"

Eddie smiles. "Don't be stingy, baby."

Francis lets out a laugh, a big, sharp laugh, and claps Eddie on the back. "I knew you would," he says. "I always knew you would. Come on."

THREE

On Forty-Fourth Street and Eighth Avenue, just a block west of Times Square and still in the glow of its lights, Francis points at a small wooden door hidden under a short flight of stairs. There's no sign on it, no address number, nothing. Just a black dot in the center and a rope-pull handle.

"Ready?" Francis asks.

"For what?"

"You'll see," Francis says. "You trust me, right?"

Eddie balks. "Wait," he says. "I don't know who you are. I don't know where I am. I don't know how we got here."

"We walked," Francis says. His face scrunches into a look of concern. "Remember?"

"That's not what I mean," Eddie says. "I mean, how did we—how did you—I mean, I was just—"

He stumbles on his words, because as soon as he chooses them, they don't make sense anymore. How can he articulate his questions, without sounding like he's lost his mind? Even the idea of saying these things out loud seems ridiculous. How did we get to 1930? Why did you keep showing up in pictures when you weren't even there in the first place? What were you doing waiting tables at the Algonquin? Why were you at the courthouse with Mae West, or at the club with Gladys Bentley? How did you know I'd be in Central Park? What happened to my clothes? Why is my camera still here, but not my sneakers? What on earth is going on? The questions are endless, but none of them make any sense at all.

Except one. Eddie steadies his breath and asks it. "Are you real?"

Francis takes a step closer. He takes Eddie's hand and presses it against his chest. "Feel that?" he asks.

And Eddie does feel it. A heartbeat. Strong and even and true.

Francis puts his own hand on Eddie's chest. "We're almost in sync," he says.

Just then, the small wooden door swings open and a pair of young men comes stumbling out, arm in arm, giggling. They look at Francis and Eddie, nod, and keep walking.

"Come on," Francis says. "Let's have some fun."

Francis grabs Eddie's forearm and they duck through the door and into a dark, narrow hallway. Eddie can't see a thing. He churns with excitement and anxiety. From deep inside the building, Eddie can hear music. It's muffled, distant, but he hears a piano, drums, and, is that a clarinet?

They approach a second door. Francis knocks twice. The door opens a crack. Music spills out.

"Speak," a voice, sharp enough to cut through the din, says.

"It's me," Francis says, leaning toward the door.

"Me who?"

"Me myself and I," Francis says. "And I brought groceries." He tips his head toward Eddie.

The door slams. Eddie turns to go, but Francis tightens his grip. "We're in," he says, grinning.

The door swings open and a pair of thick arms sweeps them inside. Their owner, a burly man with a mustache that connects to his sideburns (no beard), reaches from the stool he's sitting on to touch the Polaroid camera hanging over Eddie's shoulder. "What is this?" he asks.

Eddie speaks quickly. "It's kind of like a camera, it makes instant—"

"Camera?" the burly man says. "No. Not allowed."

"But it belongs to my—"

"No."

"Don't worry," Francis says. "We can leave it here with Link. It will be safe. I promise."

Eddie hands the camera to Link, who stashes it on a shelf behind his seat before leaning back to pull open a pair of heavy red curtains, revealing another door. "Push," Link says, and Francis pushes, and suddenly the music is much louder, the laughter, too, and the air is dense with cigarette smoke. The lighting is very low, but Eddie can see dozens of bodies, dancing and singing along to a song by, yes, once again, Cole Porter. *Let's be outrageous / Let's misbehave!*

The center of the room whoops and spins, while around the perimeter clusters of people chat and laugh and wave their hands in animated gestures. Men in black, brown, and gray suits mostly, hats cocked or discarded altogether, some with stained lips or lined eyes, others with slicked hair and sharp brows, still others rough and scarred like boxers. A few women, too, in bright, elaborate dresses and drawn-on beauty marks. At the far end of the room, a few musicians sit on rickety stools, playing joyously, toes tapping, while a man struts between them, singing over the bouncing tune. Francis tugs him toward a waistcoated waiter and plucks two glasses off his tray.

"Seltzer," the waiter says, rolling his eyes. "The bootlegger couldn't make it today." He walks on.

"Seltzer is very in these days," Francis says. "The latest thing." Eddie sips, savoring the needles and pins on his tongue.

Just then, a voice from across the crowd, high-pitched and dramatic. "Francesca!" Within seconds, as if a gate had been unlocked, Eddie and Francis are swarmed by young men in slim jackets and foppish hair, their faces glistening. All about Eddie's age, or maybe a year or three older.

"Francine, where ya been? We thought you'd been hauled off to Welfare Island!"

They laugh, surrounding Francis and covering him with sloppy kisses on the cheek.

Francis accepts all their kisses, then holds up a hand. "Enough!" He takes Eddie's arm and announces, "Boys, girls, et cetera. Meet Eddie. He's not from here, so behave. Especially you, Gene." Francis winks at a tall, husky young man in a black tuxedo with heavy rouge on his cheeks.

"Moi?" Gene responds, dramatically touching his chest with outstretched fingers.

"Vous," Francis says.

Gene bows to Eddie. "Welcome to my resort," he says.

"Hello," Eddie says, but it's a timid hello, not loud enough for anyone to hear over the music. He clears his throat and tries again. "Hello!" but he chokes when he says it. He tries a sip of seltzer to clear his throat but in his nervousness, he swallows it wrong, choking even more. Soon he's coughing uncontrollably, eyes watering and cheeks going red. He turns away from the boys, embarrassed. He hears them laughing nervously, making it even harder to catch his breath.

"Sounds like you after your last first date, Buzzy!" one of the boys says.

"Oh please, Buzzy hasn't had any reflex of that sort since 1922," says another.

"Shut up!" says a third, probably Buzzy.

Francis claps Eddie's back gently. "You all right?"

"I think so," Eddie chokes.

"Good." Francis's voice is close. Eddie feels his breath on his ear. "I thought we might lose you. Now come meet these animals. I promise they're good guys. Just a little, you know, quippy."

Eddie regains his breath and turns back to the boys. "Hello!" he shouts, clearly this time. "I'm Eddie!"

The boys cheer, swarming around him and kissing his cheek.

"Nice to meetcha!" chirps a boy. "My name's Vincent."

"He means Vincenza," says a boy named Georgie. "Welcome to the club, Eddie!"

"One more pansy for the patch!" says Gabriel.

"You single?" Vincenza asks, tugging at Eddie's sleeve.

"Hands off!" barks Georgie, taking Eddie's other sleeve. "He's mine!"

Francis swats Georgie's and Vincenza's hands away and takes Eddie's arm. "Don't mind them," he says as they step back from the gaggle. "The boys always get excited when someone new comes around. They'll settle down soon enough. Before you know it you'll be old news, just another nickname."

"Nickname?"

"Everyone gets one eventually." He holds out a hand to shake. "Nice to meet you. I'm Francesca." Eddie takes his hand, and Francis leads him across the room.

They find a corner where they can lean against the wall and watch the crowd. "They say that Prohibition will end soon, and that places like this won't be illegal anymore," Francis says. "I guess that's good, even though I kind of like the cloak and dagger of it all, you know? It's exciting being an outlaw. But I suppose that feeling will last, one way or another. Not for everyone, of course. But for people like us, yes. We will always be outlaws. Sometimes more so, sometimes less. But it will always be there. You know what I mean?"

Eddie nods like he understands, because he does.

Standing next to them is a pair of men in a tight embrace. They begin to kiss. Right on the lips! Eddie looks around nervously, then back to the couple. They kiss again. And again! Eddie is amazed, and enthralled. Kissing! Right here, in public! He turns to Francis in disbelief, but Francis isn't watching the men. He's craning his neck above the crowd, straining to see the stage.

"It's time for Gene to sing," Francis says, pointing to the tall, husky man with the rouged cheeks, who is stepping onto the bandstand.

"Is that—"

"Yes. You just met him. Gene Malin is his full name. Although sometimes it's Jean Malin. Other times Imogene Wilson. Depends on where he's performing and what mood he's in. He hit the big time recently, but we still call him Gene."

Gene Malin stands with one hand on his hip, and his other hand holding a cigarette. "Hello, pansies," he purrs into the microphone. "I've got a new song for you."

The crowd groans. "We like the old ones!" someone shouts.

"Hush, you," the diva scolds. "This one's called 'That's What's the Matter with Me' and I think you'll see . . . it's ducky!"

The band starts, and Gene Malin begins to sing.

I don't know whether I'm mister, miss, or missus | I'm on the spot as you can plainly see

His voice is rich and musical, but also light, as if he's not just singing the words, but reciting them, in a way that's both comic and pensive. The crowd laughs at the line about *why does that fellow act that way* and gasps at the line, *this thing is breaking up my life*. But Gene Malin finishes on a happy note, posing demurely, and also dramatically, as he delivers the final phrase: *And that's what's the matter with me, that's all.* The audience claps and cheers, prompting Gene

Malin to reprise that final line. And this time, everyone sings along, even Eddie.

And that's what's the matter with me, that's all!

"That's all!" Buzzy shouts.

"That's all!" the other boys shout.

"Now we dance," Francis says.

"Dance? But I don't know how to—"

Francis leans closer to Eddie and whispers, "No one cares."

His eyes are more colorful than they've ever been before, and Eddie dives into them.

FOUR

It's late, long after dark, and Francis and his friends are doing their best to teach Eddie the dances: the Varsity Drag, the Turkey Trot, the Peabody, even the Texas Tommy. Eddie, of course, struggles. He can barely step back and forth at a school dance, let alone shimmy like a flapper on a speakeasy dance floor. But there's something about the music here, about the boys, about being so far away from Mesa Springs and the twenty-first century, about Francis, that seduces him to go for it anyway. Here, on this dance floor, his clumsiness is seen, mirrored, forgiven, even celebrated. It fits. He fits.

Francis trips through the dances effortlessly, without appearing to concentrate at all, switching from a two-step to a slide as easily as he crosses a street or a threshold. A new tempo, a cross-rhythm, a burst of syncopation—Francis seems to anticipate them all, never straining, always exactly on the beat. "I could do these dances in my sleep," he says, swinging his arms to one side as a new song starts. "We've been doing them for five, six years now. I suppose they are a little passé. The Bright Young Things over in jolly olde England would turn up their snooty noses. But we still love them. Of course, five years isn't a very long lifetime for a dance, if you think about it. Do you ever think about it?"

"About dancing? I'm trying to!" Eddie catches one foot on the other as he swings it backward, trying hard to follow Francis's lead. He lands on the opposite foot, clumsily, breaking their rhythm. "Sorry!"

Francis throws an arm around Eddie's waist and shouts over the music. "Wanna go upstairs? Get some air?"

"Yes please!" Eddie shouts back, although he has no idea what's upstairs.

Francis leads the way. They make their way back through the front door, grabbing Eddie's camera from Link on their way, then around to the back of the building. Francis boosts Eddie up onto the iron fire escape, then leaps, grasps the bottom step with his fingers, and, in a single gymnastic motion, swings himself up behind. Eddie marvels silently at Francis's lean strength. He'd never be able to do that.

They climb seven flights, to the roof, where they can see the whole city. Times Square to one side, distant downtown to the other, and the Hudson River to the west. Francis walks to the edge and peers over, down to busy Eighth Avenue below.

"Yikes!" he yelps, before taking a step backward. He grabs Eddie around the waist and buries his face in Eddie's neck. He has to bend down to do it, being a half-head taller. "Afraid of heights!"

"I remember," Eddie says, and Francis looks up at him and smiles.

Oh, that smile. It's nearly as magnetic as his eyes, now half-hidden behind the sharp locks that came loose on the dance floor. They hang almost to the bridge of his nose, grazing his eyelashes. Francis laughs, squeezes Eddie's ribs, then sits on the edge of the roof, his boots dangling over the edge.

"Come sit with me," Francis says. "I'm afraid of heights, remember?"

Eddie laughs and sits down next to Francis. They're facing west, away from Times Square, and if you were to look at them from in front, they'd look like angels against the skyline, their shapes just shadows, surrounded by the glow of the city. Eddie grips the edge of the roof.

"You can see all the way across the Hudson from here," Francis says. "All the way to New Jersey. On a clear day, you could probably see all the way to California, if you squint really hard. Just don't lean too far forward."

To see as far as California, Eddie imagines, you'd have to look straight over Colorado, straight past Mesa Springs. He wonders what Mesa Springs looks like right now, in 1930. Probably dusty and rough, if it's even there. He feels so far away from that place. It is, at best, a distant memory from far in the future, a place he barely ever knew at all. And a time that, right now, he doesn't miss at all. Here is where he wants to be. Here and now.

A tiny, mischievous smile curls at the corners of Francis's lips. "I'm not actually afraid of heights, you know. I just want you to hold my hand. Will you hold my hand?"

The words move slowly through the air, surrounding Eddie, seeping like warm syrup through his ears, curling into his chest. He knows Francis is just flirting, of course. He's surely said this to a dozen boys before, a hundred. But still, no one's ever said anything romantic to Eddie before, and it feels so, so warm.

Why me? Eddie wants to ask. Why did you want to find me? But he doesn't ask, because he's afraid that Francis's answer will pierce this beautiful balloon, revealing it to be only a fantasy, not real at all.

Besides, he can't ask that question. Not now. Not while Francis is laying his hand over Eddie's, threading his fingers through Eddie's, pressing his palm against Eddie's like it belongs there, sending waves of dopamine coursing through Eddie's body. He shivers.

"Can I ask you something?" Francis says.

"Okay," Eddie says.

"Who are you?"

"What do you mean? I'm Eddie."

"No," Francis says. He raises Eddie's hand to press against his lips. "I mean who *are*—"

But before Francis can finish the question, a car on the street below, a Duesenberg perhaps, or a Chrysler or a Ford, careens around the corner and rams into a streetlight, knocking it over with a colossal crash and sending a stream of sparks high into the air. Eddie startles and jumps, nearly losing his balance on the roof edge. But Francis is there, to grab him and yank him away from the edge, to toss him, as if he were weightless, to safety. Eddie lands with a thud, and everything goes dark.

FIVE

Sometimes when a light is too bright, it doesn't illuminate. It obscures.

Eddie is standing on Forty-Fourth Street, alone in the sunshine. The light is searing out here, and the world around Eddie feels cold in it, exposed, like the sun isn't a star but a harsh overhead spotlight, a stadium light, flattening everything around him into nothing. It scorches his eyes, obliterating the mystery and romance that defined his world just a moment ago, rendering them invisible, gone.

He blinks against the light, shades his eyes with his hands to search for a shady spot. He sees one across the street, a bit of scaffolding to tuck himself under. He stumbles across the street and into the shadow, steadying himself on the cross of metal bars.

The night is gone. The speakeasy is gone. The party is gone. The band is gone. Gene Malin is gone. The boys are gone. Eddie's trousers and boots are gone.

Francis is gone.

A man on an electric bike zips past, an SUV honks, a woman jaywalks in a cropped T-shirt, a billboard above him advertises a Broadway revival of *42nd Street*. It's 2023 again.

He raises the camera and takes a photograph of the building he thinks he was just in. It develops perfectly, smoothly, nothing strange, just an unremarkable building with a semi-obscured door that says EMPLOYEES ONLY. He points the camera at the sky. The photo develops perfectly, smoothly, nothing strange, just a blue sky and the side of a glass building with two window washers in safety harnesses hard at work. He flips the flash on and off and on again, then snaps. He covers the lens with his hand, then snaps. Nothing works. Nothing takes him back to Francis.

He shouts, "Take me back!" startling a few people across the street, but nothing happens. He does a few steps of the Turkey Trot on the sidewalk, but nothing happens. He knocks on the Employees Only door, but nothing happens. He covers his face with his hands, straining to rebuild the world he was just expelled from, but nothing happens.

Just because something feels real doesn't mean it is real. We've all been fooled before. A scent you're sure is a baking pie, but it's just burnt sugar at the bottom of the oven. An embrace that feels like love, but it's just pity. A camera you think is magic, but it's just a camera. It's not special to be fooled.

Deflated, Eddie sinks to the sidewalk. The whirl of elation was so real, so saturating, like the dances themselves, and now all he feels is empty.

A flashing clock on the corner displaying the time and temperature says it's only one o'clock. He's had a day in the city and a night at the speakeasy and traveled from Central Park to Times Square and beyond, and it's still only one o'clock. Time stopped while he was away.

But if time stopped, shouldn't Eddie still be in Central Park? Wouldn't that make more logical sense?

Logic, Eddie? Really?

Eddie stands up. He has plenty of time before four o'clock. Plenty of time to keep his promise to never miss sherry hour.

Soon he's back downtown, outside the Jefferson Market Library. He decides to try the camera again, aiming the Polaroid at the sky. But nothing happens. Just a picture of the sky. He tries again, nothing. Just a picture of a taxi. And again, and again. Nothing, nothing.

Maybe it will work inside the library, he thinks, reaching for any twig of hope, and so he goes inside. He remembers to turn off the flash before he shoots a photograph of the check-out desk. Nothing. He takes a photograph of the fiction section. Nothing. The computer banks. Nothing. He wanders the stacks, snapping indiscriminately, exchanging the film cartridge twice. Still nothing. Nothing but pictures of books.

He lingers in a section of shelves filled with books about New York City history. His hand lands on one, a weathered old volume of New York City photographs from the 1920s and 1930s. He pulls it down and sits at a small desk next to a window overlooking Sixth Avenue. Flipping through, he sees some of the places he'd just been: Fifth Avenue, the public library, Forty-Second Street, Times Square. He turns the pages slowly, lingering on a photograph of the unfinished Empire State Building, scrutinizing a street filled with Duesenberg sedans and city buses. He counts one nickelodeon, one gambling parlor, two shoe shines, one candy shop, and one bread bakery. He sees overcoats and fedoras and travel suits and swinging handbags. He even spies, in the corner of one photograph, Greta Garbo kissing Clark Gable, the very same movie poster he'd seen on his walk through the city with Francis.

His walk through the city with Francis. How easily that phrase pops into his head. Not his imaginary walk through the city with Francis. No. Not his dream of a walk through the city with Francis. Just his walk through the city with Francis. Because he was really there. It all seems so easy to accept now. So easy to believe.

He turns to a two-page photograph of Herald Square at

Christmas time. It's dated 1930. The sidewalk is packed with shoppers crowded around the Macy's holiday windows, filled with evergreen trees draped in silver tinsel and red velvet bows and flanked by giant nutcrackers in gold jackets with fringed epaulets. A Santa Claus stands on the corner with a cowbell and a Salvation Army bucket. He looks uncharacteristically skinny to Eddie, his suit sagging off his frame. He studies every face, searching their expressions, trying to imagine their stories. Face to face, story to story. But he can't seem to formulate a single one. The more he stares at the faces, the more distant they grow, like they belong to another world altogether. A world he can't recognize, can't understand, can't imagine. The more he looks, the less he sees.

He is so tired. He lays his head on the cool paper and closes his eyes.

The dream comes quickly. He is with Francis and they are dancing, then walking, then climbing stairs, then entering a little flat overlooking the river with a bathtub in the kitchen. They're bathing each other, they're climbing into a big fluffy bed together, they're curling into each other, holding each other, pressing into each other, closer, closer, whispering, sighing, welcoming, accepting, making promises. There is no fear, here. There are no secrets. Francis knows who he is, and he knows who Eddie is, and he loves them both.

It's all a beautiful world, saturated with color and desire and absolute belonging. It's a place (time?) where Eddie feels aware, where he feels alive, where he sees (knows?) who he really is (wants to be?). This tiny world, this infinite world, Francis's world, where he sloughs off his calcified inconspicuousness and is finally, entirely, seen.

After a few minutes, Eddie stirs and opens his eyes.

Francis is there with a hand outstretched.

"It's beautiful out," he is saying. "What are you doing in a library? Let's go to the beach."

SIX

A soft midday haze filters the sun as they disembark the ferry at the edge of Jamaica Bay, then hike over to the boardwalk at Rockaways' Playland. They weave through a commotion of amusements and thrill rides—roller coasters, carousels, games of skill, curiosity shows. Kids run barefoot through the crowd with no obvious guardians in sight, laughing as they're chased by leashless dogs with hungry looks. Peacocking young men walk arm in arm, singing drinking songs and gawking at women, who point and laugh derisively. There's a long line for the Atom Smasher roller coaster, which Francis says he prefers to Coney Island's Cyclone, and lots of customers milling around a row of toffee vendors, which Francis ranks from worst to best as they pass.

A sign advertises an elephant show. Eddie doubts they have a real elephant, until Francis confirms it. "And monkeys, too," he says. "But for a bearded lady, you gotta go to Coney."

They scramble off the boardwalk and onto the beach, populated by sunburned men with big bellies, women under wide-brimmed hats, and wiggly groups of squealing children toting buckets. Most seem to stick close to the boardwalk, close to the concessions. But the sand stretches east and west as far as Eddie can see. He peels off his worn black boots and rolls up his trousers to walk in the sand.

"We can do better than that." Francis smiles. He holds up two pairs of black bathing trunks.

"Where did those come from?"

"Never know when you'll end up at the seaside. Let's go change." Francis points at a big stone bathhouse just beyond the racetrack.

Inside, Eddie looks for a place to hide, to conceal himself as he changes. He opens a low locker door and awkwardly tucks himself behind it before swiftly dropping his trousers into a heap on the floor and stepping into the trunks. He is relieved once they're on, and that somehow, they fit perfectly. Francis doesn't hide, and he doesn't rush. He slowly removes his clothes—all of them—carefully folding his shirt and socks and underwear neatly into a locker. Naked, he crosses the small changing room to a sink where he rinses his hands and splashes his face. Eddie watches him go, marveling at Francis's body. So lean, sinewy, his pale skin smooth except for a small strip of hair just under his belly button. Droplets of water cling to his forearms, his stomach, his chin. When Francis turns, Eddie quickly lowers his gaze, as if he's looking at the floor, but slowly raises his eyes, unwilling to miss a gesture. He fights an almost irresistible urge to reach, to touch, to feel Francis's skin under his fingertips, to test the flesh of his beautiful chest, stomach, kneecaps.

Francis sees Eddie watching as he pulls up his swim trunks, not turning away. He smooths them around his waist and—still grinning—plunges his hands inside to adjust himself. "That's better," he says. "Now let's get towels and then walk up the beach a bit. The boys are sure to be here somewhere."

They hike along the water's edge, leaving the nickelodeons and food carts behind. Whenever a wave of cold seawater splashes their feet, Francis squeaks, Eddie laughs, and they trot a few steps up into softer sand until the sea retreats again. As they pass the steeplechase track and the pavilion, Francis tells stories about life in New York, about his stint as an usher at a Times Square burlesque theater and about the time he spilled a milkshake on Pola Negri when he was working as a waiter at a fancy party uptown. Eddie laughs, pretending to know who Pola Negri is (he'll ask Cookie). It feels so easy being with Francis, at least when they're talking about Francis.

But when Francis says, "Tell me about you," Eddie doesn't know how to answer. His life seems so dull in comparison. A small, dusty, nowhere town, a nonexistent social life, a dead-end job. Here is Francis, a young man whose life is full of mystery and adventure and connection—and then here is Eddie, a young man who lives with a bedridden relative and whose days are defined by running errands and sipping sherry. What could Eddie say that would compare? Why can't he mirror Francis's ease? He's spent a life creating elaborate fantasies in which he is brave, daring, desired. Why doesn't he feel that way with Francis?

Happily, before Eddie thinks up something to say, a voice from up the beach yells: "FRANCESCA!"

Francis looks up and smiles. "This way!" he says, grabbing Eddie's arm. They slip through a clutch of dune grass onto a much less populated stretch of beach, where small groups of two and three and four people with tin buckets and picnic baskets sit on blankets spread over the sand. A crowd of young men comes racing toward them.

"Gird your loins," Francis says. "We're being invaded."

Suddenly, they are surrounded by a dozen laughing young men, some in long cotton trunks, others in tanked one-piece swimsuits, waving blankets and swinging tin buckets and tossing straw boater hats in the air in celebration. One carries a kite on his back, another has a picnic basket over one arm, another has a towel wrapped around his head like a turban. They swarm Francis, grabbing his arms and kissing him on both cheeks. Eddie recognizes Buzzy, George, and Vincent, but not the others. Like birds, they chat and chirp and sing over one another, jubilant voices spiraling frenetically, a whirlwind. Eddie struggles to keep up.

"What took you so long, La Divina Francesca?" Buzzy asks. "We've been here for hours! Charlie here, I mean Carlotta, made us catch the seven thirty train."

"That's Queen Carlotta to you," says the boy Buzzy is pointing at. "And someone needed to get you fairies out here."

"Fairies on the ferry!" Vincenza shouts. "The ticket taker sneered at us. Sneered! Twice!"

"At least he was a spruce," says Georgie. "But the way you sat there batting your lashes at him, Vincent? Scandalous. No wonder he sneered."

"He loved it. He couldn't get enough of my fetching features."

"Oh, Vincenza. Not everyone's a fairy, dearie."

"They are once I get to 'em!"

"Gabriel here says he saw the same guy at Webster Hall last Thanksgiving."

"Really, Gabby? The night when you wore that majestic Diamond Lil getup?"

"Oh, don't remind me!" Gabriel, or Gabby, responds. "But I did see him there! He looked ducky."

"I hope he comes to the next ball. I will sing to him, until he falls in love with me."

"Oh, Vincenza. You can't even catch a tune, let alone a man."

"Now, Carlotta, be sweet to our Vin. He's just had his heart broken again. Third time this week."

"By the way, has anyone heard from Clem? I haven't seen him in an age."

"Clementine? She went to Boston, remember?"

"Boston? Humph. Never heard of it!"

"It's just past the Bronx. And she had to go somewhere after the brawl at the automat! Nearly killed that man who propositioned her, you know."

"She did not. She just knocked him out, that's all. A mere Jack Dempsey uppercut to the chin."

"I heard her gown was ruined."

"What's a gown when virtue is at stake?"

"Gowns are all that ever matters, dearie!"

"By the way," whispers one boy. "Did you horties hear about Robin? Welfare Island for a week!"

"What do you expect? He made a pass at that sailor down at Frank's Place!"

"Oh please, Frank's is right next to the Navy Yard. Sailor trade is the whole point of that place."

"Until the sailor changes his mind."

"Enough!" Carlotta says in a forceful voice. This time the breathless banter stops for good.

Eddie welcomes the pause in the action. All the names! All the slang! And she is he and he is she and this one met a sailor and that one skipped town and someone wants to sing to a bus driver and whew.

Suddenly, all the boys are looking at him, as if they'd just noticed someone new was there.

"And who is this?" someone asks in a bemused tone.

Eddie feels the cool scrutiny underlying the question. There is a right answer, he suspects, and a wrong one. But what is it? "I, um," he starts.

"Well?" It's the one called Carlotta, hand on hip.

Francis, sensing Eddie's anxiety, leaps into the moment. "A friend," he says. "A friend from out of town. You met him the other night, Buzzy, and so did you, Vincenza. Don't you recall? This is Eddie."

Silence. Everyone stares. Eddie swallows.

Francis breaks the silence a second time. "Isn't he charming?" His voice is tinged with authority, and in response, the boys melt around Eddie, clapping his back and tugging at his hands.

"Welcome, Edwina!" they shout in unison, and Eddie, belonging to them now, belonging here now, bows in response. They form a ring around him and dance, just like the girls he saw playing outside Jefferson Market. *Spanish dancer, turn around! Spanish dancer, touch the ground!*

SEVEN

Just look at those beautiful boys, Eddie and Francis, chest deep in the sea, splashing in the cool, rhythmic waves. The afternoon has stretched on slowly, lazily, perfectly. He doesn't want it to end, doesn't want this spell to break. He knows that when it does, it will happen suddenly, without warning, and he will ache with loneliness again, just like he did out on the street after the speakeasy.

What is it about a crush that feels so fragile? How can the investment be so deep, so soon? You see somebody a handful of times, and then you meet them, and you talk and walk and dance, and then suddenly you realize that even though he is right here treading water a million miles from anywhere else, just you and him, both of you moving closer to each other with every shallow wave, hands grazing underwater, eyes locked, then averted, then locked again, everything just as you'd dream it, if you'd dreamed it, but all you can think of is how it will end, when it will end, and how you'll possibly survive.

Crush? What a small word. It sounds cute, inconsequential, sweet. That is not this, Eddie thinks. This is a fire.

"What are you thinking?" Francis asks, reading Eddie's mind. The sun sparkles off the waves around him.

"Nothing," Eddie lies, sensing a trap, certain that if he told the truth, this would all disappear and he'd be back in his sneakers and jeans. He takes a stroke away from Francis to escape the question. He dives and resurfaces, dives and resurfaces, shaking water from his hair. A distant, delighted scream from the Atom Smasher rises from the crowded boardwalk, a thousand miles away. Relax, he tells himself, feeling the undertow at his feet. You're in the water. Far away. Everything is different out here. You can be, too.

"You swim like a dolphin," Francis says.

"I love the ocean," Eddie says.

"It doesn't scare you?" Francis teases. "Man-eating sea monsters and stinging jellyfish?"

"I got stung by a jellyfish once," Eddie says. "On Padre Island in Texas."

"When was that?"

"I think I was eight or nine," Eddie says. "So about ten years ago." Or ninety years in the future, he thinks, depending on how you look at things.

"Did you pee on it?"

"What?"

"That's what you're supposed to do," Francis says. "Pee on a jellyfish bite to take the sting out."

"You're making that up."

"I'm not! I'm an old sea dog, I know all about it."

"Shut up," Eddie says, splashing him.

Francis floats on his back. "This is the only ocean I've ever seen," he says. "This and Coney Island. I'm a city boy."

"Aren't city boys afraid of the ocean?"

Francis rolls like a kayak, spouting a mouthful of water into the air. "No way," he says. "We're not afraid of anything."

Eddie widens his eyes and points out to sea, behind Francis's head. "Shark!"

Francis spins, startled, and Eddie laughs, proud of himself for being playful.

"Got me," Francis says, splashing Eddie. "Square state boy."

"How do you know where I'm from?"

"Lucky guess, I guess."

"Pretty obvious I don't belong here," Eddie says.

Francis spins up and faces Eddie. "Hey. You do belong here. Where you're from doesn't make any difference. You're here now, so that must mean you're supposed to be. Right?"

Eddie doesn't know the answer. Where is *here* anyway? He looks back toward the beach, where the boys are attempting to form themselves into a pyramid. "Are they all from New York?"

"Dunno," Francis says.

"You never asked?"

Francis takes in a mouthful of seawater and spits a spout into the air. "Everyone's from somewhere."

"But aren't they your friends? How long have you known them?"

"Look," Francis says. "We don't ask a lot of questions around here, these days, because everyone's got a past, you know? Especially us. Like, those boys up on the beach. George and Vincent and Buzzy and the rest. They're good people, of course. I only associate with good people. But they are also runaways, maybe also thieves, hustlers. Not because they want to be, but because they had to be, to make their way. That's what the world is for fairies. You can't survive in this world without bending a rule every now and then. Maybe that's why they call us bent."

Buzzy, the smallest of the boys, is clambering his way to the top of the pyramid. The others shout just as he reaches the apex, then squeal as he starts to lose his balance, then all tumble together into a heap of laughter and whoops.

"They don't seem like criminals—"

"Maybe they are, or maybe they aren't. I don't ask. I know all I need to know. They have good hearts, and we are friends. Mates. Family. We take care of one another, we do the best we can. And besides, you can't have a future without a past."

Francis dives under. He disappears into the darker depths, so deep that Eddie can't see him. The sea grows still around him, and quiet. A moment passes, and then another, and then, just when Eddie starts to wonder if he'll ever surface, Francis shoots up, his black hair slicked back off his face. Tiny drops of water fall from his eyelashes, to his collarbone, and down his chest. Eddie watches each drop, wondering what it would feel like to slip down Francis's skin like that. He wants to run a finger across his neck. Down his back. Across his—

Eddie takes a sharp breath, holds it, and exhales.

"What about you?" he asks.

Francis cocks his head quizzically. "What about me?"

"Do you have a past?"

Francis opens his mouth, as if to speak, then abruptly dives under again. A moment later, suddenly, he surfaces just behind Eddie. He wraps his arms around Eddie's shoulders and presses his chest against Eddie's back, his hips against Eddie's hips. Breath grazing Eddie's earlobe, he whispers, "Don't we all?"

And then Eddie feels Francis's lips at the nape of his neck. Soft, careful, the tiniest kiss, hardly any pressure at all, but he holds it there, right there. And then, just as suddenly, he dives back under and away, swimming back to shore, taking Eddie's waterborne boldness with him.

EIGHT

The afternoon sun is heating up, so the boys have gathered closer to the boardwalk, taking refuge in its shade. They cluck and giggle and spar, sometimes sweetly, sometimes sharply, each taking his turn as the target of the group's barbs. But the ritual is never cruel, only clever, and running under it all is a current of committed friendship that Eddie can feel. Thankfully, they never toss their darts at Eddie. Maybe they're treating him gently because he's new. Maybe because he's here with Francis. Or maybe it's just luck.

Whatever the reason, he's grateful. He doubts he'll ever be able to keep up with the pace of their wit even if he did know all the slang and shorthand, which he doesn't. For now, he's happy to listen, spread out in the shade, just a few feet away from the boys.

Currently, they are arguing about when exactly the bathhouse and concessions opened out here, and when the ferry started running, and what was here before all of that. It was a fishing village, Buzzy says, and oystering. No, not oystering, Vincent says (at least Eddie thinks it's Vincent, but he doesn't look over so he can't be sure). Oystering's been banned out here for thirty years. Not so, says Charlie (at least Eddie thinks it's Charlie). That ban was only for the Jamaica Bay side, not out here. And besides, who ever did any oystering here on the ocean side? The waves and currents would make it almost impossible. But Charlie insists that he's right, because his father was an oysterman. I always knew you were an oyster princess, Gabriel says. Oyster queen, Charlie corrects, and collector of pearls. More like pearl necklaces, Vincent says, and everyone laughs. Even Eddie understands that joke.

After a while a few of the boys race down to the water, and the others climb up onto the boardwalk to chase down a man selling cupfuls of water from a cart for a penny. They deputize Eddie to stay put and keep an eye on the blankets and buckets.

Eddie turns onto his side and notices a small group of people on a blanket down the beach, not too far away, gathered around a small patch of dune grass. Maybe thirty yards off. A family, it looks like. A different kind from the one he's sitting with right now. A more typical kind. A woman, a man, and three kids. The man and woman are leaning up against each other, back to back, as the young ones play in the sunshine. They look so peaceful, Eddie thinks. Happy. He closes his eyes.

Soon he feels a sprinkle of sand on his foot. Just the breeze, he figures. He reaches down to brush it off without opening his eyes. Another sprinkle, another brush. Eyes still closed.

Another sprinkle, only this time, it's accompanied by a giggle. So he looks up. It's a little girl, no more than seven, wearing a blue-and-white-striped swimsuit, tank-style with a skirt to her knees. She has a white swim cap on, with a daisy appliqued on one side, but it's much too big for her. A wild poof of red hair spills out over her neck, half-wet curls reaching past her shoulders. She looks mischievous, delighted with herself, holding one hand over her mouth to muffle her laughter. She is adorable, and Eddie can't help but grin back at her. He sits up.

"Hello," he says. He looks around for the others. "Are you lost?"

"No," she says. "My name's not Lost. My name is Lenore. What's yours?"

Eddie sits up. Where are the other boys? Where is Francis? What is he supposed to do with a wayward little girl? Should he take her to someone with authority? Or just let her roam free, like the kids he saw up on the boardwalk? Then he remembers the family on the blanket he noticed a few minutes ago. They are still there, only there are just two children now. "Is that your family?" he asks, pointing.

"Yes," she says. "Mother and Father and my silly brothers. What's your name?"

"I'm Eddie."

"Where did your friends go?"

"Here and there," he says. "Some of them went swimming."

"They should be careful," she says. "There are whales out there. Whales as big as the bathhouse! They could be swallowed whole, and then what will you do?"

"Really!" he exclaims, playing along. "I didn't know whales eat people."

"Oh, they do," she says. "But they won't eat me because I have a flower on my head." She points to her daisy. "They'll say I'm too pretty."

Eddie laughs. "Well, they wouldn't be wrong."

Just then Francis and Gabriel and Charlie come scrambling up the boardwalk, laughing and shouting and throwing peanuts at one another. "Hello!" Francis says, jumping down into the sand. He smiles at the little girl. "Who are you, magical creature? Where did you come from?"

"I'm Lenore," she says. "I came from over there." She points at the family.

"Uh-oh," Vincent says, strolling up from the water. "Look alive, boys. Remember what happened to Sebastian and Gerald, when they found those lost kids at Coney Island and took them to the precinct, trying to be Good Samaritans. Four days in the clink for conduct unbecoming."

Francis waves Vincent's comment away. "She's not lost," he says, then turns to Lenore. "Your swimming costume is exquisite, Lenore."

"It is?" she says.

"Very elegant," he says. "Now, tell me, which country are you the princess of?"

"I am a princess?" she asks, tilting her head in amazement.

"Yes, I believe you are," he says. He strokes his chin thoughtfully, looking intently at her. "In fact, I believe you are the princess of the fairies!"

"I love fairies!" she exclaims, and the boys all look at one another and try not to laugh.

"Your grace," Francis says, his voice suddenly serious. "Your daisy is quite fetching, but you seem to have lost your crown."

She puts her hands up to her head, feeling for a phantom crown.

Francis looks around and gathers a few stray strands of dune grass. "I will fashion one for you, if your grace will permit me."

Lenore watches closely while Francis weaves a rough wreath from the grass. When he's done, he places it on her head, carefully resting on the daisy. "I pronounce you Princess Lenore of the Fairy Kingdom, and I am your liege!"

"My what?"

"Your liege. It's kind of like, well, kind of like a best friend who you can command."

"My best friend," she repeats, and Francis bows theatrically. He motions for the other boys to bow, too, and they do.

"Now, your highness, won't you favor us with a twirl?" Francis asks, and Lenore does, watching her skirt as she goes to make sure it's spinning out like a ballerina's.

"The belle of every ball!" Francis shouts. "Princess Lenore!"

Lenore, overcome by giggles, runs back across the sand to her family. She beams as she goes. They welcome her back, and clap as she spins some more. She takes off her crown to show them. The man, presumably her father, looks over at the boys and springs to his feet.

"Shit," Vincent says. "He sees a bunch of fairies. He's coming over."

"We're not all fairies," Charlie says. "Some of us are pansies."

"And some of us are queers!" Gabriel says. "And queens!"

"You and your words!" Vincent says. "What are we going to do?"

But the man doesn't come over. He just throws up a hand and waves, his grin visible from all the way over here. "Thank you!" the man shouts at the pansies and fairies and queers and queens.

"All hail Princess Lenore!" Francis shouts back, and the rest of the boys shout it, too, even Eddie. "All hail Princess Lenore!"

NINE

The pack of men in loosened vests and cockeyed hats, carrying bottles and shout-singing a drinking song, stumble up the boardwalk toward the boys. They are rowdy, punching one another in the shoulder and thwacking one another on the back. A biplane putters in the sky above them, and one looks up and points at it, stopping the others. "The Red Baron!" he shouts, and the other men shout, too. "Shoot it down! Shoot it down!" Looking skyward, they seem to lose their balance on the boardwalk, stepping dangerously close to the edge, until the biggest one, with a mustache that extends beyond his chin, takes one step too far and falls over, landing next to Eddie with a thud. The impact kicks sand into Eddie's eyes. He leaps up blindly, banging his head on the edge of the boardwalk.

And then, just as suddenly as they appeared, the men are gone. The boys are gone, too—Francis and Vincent and Charlie and the rest. The little girl is gone. The attractions are gone, the roller coaster, the bathhouse, all gone. Eddie is once again in his sneakers and jeans, sitting on the beach beside the boardwalk, his Polaroid at his side. Below him, a small group of seagulls fights angrily over a bare chicken bone in the sand, their flapping wings knocking against an empty beer can, *ting ting, ting ting.*

"Shit!" Eddie spits. He was having such a good time. Feeling so brave. Like he belonged.

And now he's alone again.

He has no idea how to get back to the city, or how long it will take. Not that he wants to go back there anyway, unless it means finding Francis again. But he can't just sit here. He's back in a time when time moves, and Cookie will be waiting.

The boardwalk, so vibrant and active just minutes (decades, a century) ago, is splintered and faded now, quiet, melancholy. Only a few weatherworn shops are open, lazy vendors selling tie-dyed T-shirts and steamy hot dogs. The sun is too bright again. He sees a stand selling cheap sunglasses, just five bucks a pair, but his pockets are empty.

Off to his left, a sign for the A train points the way. If it comes quickly, he'll be back in the Village before long.

The station is empty, so no one notices Eddie slipping through an open exit door and onto the platform for free. He thinks of Francis when he does it, of the thieves and hustlers. Now he's got a past, too, however small.

Soon he's in a train car, sitting across from a woman with pink hair and a cat in a carry-cage, his desperately sleep-deprived head drooping to his chest as they roll across the bridge over Jamaica Bay, bound for Manhattan.

TEN

Have you ever heard a fire alarm on a subway train? Eddie hadn't, either, so when the screeching bell wakes him from his train-nap, he leaps to his feet. He and the other passengers look around, frightened, as the train pulls into the Canal Street station. They push at one another as the doors open, shouting in panic, desperate to get off the potential death trap. Eddie's caught in the crush, pushed out onto the platform. He races with the others toward the Exit sign.

"Don't worry," Francis says, suddenly at Eddie's arm as they sprint up the stairs and out onto the street. "There's no fire. But I had to wake you up somehow. We have a ball to get to."

"You could get arrested for that," Eddie says.

"Not if they can't catch me," Francis says.

It's dark out here, so it takes Eddie a minute to recognize where they are, and when they are. The old cars, the old taxis, the horses and elevated trains and billboards advertising tobacco and coffee and Broadway shows like *Girl Crazy* and *Whoopee!* tell him: They are back in 1930. Eddie's in his scuffed boots, Francis in his newsboy cap.

But it's nighttime, and Eddie is worried about Cookie. "What time is it?" he asks, looking uptown, toward Cookie's neighborhood.

"Don't worry about time, remember?"

"But—"

Francis touches Eddie's cheek.

"Have I ever lied to you?" he asks, and in another mouth the words would sound loaded, even sinister. But in Francis's warm, careful voice, they sound like a safety net, a seat belt, a hand pointing the direction.

They walk along Canal Street, past Broadway, and up through Little Italy to Eldridge Street. They hear so many languages as they cross this part of Manhattan: Chinese, Polish, German, Portuguese, Greek. Francis knows how to say hello in most of them, greeting street vendors and shopkeepers as they go. "Ni hao! Witam! Guten Abend! Ola! Yia sou!"

"Don't be fooled," Francis says. "I can't really speak any of these languages. A little German maybe, a few words in Italian. But it helps, especially down here, to know a word or two. You never can tell where the next person you meet will be from. That's New York, you know? Ah, here we are."

They stop outside a large stone building with an arched doorway, flanked on both sides by tenement stacks. It looks grand but deserted.

"Really?" Eddie asks, skeptical. He's not sure what he expected, maybe a red carpet or a marquee or something to indicate there was a big event happening inside. But the street out front is quiet.

"Dull outside, dazzling inside," Francis says. "New York is a city of hidden depths, you know. Kind of like some people I know." He elbows Eddie in the ribs.

Eddie stiffens at the implication, the idea that Francis can see something inside him. It's the thing he's worked so hard at, to keep what's inside hidden, camouflaged. But after a breath, he relaxes. This is Francis. This is 1930. You're okay here. Be braver.

"Dull?" he flirts, reconjuring the feeling of being in the water.

He takes a step back and spreads his arms to show off his outfit, just a simple black jacket and trousers. "You call this dull?"

Francis laughs. "Don't worry, you look perfect," he says, sweeping the dust from Eddie's shoulders. "You don't want to look like you're too rich, you know? We all hate rich people these days, and they don't know how to have a good time anyway. Besides, wearing all black is a favor to the queens. We look dull so they shine brighter. We're guests, not brides. Know what I mean?"

"If you say so," Eddie says.

"I do." Francis tugs at Eddie's jacket hem and straightens the lapel. "There. Look at you. You'll be the handsomest boy at the ball."

Eddie doubts it. He's not even the most handsome boy standing here on this sidewalk. Not next to Francis, anyway. He steps toward the arched doorway, but Francis stops him.

"No, this one," he says, pointing at another, smaller door off to the side. He guides Eddie inside, and then through a second door, and then into a lobby with faded red carpeting on the wall. "Keep going," he says, nudging Eddie toward a green curtain at the far end of the room.

Francis pulls back the curtain, and together they step into the vast ballroom, crowded with people. The ceiling towers over them, two or three stories high, with a giant chandelier in the exact middle of the room, hanging over a swing band playing, would you believe it, Cole Porter. They play vigorously, music bouncing through the air, as a man with a raspy voice sings in syncopation: *Let's fly away / And find a land that's warm.*

Laughter pierces through the room, mingling with the music as Eddie takes in the scene. There are a hundred, maybe two hundred couples dancing around the band, men in tuxedos dancing with drag queens in stoles, women in tuxedos dancing with women in shifts, young men in ragged suits dancing with other young men. Eddie watches them spin and laugh.

"Is everyone here—" he whispers.

"Yup," Francis says, not needing the rest of Eddie's question to answer with confidence. "Everyone."

They do a lap around the room, Francis leading the way. He seems to know everyone here. He points and nods as he goes, saying hello to this one, giving a peck on the cheek to that one. They all look Eddie up and down, some smiling warmly, some squinting suspiciously, others quickly averting their eyes. Kind of like in real life. (Is this real?)

Francis grabs Eddie's hand and pulls him off to the side of the room, where a bench lines the wall. He climbs up onto it, standing a head above everyone else, then helps Eddie up beside him. From here, they can see the whole room. The crowd seems even bigger from above, swinging tails and sweeping gowns in the center, more modestly dressed partygoers (like Francis and Eddie), mostly in black, around the edges.

"It's almost time," he says.

"For what?"

"You'll see."

There's barely enough room here on this riser for two sets of feet, so Francis stands behind Eddie and wraps his arm around Eddie's chest. He's so close Eddie can feel his breath on his earlobe, and in his mind, Eddie flashes back to the patisserie, where Theo stood behind Eddie just like this. That was only a day or two ago, wasn't it? (What is a day anymore?)

Across the crowd, standing in front of a door adjacent to the one Eddie and Francis entered, a woman in a sharply tailored tuxedo, her hair slicked back and a razor-thin mustache penciled over her lip, cups her hands around her mouth and shouts, "Let the parade begin!"

The door opens, and a very tall person in a flowing lavender gown and towering powdered wig enters, snaps open a fan, looks around at the crowd, and begins to walk. Another, in a red dress with a black lace shawl, follows. Then another, in gold sequins to the floor, and another, in a white halter dress with camellias pinned across the bust. One after another follows, and soon there are ten, twenty, fifty, more, an endless pageant of colors and sequins and turbans and boas and tiaras and corsets and capes. Eddie is astonished by the spectacle, stunned by the confidence in their walks and the complexity of their looks. Their spidery eyelashes and apple cheeks, Cupid's-bow mouths and kohl-drawn brows. Eddie wants to take a photograph for Cookie, because he knows how she'd clasp her hands in delight to see the display, but he doesn't dare. He won't tempt that particular fate. He doesn't want to be sent back to the twenty-first century, not yet. Not yet.

"The pansy parade," Francis whispers. "Isn't it marvelous?"

They watch a queen pass in an orange cape trimmed with feathers that slide across the floor behind her. Another balancing a towering headdress of paper flowers, calla lilies and gladioli. Another in a dramatic, villainesque black column with wide, squared-off shoulders and crimson-stained lips. He sees a Mae West look-alike with a cinched waist and a sprawling Victorian hat. He sees a queen that looks just like Greta Garbo, in a deep blue gown with an open back. Another who looks like Louise Brooks, with a severe black bob and ingenue eyebrows.

"See that one in the green?" Francis asks, pointing. Eddie squints, following Francis's outstretched finger. He sees a queen in an emerald satin sheath clutching a white shrug around her shoulders, platinum ringlets of hair piled high and secured with a tiara. She drags a long strand of pearls behind her, feigning a look of aloofness. She looks like a movie star, untouchable, but as she approaches, the now-familiar features come into focus.

"Is it?" Eddie asks. "Is that—"

"Yes," Francis says. "Carlotta." It is Carlotta—Charlie—and she tips her head in acknowledgment, an elegant gesture as she passes, tapping Eddie on the shoulder with one gloved finger and winking coquettishly. She is beautiful.

"Goddess!" Francis shouts. "You are Jean Harlow! You are dee-vine!"

Carlotta smiles and saunters on.

"Wait till you see Gabby," Francis says.

And then there she is. Gabby—Gabriel—in a blindingly white cape that falls all the way to the floor, her hair a haystack, powdered white. Her cheeks are rouged a shocking red, her eyes lined with green and gold, and she's dabbed a beauty mark on one cheek.

"Gabrielllllla!" Francis shouts, drawing out the Ls with so much enthusiasm his voice cracks. "You are Marie Antoinette! You are Norma Shearer! You are chosen!"

Gabby waves regally, palm facing inward as if she really is a queen. And she is followed by another queen, and another, and another. By now dozens of beautifully turned-out queens are winding through the crowd, whoops and cheers of the spectators echoing off the walls.

"One more round, ladies," the tuxedoed woman says, gesturing with her rhinestone-encrusted walking stick toward the front of the room. "And please don't rush. Let us admire you. Let us be overcome by your femininity. Let us bathe in the extravagance of your beauty."

Eddie is dazzled. He's never seen anything like this, certainly not in real life, and never in his fantasies. He doubts he could even conjure such an elaborate, colorful, creative vision. Hats, boas, big-shouldered gowns, flowing robes, intricate kimonos, corseted bodices. Red lips, tinted eyelids, pomaded curls, brows dusted with glittery mica powder. He cheers for their honesty, their bravery, their belief in themselves. Here they are, proudly sweeping through a room of admirers, forgetting (or maybe just setting aside) for the briefest moments just how impossible this should be, how impossible it is—except here. Here, in this ballroom, in the safe embrace of one another, they can open up their colors. Eddie cheers for them. He wishes it would never end.

But eventually, it does. After the parade participants have circled the room twice, and gathered to pose in the front, and after several ovations from the onlookers, the queens begin to mingle with their admirers. Francis loosens his grip on Eddie's chest and hops down to the floor, where they wander among the queens, admiring their outfits.

"Isn't it something?" Francis asks. "Seems like there's a ball every week somewhere in the city. And in Chicago, Boston, Berlin, Paris. All around the world."

"Have you been to those cities?" Eddie asks.

"Some of them," Francis says.

He plucks two glasses off the tray of a passing waiter and hands one to Eddie. The seltzer is different this time, flavored with mint and licorice, a compelling combination that lingers on Eddie's palate. "Delicious," he says.

"Drink up," Francis says, holding out his hand. "Because now, we dance."

And they do. They dance. They spin and jump and swing and Francis wraps his arms around Eddie and flings him into the air and catches him again, and Eddie sings aloud, not knowing the words to the songs but not caring, and he knows they won't stop until the sweat soaks through their shirts and their legs wobble beneath them. Oh, let this moment last. Let this ball go on forever. Don't send me back to the real world, to the other world, to my world. I want this world now. Not that one. Francis's world. Not mine. He dances faster.

Eventually the music softens to something slower. Eddie stands in front of Francis, breathing hard, sweat dripping from the ends of his hair. He pulls at his shirt, laughing. "I'm soaking wet!"

Francis reaches for Eddie. "So am I," he says, wrapping his arm around Eddie's waist and pulling him closer as the singer starts to croon: *You do something to me.*

"Cole Porter," Eddie says.

"Our best," Francis says. "Timeless. Even a hundred years from now, two hundred years from now, he'll still be our best."

"How can you know that?"

Francis pulls Eddie's head into his shoulder, where it fits perfectly, like a missing piece. "Timeless is timeless," Francis says. "We are timeless, too."

They sway through the slow song, Francis's hands around Eddie's waist, Eddie's lips pressed against Francis's neck, tasting the salt of his sweat.

When the song ends, the other partygoers—the fairies and the pansies and the queens and the queers—all start to shuffle off the floor to gather their things and head for home. But not Eddie and Francis. They stay where they are, swaying, connected, blissful, until the tuxedoed woman shouts, "Good night!" and the lights overhead burst into illumination, shocking the hall with a sudden, blinding, explosive flash.

ELEVEN

Is Eldridge Street today so different from a hundred years ago? New shops, maybe. New cars. New noises, a few new buildings. But not everything is new. Some of the stoops are the same. Some of the window frames, the rooftops, the doors. And the people. The errands are different, the clothes, the slang slung from their mouths. But not so different. The same worried looks, the same generous laughter, the same recognition exchanged between neighbors.

Eddie trots up the block, and back down again, his pace increasing from building to building as he searches for a way off the sidewalk and back to the ball. A promising door, a Cole Porter melody on the air, a glimpse of Francis. Something. But there is nothing. Nothing but a mundane overcast day at an ordinary hour, a procession of people tugging on dog leashes or mumbling into their Bluetooth earbuds or pushing bikes as they stroll, sipping coffee from paper cups.

What's going on behind the doors here now? A dance? A ball? A room full of people celebrating, dancing, sipping licorice seltzer? Remember the way it tasted, Eddie? Remember the pins and needles on your tongue? Remember the way you and Francis fit together, Eddie? The way you moved together. The way your head nestled into him, like it was sculpted just for that. But that's over now.

Vanished. Instantly, inexplicably gone, brutally gone, leaving nothing. You knew it would be, Eddie. It always ends too soon, doesn't it? But this time feels different. This time, it's not just the floor that's fallen out from underneath. This time you want to blame someone. But who? Francis? Fate? Yourself?

Have you done this to yourself, Eddie?

The thoughts feel like panic. He has to find his way back. He has to know, to see, to understand. To believe. Nothing will be right until he does.

He feels the camera hanging from his shoulder.

Maybe this, he thinks, suspending the truth, pretending he doesn't know better. Maybe this is the way. Maybe this has been the way all along.

But when he aims it at the building behind him and presses the button, nothing happens at all. Just a picture of a building. He takes another, and another, impatient for the camera to spit out every plastic card before he turns the camera on another doorway, another window. He snaps, and snaps, one after the other, hoping for something to happen, for some alchemy to occur, for that phantom boy to reappear. Another picture, nothing. Another, another. He shoots until he runs out of film, and then keeps shooting, tears leeching from his eyes.

This time, you haven't just lost Francis, Eddie. This time, you're losing hope.

People talk about loneliness like it's a slow feeling. A dragging, dull sense of missing someone you've loved for a long time, someone you've grown accustomed to, someone who's nestled into the crevices of you. But this, here on Eldridge Street, is a different loneliness, a sharp, swift, brutal, piercing loneliness, the kind you only feel when you're missing someone you've barely begun to know, when you're missing not just what was, but all that hadn't yet been. Francis was still new to Eddie—his movements, his enthusiasms, his smile, his smell. And now he's gone, and the space he's left in Eddie is too big for Eddie to fill for himself. His sense of logic won't fill it. His imagination won't fill it. Cookie won't fill it. Theo won't fill it. Only a return would fill it. But how?

I will see Francis again, Eddie tells himself. I am going to find him. I am going to prove he is real, that all of this is real. It has to be real. I don't know who I am if this isn't real.

Let me find you.

"Are you okay?" a woman pushing a stroller asks him.

How is he supposed to answer her? He's anything but okay. He doesn't know how to slow the spinning of his mind. He doesn't know where he is. But he is standing. His feet are on the ground and he's breathing. And so Eddie, conspicuous Eddie, nods. That's enough for her. She doesn't care about him. Not really.

TWELVE

Eddie hasn't said hello yet, and Cookie hasn't noticed that he's here. He watches her from her doorway. She's sitting up in bed, holding a picture frame in her lap, smiling and whispering and tapping her lacquered nail on the glass. What's that feel like, he wonders, to just sit in bed and be content, and not worry about who you are or where you belong?

Eddie is pissed off. Not at Cookie, not at anyone, really. Only at himself. There's no one else to blame for the way he feels right now, for getting so caught up in the idea of Francis. He really should know better. He's so good at staying inconspicuous, quiet, out of the way in the world he knows. Why should this wrinkle in time, this glitch in the matrix, be any different? It's just another fantasy, or maybe another reality. It's not like he's any different, right?

Yes, he's pissed off, but he can't show it to Cookie. All she'll do is ask him about it, and the last thing he wants to do is talk. He's going to have to conjure up a happy face and sip sherry and listen to her go on about whatever dead movie star she's got in her lap.

"Hello, Lollipop," she says without looking up. There's a cheerful nonchalance in her voice. "It's such a beautiful day today. When I was little, on days like this, we always went to the beach. We'd get in the car and Daddy would drive us. Coney Island, Long Beach, Jones

Beach. We'd stay all day until I was as red as a cooked lobster. Is that what you did today? I don't know why, but I had a feeling you might go to the beach. Did you? Did you go to the beach?"

Eddie answers reflexively, too quickly. "No, I didn't go to the beach," he says, but of course yes, in a way, he did go to the beach. But it wasn't today, not exactly. Or was it? "No," he says again, knowing how much energy it would take to explain, knowing he doesn't have it.

Cookie's eyes narrow, a suspicious expression. She leans back against her pillows and picks up her hand mirror. She wets her thumb and forefinger on her tongue to tend to her spit curl. "I see."

His brain is so muddled right now, his words so clumsy. But she knows he's lying. He knows he won't get away with it. Better fix it now. "Oh, Cookie. I forgot. I did go to the beach. It was so beautiful. I wish you could have been there to see it." He chirps his words, hoping to distract her from the lie he just told. "The sun was high and bright but it wasn't too hot. The breeze off the ocean was so nice. I went into the sea twice. We bought peanuts on the boardwalk—"

She interrupts. "We? We who?"

Eddie stumbles. "I mean, there were a lot of people out there and—"

Cookie lowers her mirror and looks up at him, the tiniest crinkle forming just at the corner of her eye. The beginning of a smile. "Did you make some friends?"

Did he? Did Eddie make some friends? He met some people, sort of, or something. He saw Francis again, or something. But are those friends? He shakes his head. "No," he lies again. "Not really."

Cookie sighs, returning her concentration to her spit curl. She's not convinced. He can see that.

"That's a shame," she says coolly. "Honestly, I don't know what it is with you young ones. In my day, we made friends at the drop of a hat. Just walked right up to people and said hello, and they said hello back, and that was that. Like Tallulah here." She taps the photograph in her lap. "I just started talking to her one day, and now we're bosom buddies. But you kids, I don't know. It's all different now. Everyone's scared of one another. Everyone's too busy with their little phones. Don't you young ones like people?"

Eddie tries to fake a look of indifference, but inside he's stung by what she's said. Even though she's talking about an imaginary friendship with a photograph of a dead person, he's stung.

"It's a shame you kids will never know the kind of freedom we had," she says. Her tone straddles pity and smugness, with another foot in resignation. "You'll never have that kind of fun. You could, of course, if you tried. But you don't. You won't. You don't have it in you. I guess you just like things easier."

"What is that supposed to mean?"

"I think you're scared. That's what I mean."

"Scared? Of what?"

"To let go. To be yourselves. To rebel. To break a rule every now and then. To try something you don't know anything about. To take chances. You can't even walk across town without looking at your little map things. You won't even go to a movie without checking to see what other people think of it. Not like us. We weren't afraid. Everything was new, everything was risky, no one told us what was safe, or not safe, but we went for it anyway. We weren't afraid to fail, we weren't afraid to fall. But you kids? Timid. Afraid to be different. Afraid to be yourself. Even your movie stars are boring. Carbon copies, one just like the next. It's sad, it really is."

Eddie balls his hands into fists, digging his fingernails into his palms to keep from saying something unkind to Cookie. Something like shut up.

"Don't you agree, Tallulah?" she says to the photograph in her lap. "We knew how to have fun, didn't we? The kids today, though? Not a chance. They wouldn't dare. No guts."

    This tips him. This tips Eddie into something he'll regret later. But the cynicism spills out before he can stop it, and he feels his voice rising. "Oh, of course, Cookie. Your life has been so much better than mine. Is that what you want to hear? That the way you lived was so brilliant and fearless. The way you lived was the only way. No one else will ever measure up. Is that it?"

    "That's about it," she says, smirking.

    "Except it's not the 1920s anymore, Cookie. We don't walk around wondering if someone's going to tie us to the train tracks like in a Charlie Chaplin movie."

    "That never happened in a Charlie Chaplin movie," Cookie says.

    Eddie explodes, uncontrolled now. "Whatever! It's not the 1920s! It's not the 1950s, or the '60s, or even the '80s! We don't walk around worried about switchblade dance-offs like in *West Side Story*, or catching the mumps from someone in gym class! We walk around wondering when a psychopath is going to pull out a semiautomatic rifle at school and shoot us all. We wonder how many of our friends are going to die from overdoses! We don't even know if the planet's going to be inhabitable by the time we're thirty! And that's all thanks to you! You and your fun-loving ways! Look at the mess you're leaving us! No, the world is different now, Cookie. But you, you wouldn't understand. You wouldn't be able to. You're too—" Something inside tells him to stop himself, and so he does.

    "Too what?" she snaps. "Too old? Is that what you think?"

    Eddie doesn't answer. He stares at the wall, grinding the inside of his cheek between his teeth.

    "I stand by what I said. No guts," she says. "No guts. No moxie. No imagination."

    "Says the expert on imagination!" Eddie shouts. "Says the lady who stays up all night talking to pictures in frames! Says the lady who's lived in the same apartment for eighty years! Says the lady who calls herself eccentric, but who everyone knows is nothing but crazy!"

Cookie's jaw twitches, and then her cheek. Her shoulders fall and her mouth turns down. Her gaze drops from his eyes, to his mouth, to his neck, to the floor. She looks wounded, hurt, angry. She clutches the photograph to her chest and turns away from him. "Why are you here, Eddie?"

Eddie, she called him. Not *Lollipop*. Just *Eddie*. He's so stunned to hear his real name from her mouth that he just stands, staring.

"Well?"

"I—"

"I think it's time for you to go," she says, not quietly, not loudly, just flat and clear. "I think it's time."

"Fine, I'm going to lie down."

"I said it is time to go," she says, and he can hear a finality in her voice, like a door slamming, and it shocks him. She doesn't just mean go, she means *go*.

"But," he says, choking on the words. "Where? Where am I supposed to go?"

"What are you asking the *crazy* lady for?" she says flatly. "You know everything, don't you? You've got it all figured out. You're not crazy. So go wherever you want. I don't care. I don't need you here. Just go. Just—" She grips her back scratcher tightly, knuckles whitening. "Go."

That familiar flavor of panic floods his throat, that anxious bile. He hasn't tasted it in a while, but it rushes back now, nearly choking him. He tries to swallow it, but it bubbles, like lava. "Cookie," he says. "I'm—"

He reaches for her hand but she swats him away, cold, hardened, distant.

"I said go."

THIRTEEN

I said go.
  Shit, Eddie. Now you've done it. Now you've really screwed up. What will you do now? Sleep on the street? In the park? At Port Authority? Go back in and beg?
  Eddie stands on Bedford Street, with the camera slung over his shoulder. He looks up the street, down. Which way? It doesn't matter, Eddie. Walk.
  As he walks up Seventh Avenue, he feels a plastic card in his pocket. Another picture that never developed. He doesn't even look at it. Just crunches it up in his hand and throws it in a garbage bin without even breaking stride. He won't see, of course, that it did develop, after all, but its image isn't like anything that he saw this morning. It's a photograph of a girl, maybe fourteen, maybe sixteen, sitting alone on a park bench, reading a book. *Portrait of Jennie,* the book is called, and she's nearly finished.
  It was the first time that girl ever saw her future. She knew it would come, and it did come, but it wasn't until after the war when, like everyone else it seemed, she opened a bookshop. She had no money, no experience, and if there was an entrepreneurial hair on her head, no one had ever noticed it before. But she did it, right there on Cornelia Street, dinky little Cornelia Street with its

basement laundries and corner greengrocer and three tobacco shops. And people came. It was like flypaper, her shop, collecting everyone. The poets, the musicians, the actors, the landlords, the soldiers, the cooks, the swans, the communists, the painters, the subway drivers, the politicians, the organizers, the teachers, the mistresses, the queens. Capote came, and Cecil Beaton, even the Bouviers and Paleys when they ventured downtown. Dick Avedon came to shoot photos of Dovima in the back stacks. Rosalind Russell brought Peggy Cass, Christopher Isherwood brought Don Bachardy, Cecil Cunningham brought Anna May Wong. Allen Ginsberg brought cookies from San Francisco, Jean Cocteau brought cookies from Paris. Montgomery Clift fell asleep on the floor by the poetry section, where Anthony Perkins tripped over him and nearly broke his neck. She laughed then, and so did they. Louis Falco was there, skipping school to browse the shelves, just a teenager then, so beautiful. Some people swear they saw Garbo there, but you could never be sure with Garbo, because she'd stopped looking like herself.

The men came after the bar raids. They came after the rent boy roundups. They knew the shop was a refuge. Even the down-and-outs and drunks came, to lean against the shelves and thumb through GI paperbacks. She never kicked them out, even if they never bought a thing, because hardly anyone ever bought a thing. They just talked, and argued, and gossiped, and smoked, and flirted, and schemed, and lamented, and planned, and worried, and wondered, and stayed. Everyone stayed. Oh, it was an exciting time. Like magic. She was like magic. Have you ever known a person like that? A person who everyone loved?

Even when the landlord raised the rent after the election, the big one, and she feared she'd have to close up, the people rallied. They came together and paid the rent on her shop, their shop, and they paid it over and over, year after year, until the world changed again and she locked the door behind her for the very last time.

But Eddie won't hear this story, not for a long time. For now he'll just keep walking. Who cares where? He'll walk every street in this city. What else is he going to do, besides walk?

FOURTEEN

"**H**ey!"

Eddie doesn't hear that first greeting. The rest of us do, but he doesn't. Or maybe he does, but it doesn't register. He's in a daze of anger and confusion and regret, weighted down by a searing, brutal loneliness. He's been walking, thinking, not eating, for a long time, and his brain is foggy, misfiring, exhausted. He's not paying attention to where he is. Lost.

"Eddie!"

He looks up to see a face. A familiar face, a lovely face, warm and focused, standing in the patisserie doorway. What's that on the side of the face? Oh, a dusting of flour. That's right. He's not lost after all. He's on Cornelia Street again. It's where his body seems to come, when it doesn't know what else to do.

"It's so good to see you!" Theo says, holding the door open. "I've been wondering about you. Mysterious man."

Eddie still doesn't answer. It's dark out here. No one's around, just a lonely taxicab thumping across a pothole, and Theo.

"Your timing is perfect. I was just about to roll out some croissants and I could use the extra help. Come on in, I'll get you an apron and put you to work."

Eddie doesn't move.

Theo's voice lowers. "Eddie? Are you all right? How long have you been here?"

"I don't know," Eddie says honestly. He's foggy. Maybe he got here a minute ago. Maybe an hour. Maybe a lifetime. "What time is it?" he asks.

"Three?" Theo says, though it sounds like a question. "Or just after."

"Oh." Eddie's voice sounds distant, even to himself.

Theo looks up the street, and down it. The taxi has thumped away. There is nothing here now, only a distant, blinking Don't Walk sign, warning nobody.

"Is everything all right?" he asks.

"I'm fine," Eddie says, suddenly hyperaware of where he is, and embarrassed. The last time he saw Theo was so humiliating, the way Theo had to pull him up off the curb and walk him home. "Everything is fine."

"Come inside," Theo says, gentle, soft, strong. "I'll put on some fresh coffee."

The words are friendly, but they grate against Eddie, whose fury still simmers, searching for a target, any target other than himself. Talk about what? Theo's kindness can't solve Eddie's problems. Theo's kindness can't help at all. It only reminds Eddie of how unkind he was to Cookie. How small and impatient and cruel.

"No," Eddie says. "I shouldn't have bothered you. I'm sorry."

"Eddie," Theo says, taking a step forward. "It's dark out here. I don't think you should be out here in the dark. We don't even have to talk if you don't want to. We'll play music. Or you can sleep on the cot that Gaston keeps in the back. Just come inside." He puts his hand on Eddie's shoulder.

Why is he being so nice? Eddie doesn't deserve this right now.

He hasn't earned it. What's he ever done for Theo? Nothing but be a pest. He pushes Theo away, sending the bigger boy stumbling backward into the door. It swings open behind him, ringing the entry bell, the gentle tinkle incongruous inside Eddie's stormy mind.

"What's going on, Eddie?" Theo says, his voice tighter now as he regains his balance. Is he angry? He should be. But his face says he's only concerned. Worried.

Eddie doesn't have an answer. He can't find answers for anything right now. Not an answer for what's been happening, an answer for why he's walking, an answer for who he even is anymore. He knows himself in Francis's world, but here, in this world, in Theo's world, he can't find an answer for anything. Not a fucking thing.

Oh, that acrid bile in his throat. It rises again, thick with humiliation. A toxic elixir. He is so sick of that flavor. He wants to retch, to spit, to cut off his tongue so he never has to taste it again.

"I don't know," he says, jaw clenching in resentment. How dare Theo see him like this?

"Let me help you." Theo speaks slowly. His voice is so calm. "Come inside, Eddie. Let me help you."

"No!" Eddie shouts, like a child, shocking himself with the intensity. "I don't belong here! You don't know anything about me. I don't belong in your perfect little world with your perfect little cakes! Just leave me alone!"

It's a terrible thing to say, and he knows it. But he's got nowhere else to put this frustration, this fury. So he aims it at Theo, and spins away. He trips blindly across the sidewalk, catching his foot on an empty cardboard box and tumbling into the street. He catches himself on his elbow, drawing blood, then quickly scrambles back up and, not looking back, speeds into a run. He can picture Theo behind him, watching him go, and the image enrages him even more. What a pathetic sight he must be. Weak and ugly and stupid and cruel. Exposed. Naked. Raw. Eddie.

He races around the corner and up Sixth Avenue, rageful tears streaming as he runs. *I hate myself. I hate myself. I hate myself.*

FIFTEEN

Eddie hangs his head, ashamed as he replays the last twenty-four hours. How unfair he was to Cookie. How unkind he was to Theo. And what's happened to Francis? Did he fuck that up, too? Maybe this is just who he is—a terrible person, someone who takes people for granted, someone who says cruel things, someone unreliable and ugly who trashes everything good. There's hardly anything left to destroy now.

He should be more tired than he is. He hasn't slept. He walked through the night and the day, up to Central Park, back down to the Battery, and now to the Christopher Street pier. It's dark again. It feels like days since he's been to bed. Years, centuries. Too many to count, too many to contain. He can't hold it all, can't control it, and he's never been out of control before. Not since he learned what control means. Not since he learned how important it is, to enter a moment on your own terms, to exit whenever you wish. Maybe he was bored in Mesa Springs, but he had control. Nothing happened that he didn't ask for. No surprises. Even his dull clothes, his dull job, his low expectations—all just expressions of control, nothing more. Even the fantasies, the illusions. He directed them, like movies, taking them where he wanted them to go, and no further.

But that's all gone now, and he can't predict from breath to breath what's happening, what might happen, what will happen. It's like he's being knocked around like a steel marble in a pinball machine, bouncing from the past to today and back again, from exhilaration to despair and back again, from belonging to not belonging and back again. He can't even retreat to his imaginary worlds inside. He barely recognizes them anymore. Foreign lands, created by someone else. Only strangers there now.

Now.

He scoffs at the word. What does *now* even mean? Is it the opposite of *then*? Is it the end of *then*? The beginning? He always thought that time is meant to move in one direction, a steady tick-tock from early to late, from before to after, from yesterday to today to tomorrow. Then is then, now is now. Simple. But now, nothing about time makes sense. It slips. It stalls. It sprints, stumbles, stops. It falls away, doubles back, burrows, hibernates, deceives, dissolves, explodes, fades. We pretend we can measure it, but we can't, not really. Clocks tick and turn, measuring minutes and hours. But minutes and hours are not time. They are just words, invented ideas, clumsy attempts to suggest structure, false promises claiming to be truth. But they are not time. Time can't be captured by a clock. Or a person.

Eddie stares across the black river as the questions he's faced over the last few days speed through his mind. What are you afraid of, Eddie? Why are you here, Eddie? Who are you, Eddie? What do you want, Eddie?

What do you want?

The question echoes inside, over and over, a rhythm, a chant, an insistent, demanding beat.

"Shut up!" he shouts, to no one.

He kicks a rock off the edge of the pier, because nothing makes sense. And then another rock, and another, but the splashes they make in the thick, slow-moving Hudson don't satisfy him at all. They just tuck themselves into the inky waves and disappear. Unfelt, unheard, unseen, unimportant. Inconspicuous. These rocks mean nothing to this river. He kicks another one. It is absorbed into the black.

It was so easy to be with the boys at the speakeasy, at the beach, at the ball. It was so easy to be with Francis. Eddie was comfortable there. He could breathe. No bile, no fear. He was where he belonged, for the first time in his life, even though he'd never been further from home.

Is that the answer to the question, Eddie? To belong?

He opens the camera and points it aimlessly across the river, at nothing. He snaps, and when the camera whirrs, it sounds like more words: *Let me find you.*

Eddie rips the photograph from the camera and stares at it. But it is a dud, blank, just a black square. This stupid camera, he thinks. This stupid piece of junk. He believed it was special, but it is not. He throws it to the ground in anger, instantly regretting it as he hears it scrape against the cement. He steps forward to pick it up.

And just then, a voice.

"Hiya."

Eddie spins to see Francis, arms wide open.

For a moment he freezes, stunned to see the boy he's been so desperate to find. His presence shocks Eddie, sparking adrenaline. He throws himself against Francis with all his weight and strength, nearly knocking the boy over.

"Whoa!" Francis laughs, struggling to stay upright against the force of Eddie's lunge. "Easy!"

But Eddie doesn't ease up. He drives into the boy, gripping his waist tighter, tighter, a frantic clutch. Oh, this urgent impulse to grasp, to hold, to squeeze, to possess . . . how close it feels to violence.

Nothing matters but contact. Eddie pushes deeper into Francis, fusing them together.

Francis squares his feet to stop his backward momentum, steady now. He wraps his arms around Eddie's back. "Hey," he says softly, taming the beast. He reaches up to cradle the back of Eddie's neck with one hand. "It's okay. It's only me."

Only you? Eddie thinks. *Only you?* He looks down at the ground, at Francis's Nike sneakers. "Where did you—"

"Shh," Francis says, caressing Eddie's nape. "You're all right."

Eddie burrows closer, pressing his face against Francis's chest, fighting tears, gasping like a little boy trying not to cry. "I didn't know how to find—"

"Shh," Francis repeats. He rests his chin on Eddie's head. "Everything's okay. I'm here, you're here. We're here. We're okay."

After Eddie finds his breath again, he exhales and relaxes his grip. But he doesn't let go. "I'm sorry," he whispers. "I'm sorry. Fuck."

Francis draws his head back and raises an eyebrow. He smiles, eyes shining. "You kiss your mother with that mouth?"

Eddie looks back, feeling a sense of comfort wash over him. That now-familiar feeling of belonging that seems to come when Francis is around. "I guess I do," he says.

"Lucky mother," Francis says, pulling him close again.

Eddie closes his eyes and they stay there for a few minutes, or maybe longer (what is time?), before Francis speaks.

"Let's go," he says. He turns and starts across the West Side Highway. As he walks, he kicks up a cloud of dust, and through it, Eddie sees his sneakers morph into scuffed work boots, his jeans into nubby gray trousers. The trees along the pier-path fold into themselves, disappearing. The skyline draws downward, sinking into towers of stone, not glass. The cars spin from SUVs into sedans.

Even the distant music changes into a wistful crooner's love song. It's all a peaceful transition, nothing more than a breeze, but in it, everything changes. Everything except Francis himself.

Francis turns back and beckons Eddie. "Come on," he says, and without asking where, or why, Eddie follows.

SIXTEEN

If you were to ask Eddie how he and Francis got from the downtown piers in 1943 to the marina all the way up on Seventy-Ninth Street along the Hudson River in 1930, and did it all in the course of just a few minutes (hours, decades, lifetimes), this is the answer he would give you:

First, they walked through 1943, from the pier over to Houston Street, where, after the boys narrowly missed a loud but not especially destructive collision between two bicyclists, it was suddenly 1892. Francis waved down a hansom cab, and the driver slowed the horse just enough for him to boost Eddie aboard and scramble on himself. They rode up bumpy Sixth Avenue, its dirt heavily grooved by endless carriage wheels, all the way to Eighth Street, where a pothole knocked the boys out of the cab and onto the ground.

When they dusted themselves off it was 1909, and a hand-cranked motorcar came careening around the corner, narrowly missing the boys. The driver, a young man with deep red curls and a deeper brogue, apologized and gave them a lift to Fourteenth Street, where he sputtered out of gas and it was 1963.

Francis and Eddie, like athletes on a football field, darted through the Sixth Avenue traffic, weaving and dodging all the way up to 1938, Twenty-Third Street, where Francis shouted, "Bus!" and the boys leapt onto a moving city bus, grasping at the window frames to hang on for as long as they could.

They held on as far as 1952, Thirty-Fourth Street, when the bus came to a grinding halt at the end of its line, 1977, Herald Square. The air was filled with disco music and the sidewalks were thick with bellbottom slacks and stack-heel sandals.

And so on, and so on, up through the city and through the years. To 1940 on Forty-Second Street, to 1916 on Forty-Ninth Street, to 1968 on Fifty-Seventh, where they caught a lift on the roof of a camper van.

They hopped across the city like frogs across a pond of lily pads, leaping through neighborhoods and time as lightly as dancers. Finally, at Seventy-Seventh Street, Francis yelled, "Jump!" and the boys tumbled off the back of the milk-delivery truck they'd boarded at Amsterdam Avenue. Francis laughed as they landed and rolled, breathless but unharmed, in 1930.

"Welcome home," Francis said as he swept dust from Eddie's shoulders.

And now here they are, standing by the Hudson at the end of Seventy-Ninth Street, breathing in the humid evening air. They stand with their arms by their sides, knuckles faintly grazing each other's, looking out over the unusually calm water at the half-moon over the shadowy Palisades rising across the river.

Francis breaks the silence. "I have an idea," he says, pointing at a small skiff tied up at one of the docks in the marina below.

SEVENTEEN

Eddie is grateful for the stillness of the water tonight. The vision of the river's angry dark waves swallowing stones just an hour (day, generation) ago has been eclipsed by the placid current now. Francis steers the skiff by its small, sputtering outboard motor through the slow waves, snaking out of the marina and into the open water. It's a small thing, this boat, maybe ten feet long, with two slats of wood spanning across the hull, one in the back by the motor where Francis sits, and one in the middle for Eddie. A small tarp covers most of the front half of the boat, or as Francis says, bow.

"The front is the bow. The back is the stern. The left side is port and the right side is—" Francis stops, raising his eyebrows to invite Eddie's guess.

Eddie shrugs.

"Starboard," Francis says.

"You sound like an expert."

"I used to drive an oyster boat in Jamaica Bay."

Eddie's mind flashes back to the conversation at the beach, the other day in 1930, when Vincent and Charlie were arguing about the ban on oyster fishing in Jamaica Bay. They said it took effect thirty years before. Which means Francis must have somehow— Eddie's mind tumbles.

"We don't have boats in Mesa Springs," he says. "Other than a kayak or two on Rifle Creek."

"I've always wanted to see Rifle Creek," Francis says.

Eddie's eyes widen. "You've heard of it?"

Francis laughs. "Of course not."

Eddie swats his shoulder.

"Ouch!" Francis yelps, then turns to the river. "Tonight, we will have to settle for the mighty Hudson. Not a bad stand-in, I'd say."

Eddie watches Francis's eyes as he steers the boat confidently into the center of the river to catch the current. It's lazy, but still strong, drawing them down toward the tip of Manhattan.

It's warm out here on the water, warmer than you'd think from shore. Even with the breeze, the midsummer air is thick. Eddie drapes an arm over the side of the boat and drags a finger in the cool water, watching the reflected lights from the city and the moon glimmer in the tiny wake. His mind begins to churn again, trying to make sense of all this, but it only goes in circles. *Stop trying to explain it all, Eddie. Don't quash the magic. It feels good to be here, doesn't it? Wherever, or whenever this is. It feels good. Maybe that's enough.*

But he doesn't listen to himself. He has to ask. "How do you do it?" Eddie asks.

"Do what?"

"Travel? Move? Slip through? I don't know the word to use. Whatever you call it. How does it work? How do you get from then to now? From there to here? How is it possible?"

"I don't know," Francis says, with something like wistfulness. "It's almost like this current. It just sweeps you along, whether you want to go or not. You just go, and you end up where you end up. If you're lucky, it's a place you want to be."

"But what if it's not a place you want to be? How do you get back to—" Eddie stops himself. Back to where, Eddie? Where does Francis belong? Where is his home? "Back to somewhere you want to be?"

"I want to be here," Francis says. "In our boat."

"But I don't know where you're from. I don't even know how old you are."

"Not everything has an explanation. Some things you just have to trust. I've learned this."

"Like what?"

Francis flips a switch and the outboard motor sputters once more, then stops. They are only drifting now.

"Like I am here. Like you are here. Like we are together, and time is on our side," he says. He pulls his shirt up over his head and tosses it to one side, then scoots down to the base of the boat, onto his back, halfway under the tarp. "Come," he says.

Eddie, drawn by the glow of Francis's skin, slips off the slat and next to the beautiful boy. Soon, his own shirt is off, and they are kissing, slowly at first, taking their time, and then more urgently. Francis's kiss tastes like caramel, like chestnuts, like seawater, like licorice, like all the flavors they've known together, like skin. Eddie takes greedy mouthfuls, hands grasping.

"Easy," Francis says, steering them. "Let's not rush. Let's never rush."

They move slowly. Somehow Francis knows to meet every one of Eddie's gestures, and somehow Eddie knows to answer back, every motion a perfect synchronicity, every touch bringing them closer. Eddie's hands around Francis's shoulders, fingers interlocked behind him. Francis's arms around Eddie's waist, resting at the coccyx, just there. They whisper, and laugh, and ask, and answer, and when the feelings overwhelm them they shudder, each holding the other, protective, steadying. Lips pressed against ears, tiny sounds, the soft *tap, tap, tap* of the waves against the skiff, the distant hum of the city.

I am here. You are here. We are together.

How natural it all feels, how easy and relaxed, like a seamless recitation of a passage Eddie didn't even know he'd memorized. He's wondered about this moment for years, about what to do, about how he'd look, about what he'd feel, about bravery. In Francis's hands, beside Francis's body, following Francis's lead, Eddie feels no doubt, no fear, no hesitation, no shame. He feels only alive.

"Is this a dream?" Eddie asks, curling over and on top of Francis. "Are you real?"

"Are you?" Francis replies, his voice a vibration as he wraps his legs around Eddie.

Eddie's hands grasp at the boy beneath him, clutching hungrily at his waist, his thighs, his hands. "Yes," he answers. "I am."

EIGHTEEN

After some time (what is time?) they come up for air, leaning into each other and watching the lights of the city from the river. At first, the skyline is low, with only the Empire State Building and Chrysler Building standing above the rest.

But as they drift, the skyline changes. Buildings rise, and fall, and rise again. Eddie recognizes some—the World Trade Center, the towers of Madison Square, Hudson Yards. They sprout like flowers, then recede like vapor as the boys float downstream and around the Battery. Francis steers them up the East River where the Brooklyn Bridge appears and then vanishes. And then the Manhattan Bridge. And the Williamsburg Bridge. The Domino Sugar building, the UN building, the Queensboro Bridge. One after the other they appear and disappear, rising and falling, like time.

Francis whispers, "What do you want, Eddie?"

It's that question again. That relentless, unanswerable question, that plague. Except from Francis's lips, the question doesn't scare Eddie. Here, now, for the first time, he has an answer.

"I want this," Eddie says, burrowing into Francis's chest. "I want forever."

But you already have forever, Eddie. Can't you feel it in your hand? It's not an impossible possession. It's not off in the distance, not a limitless expanse. It's not even big. Forever is small. It begins and ends before you can even say its name. Forever is *this* instant, *this* thought, *this* breath, *this* pulse, and it is everything, the only thing. The future, the past—these are only ideas. The breath you just took is only a memory, your next breath only a possibility. They don't exist, because they are no more, or they are not yet. There is only here, and here is everywhere. There is only now, and now is forever.

There is only us.

With Eddie's head in his lap, Francis blinks up at the stars, watching them churn in the sky, marking the years, the decades, the generations, time and light and infinity, everything he knows and doesn't know.

"Yes," he says. "Forever."

They pass silently under the bridges, up the Harlem River, back into the Hudson, floating slowly, gently, safe in their skiff. They skirt a city of millions, unnoticed, the only two people in the world.

PART FOUR

ONE

"Wake up!"

Eddie snaps into consciousness with a yelp, eyes wide to see Albert standing over him, panic in every crease on his ashen face.

"She's not breathing!" Albert shouts. "Do you hear me? She's not breathing! Get up!"

Eddie springs off the fainting couch and pulls on his jeans.

"I called 911." Albert's voice is shaking with worry. "The emergency crew is on the way. Now go pack a bag for Cookie. Change of clothes, her hand mirror, her lipstick. A beret. What am I forgetting?"

Eddie races to the little closet in the hallway where Cookie keeps a small faux-crocodile valise. Before he can extract it from the stacks of coats and shoes and boas and capes, a trio of EMTs comes crashing into the apartment.

"Move!" they shout as they sweep down the hall pushing a gurney, knocking knickknacks onto the floor and pushing him out of the way. "We don't have much time!"

In moments, they sweep past again, with Cookie strapped atop the gurney now. Her head bounces like a doll's as they bump across the floor, around the living room furniture, across the threshold, and out the front door.

"Her bag!" Albert shouts when the door slams shut behind them. "For Christ's sake, what are you waiting for?"

Eddie finds the valise and stuffs in a polka-dot dressing gown, a pair of green-striped sateen pajamas, a blue marabou boa, and a giant floppy sunhat. Why a sunhat? He's not thinking clearly. He reaches down for a pair of faux fur–lined mules, just in case—

—and there it is.

His phone.

He freezes for a moment, looking at the forgotten object, the foreign, ancient relic that's been eclipsed a thousand times over since he last saw it. Has it been here all along? He taps the screen. Miraculously, it somehow still has sixty percent battery power. How can that be, if it's been missing all this time?

No time to think about that now, no time to wonder. He slips it into his pocket and dashes into Cookie's room. He grabs everything Albert mentioned, plus her back scratcher, a handful of bangles, and the photograph of Tallulah Bankhead. He reaches for the photograph of Bette Davis, but then remembers she and Tallulah don't get along, so he grabs Dorothy Parker instead.

Albert's in the kitchen, inspecting the little plastic containers of prescription pills on the kitchen counter. His face is ashen, panicked, so Eddie reaches over and sweeps the whole lineup of drugs into the valise.

"Let's go," Eddie says, leading Albert out the door, but just after he steps out into the hallway, he remembers something. "Wait!"

He runs back inside for two things, the Polaroid camera and Francis's note. The first thing is easy to find, sitting right there on the fainting couch. He drops it into a tote bag—a Mostly Mozart bag from the New York Philharmonic—along with a couple more cartridges of film.

The second thing is not easy to find. In fact, he doesn't find it at all. He searches his pockets, looks under the pillows on the fainting couch, scans the floor. Shit. He knows it's here, somewhere, sitting among the books and figurines and cuckoo clocks and photographs. He'd never lose it for real. But he can't search now. There's no time. He has to go.

Eddie and Albert cascade down the stairs and race up the block to Sixth Avenue. They dive into a taxi to chase the ambulance.

"Not her," Albert chants as the streets tick by. "Not her. Not her. Not her."

Eddie grips the suitcase tightly on his lap, watching the city whiz by. He sees the Empire State Building gleaming in the morning sun, reminding him of his night with Francis. He should be relishing the memory today, replaying every movement and breath over in his mind, thinking intensely about what they said, what they did, how it felt, what it meant, when they'd see each other again.

But the jolt of this morning leaves no room for those thoughts. Eddie will lock last night away, like a jewel in a safe. All he needs to think of now is Cookie. He has to get to her. He was unkind to her the last time they spoke. They argued, and he left. And now, he may never have the chance to make it right.

Hurry, taxi driver. Hurry, hurry, hurry!

TWO

Albert's hands shake at his sides as he and Eddie stand outside Cookie's room, in the hallway of the intensive care unit, surgical masks over their mouths and noses, watching her through the little window in the door.

Her room is dim—lights low, shades drawn—and they've erected an oxygen tent around her, really just a clear plastic canopy over her top half. She looks like a museum exhibit, Eddie thinks, like a relic sealed off from the world, something to be protected, untouched. She is asleep, hooked up to a thousand wires and tubes, her blood coursing with who knows how many medications. If you squint your eyes, blurring everything around her, she looks almost peaceful in her slumber, but then every now and then her body twitches and the machines beep and you're reminded where she is, where you are. What is she dreaming about? Is she dreaming about her life? Is she dreaming about her death? Is she conjuring a friend—Dorothy, Tallulah? Is she dreaming about Eddie?

"I hate this place," Albert says abruptly. "I hate hospitals. Hospitals are where you come to die."

A day ago (week, decade, century) Eddie would have found a reason to leave Albert and go walk around, but today Eddie stands next to him. They are partners here.

"Is that my tote bag?" Albert snaps.

"Is it?" Eddie answers.

"Chrissakes," Albert says, then turns back to Cookie.

They stand and watch, counting Cookie's slow breaths. One, two. One, two. One—

She twitches, losing her breath for a beat, then settles back into a rhythm. One, two. One, two. Her breaths seem to sync with the clicks from Albert's watch. One, two. Tick, tock. One, two. Tick, tock.

"The oxygen will help her," Eddie says, in response to no one, because it feels like he should say something optimistic, if only to soothe himself.

"Thank you, Doctor," Albert says, sarcasm thick in his voice. An orderly pushes past with a pair of IV towers in tow, brushing against Albert.

"Excuse me," the orderly says without slowing.

Eddie can almost feel a retort rising in Albert, and is relieved when it doesn't come. The last thing they need is to cause a scene in the ICU.

"I can't stand here staring at her anymore," Albert says. "I'm going down to the waiting room."

Eddie stalls for a moment, unsure if he should follow. What if something happens?

"They'll call us if anything changes," Albert says, reading Eddie's thoughts. He points to the stairwell. "Come on."

They descend to the fourth-floor waiting room, which is nearly empty. Albert falls into a cast-plastic chair with a dramatic sigh and a heavy thud. Eddie chooses a seat nearby but not too close, leaving a few empty seats between them. He stares out the window and across the linden trees lining the avenue.

Neither of them says anything for a while, until Albert breaks the silence.

"I'm breaking a promise today," Albert says, his voice soft with sorrow. "A promise I made forty years ago, never to spend a single minute in a hospital ever again. We thought hospitals were just a place you'd go to die. I meant it when I made it, but now look at me, strapped into this mask that doesn't even match my tunic, like an extra in a low-budget hospital melodrama, breaking that promise."

Albert's pensive tone disorients Eddie, because he's so accustomed to Albert's bitter mode. There's something unsettling about it. But they're here in a hospital, just the two of them, and Eddie feels a responsibility to respond.

"Who did you promise?"

"Someone I loved. Someone who loved me. But he is gone now. Just a memory."

Eddie blinks out at the linden trees. What if Albert was right? What if hospitals are just a last stop? What if Cookie is only here to die? "You didn't break your promise on purpose," he says. "You had to be here, for Cookie. He would understand."

"He loved Cookie almost as much as I did," Albert says, his voice breaking. "She took him in, just as she took me in. Lyle, Lyle, Crocodile, she called him. She loved us both, and never stopped."

"She still does," Eddie says.

They stop talking again. Albert checks his watch every few minutes, sighing aggressively. Eddie taps his foot slowly, rhythmically, like a metronome. He doesn't realize he's doing it. It's warm in here. If only he could open the window. Fresh air. He closes his eyes, trying to conjure the memory of being on the river with Francis. It was just last night (year, lifetime), but it doesn't work. The vision won't come into focus. The hospital—the buzzing fluorescent lighting, the strange beeps of distant machinery, the hurried footsteps of nurses and orderlies—all intrude on his imagination. He can't picture Francis. All he can picture is Cookie, alone in a room upstairs.

He's been trying to remember, in detail, that last conversation with Cookie. He's trying to remember exactly what he said, and exactly how he said it. He's sure it was worse than what he remembers. He's certain he hurt her. His worry and guilt tangle together, strangling him, and sitting here in silence only tightens the knot at his neck.

"I have to apologize to her," Eddie blurts abruptly, surprising himself. Saying it out loud loosens the knot, just enough for a breath.

Albert arches an incredulous brow. "Apologize? For what?"

"Forget it," Eddie says, realizing that he doesn't actually want to talk to Albert about it. Thoughts of Francis keep seeping out of the safe where Eddie's tried to lock them. Just hours (years, decades) ago they were entwined, connected, safe. And then, suddenly, it was over. Shouldn't Francis appear? Send a message? Do something to reach Eddie, to explain the abrupt ending, to ask when they can see each other again, to see if Eddie's all right? Maybe in a normal world. But Francis is not part of the normal world. And maybe, neither is Eddie. Put him back in his safe, Eddie. Take control and put him back.

"Apologize for what, Eddie?"

"Nothing," he lies.

"Oh, relax." Albert fumbles through his shoulder bag. He pulls out a package of Juicy Fruit, unwraps a stick, and folds it into his mouth. He doesn't offer a stick to Eddie. "Whatever you said to her, she'll get over it. She probably already has. That's how she is. I know this about her. She is my wife, after all."

Eddie pretends not to hear him. He doesn't want to talk to Albert right now. Conversations with him never go well, and his mind is tangled enough already.

But he feels Albert studying his face intently, searching for curiosity, looking for an opening. He's not going to let go.

"Did she ever tell you how we met?" Albert asks.

Eddie shakes his head, eyes fixed on the window.

"Well?" Albert says.

"Well what?"

"Well what? Aren't you curious? Don't you want to know how the queeniest queen in Manhattan ended up marrying your great-aunt Cookie?"

Eddie doesn't answer.

"He's not interested," Albert says to the air as he fiddles with his watch. "But he doesn't have anywhere to go. He's stuck here just like I am. So I'm going to tell him anyway." He clears his throat, and Eddie listens.

THREE

"I knew I was a terrible actor," Albert says. "I was unable to remember my lines, I felt awkward in costume, and I couldn't sing a note, which obviously matters on Broadway. But I was determined to get onstage. I was determined for people to cheer for me, even if I didn't have much to offer. So I went to every open casting in the city, and never booked a single show.

"Of course, I convinced myself that it wasn't my lack of talent that kept me from nailing my auditions. I was certain that the reason was that I was, you know, a confirmed bachelor. That's what they called it back then. Wink wink, nudge nudge, this guy's never getting married, know what I mean? I asked my agent what he thought, and he said it couldn't hurt. Which was really his way of saying that my bachelor status wasn't the problem at all, that it was my utter mediocrity that was the problem, but he was a nice guy. I left that conversation with a mission to get married as soon as possible.

"That's what was in my head when I walked into the Contrarian. I was looking for a book that would help me find a wife. Which, of course, is idiotic, because a book can't help you find a wife. But I was nineteen, what did I know? The woman working there asked if I needed help, and I said no, I needed a wife. And she said why and I told her why and she said, 'What about me? I've always wanted to be a beard.' You know, a person who goes out with someone of the opposite sex to give the world the impression that they're both straight. And sometimes not just go out with, but marry. That's what the nice lady at the bookshop offered to do. Marry me."

"Cookie," Eddie says.

"And she meant it. I even told her that I had a lover, a very talented actor who was starring in a show that I'd been rejected from. And she said she didn't care, that she knew just from looking at me that we'd make a great pair. She put a sign in the window that said *Out to Lunch* and we took the subway straight down to City Hall. And that same night, we went to Rudy's cast party as a married couple. Sure, a few eyebrows went up, especially Rudy's, but from that moment on, well, everything changed. I gave up acting—I was not missed—and I started working at the bookshop. It was already the talk of the town by then. Cookie was a magnet. She attracted everyone."

Albert's voice lightens as he speaks, and his eyes glaze, as if he's not here in this waiting room, but somewhere else, somewhere happier, a different place and time.

"In those days, everyone wanted a weird counterculture couple at their parties, so for a while, we were invited everywhere. Of course, she was the one they really wanted. I was just part of the bargain. Everyone knew we weren't married married—we both had reputations and believe it or not, no one mistook me for straight—but for a time, we were on every list, at every party. Roddy McDowall, Candy Darling, Diana Vreeland—they all wanted us around. Even Anthony Perkins and Stephen Sondheim would have us over—oh, Anthony was so cute. The hands on him! I had to swat him away from my business again and again. 'Perkins!' I would shout, and he'd just giggle like a maniac."

"I don't know who that is—"

"You've never seen *Psycho*?"

"No."

"Honest to god," Albert says. He stands up and begins to pace. "You kids. The point is we were everywhere. We were at the old Loew's State Theatre, where all the Marilyn Monroe impersonators showed up for the premiere of *Some Like It Hot*. What was that, 1958? 1959? Oh, and the Copacabana Club, where Cookie saw Little Richard from across the room and wouldn't leave him alone until he joined us for a drink."

He speaks fast, the names all running together, a blur in Eddie's ears. These words, these people, these places—Albert says them as if everyone knows them, as if everyone should, but Eddie doesn't. He remembers his phone, takes it out, and marvels again at the sixty percent power still remaining. He starts tapping out a list of the names and places Albert is saying. If they are important to Albert, here in this waiting room, then they must be important to Cookie, too. He's certainly misspelling them, but he can figure that out later. Right now, he just listens and types.

"We waited at Lincoln Center with every queen in the city for Maria Callas tickets in 1965. We stood outside the Plaza to watch the swans arrive for Truman Capote's Black and White Ball in 1966. We hit Studio 54 in the 1970s, where I stood off to the side flirting with Joe Dallesandro and she wore sequins and danced circles around Bianca Jagger, no matter that they were all twenty years younger than she was. And of course, we lived at Mr Chow in the 1980s, eating dishes of dumplings and talking about our real love lives while the supermodels sashayed around us. Iman, Lisa Taylor, Pat Cleveland. And somehow Cookie always got someone else to pick up the check. Oh, she loved this city. Even when the city wasn't good to her—even through the Depression, the war, the burglary at the Contrarian, the raids, the lean times, the dark times—she loved this city."

"Loves," Eddie corrects. "She loves this city."

Albert sets his weary eyes on Eddie. "Yes," he says. "Loves."

Eddie looks up to see Albert shift his focus from Eddie to the linden trees outside. A mist comes over him, and his breathing slows. The circles under his eyes are dark, and the lines on his forehead run deep. He looks so, so tired. Eddie feels something like tenderness for Albert in this moment. Seeing this man, this unkind, bitter man in such a cloud of sorrow, of despair, makes him want to reach forward, to offer a hand. He does, taking Albert's hand just as his knees start to shake. He puts another hand around Albert's back, steadying him, and an image enters his mind: Theo. This gesture is just like Theo's that day on the curb. Protective, supportive, kind. "I got you," he whispers, remembering.

Albert sits again. He speaks quietly. "Mr. and Mrs. Gagné were the toast of the town."

"I've never heard of them, either," Eddie says, sounding apologetic.

"But you have, Eddie. Gagné is my surname. And according to the official wedding registry on file at City Hall, it's Cookie's surname, too."

"Mr. and Mrs. Gagné," Eddie says, trying it out.

FOUR

Have you ever tried to sit in a hospital, just waiting? And not knowing what you're waiting for, while the person you love just . . . sleeps? It's a unique torture, one that twists your heart like a sponge and rips unfixable fissures through your brain. It makes you want to pace the hallway in fury, stare at the heart monitor for clues. Scowl at strangers, spit at your reflection in the bathroom mirror, bite the inside of your cheek until it bleeds.

"We'll keep her under sedation for at least twelve hours" is all the doctors will say. "We'll update you when we know more. But for now, all we can do is wait and observe."

And Eddie can't stand it. What is happening inside Cookie's body? What are all those tubes and monitors doing? What is she thinking? Is she thinking? When will she wake up? Will she wake up? Why can't anyone tell him what will happen?

"Observe what?" Albert is saying, his nose pressed against the glass like a child at the aquarium. "Observe her sleeping? Is this a sleep clinic now?"

Eddie can see that Cookie's bright orange hair, which he's so rarely seen without her beret, has dulled over the past few days, and for the first time, Eddie notices her gray roots standing starkly out from her scalp. He hopes she didn't catch sight of that in a mirror. She'd hate it.

"Those damn roots. She's been bugging me to touch them up for two weeks, and I kept putting her off. And now—" Albert stops abruptly, as if he's lost his breath. "I'll touch them up when she's back home."

"When will that be?" Eddie says.

"How the hell should I know?" Albert snarls. He's ricocheted back to rude, and it's strangely comforting to Eddie. Like a rebalancing, like order. "All I know is she can't wake up here. I just don't want her to wake up here. There is nothing about this hospital that feels like New York City. Beige walls, ugly floors, ugly scrubs, mortifying lighting. We could be anywhere. We could be in Minneapolis, or Missoula, or even your silly little town. What's it called?"

"Mesa Springs," Eddie says.

"Mesa Springs," Albert says, mocking. "She deserves better than Mesa Springs. When she opens her eyes she has to know that she is exactly where she belongs, in New York Fucking City. I need coffee." He sweeps off toward the Exit sign in a gust of sour sandalwood.

. . . exactly where she belongs, in New York Fucking City, in New York Fucking City . . .

The words echo through Eddie's head, and suddenly, he knows exactly what to do. "I'll see you later," he says to the glass separating him from Cookie.

FIVE

The internet is amazing. Now that he's got his phone back, Eddie's remembering how useful it can be. With just a few taps he's able to find the addresses of all the places he'd typed into his notes app, even those places that have long since shut down. He pins them onto his map app, checks to make sure the extra film is in his tote bag, and heads out. He's got places to go, and pictures to take.

His first stop is Chelsea, where he stands outside the townhouse where Stephen Sondheim and Anthony Perkins used to host those parties that Albert mentioned. Eddie's disappointed to see that it's a pretty drab brownstone with a brand-new New York City garbage truck parked out front. Two men are tossing black plastic bags into the truck's giant maw at its back. Eddie wishes they'd finish up and pull the truck away so he could get a better picture of the building, but they don't. He snaps a Polaroid, hoping she'll at least recognize the building itself. Click.

Next, he heads up to Times Square, to 1540 Broadway, where the old Loew's movie house used to be. The theater was torn down many years ago, and the address is just a big boring glass skyscraper now. But he steps back across the street to try to get as much of the building into the frame as possible. He tries to capture the tourists and Spider-Man-clad buskers milling around on the street. Click.

Eddie checks his map app and heads up to Lincoln Center for a photograph of the iconic Metropolitan Opera building, where Cookie and Albert waited for tickets to see Maria Callas sing. It's a beautiful building, but there's not much happening outside today. Then, it's over to Sixtieth Street, just a half block from Central Park, to find the Copacabana Club. Of course, it's not there anymore. Just a boring old limestone office building. He takes the picture anyway. Click.

He circles back to the corner of Fifth Avenue and Central Park South, the Plaza Hotel. According to Albert, this is where Truman Capote hosted the famous Black and White Ball in 1966. Eddie's not sure which side of the building he should include in his photograph, so he chooses the grand front entrance, where two bored doormen stand with scowls on their faces. Click.

Next stop: Mr Chow on Fifty-Seventh Street. It's still there! Eddie's not sure if he's pleased to find the restaurant still open, or if he wishes it, too, had turned into something else—change is life, after all. But it doesn't matter. Cookie will enjoy seeing it anyway. He waits, in case a waiter comes outside for a cigarette or something, but nothing happens. Oh well. Click.

The sun is starting to fade, giving the city over to the long summer twilight. Eddie checks the time. Still a few hours before Cookie will wake up, but he should go back to the hospital anyway. Maybe there's news. Maybe it's good.

SIX

"Where the hell have you been?" Albert bellows, crashing through the front door of the hospital just as Eddie arrives. "And where the hell do you think you're going?"

Albert's tunic has wrinkled, and the lines on his face seem deeper than they did this morning. He looks like a man who has been grinding his teeth all day, a bald, bejeweled ball of freewheeling anxiety who's lost all sense of time and gravity, ceding them to worry while flitting from hallway to hallway in the hospital, searching, waiting, for information that never came. He looks terrible.

"I was going up to see Cookie," Eddie says.

"It's after eight, you idiot. No visitors after eight."

Eddie's shoulders slump, so low that he almost loses his tote bag. "Oh," he says, dejected.

"I repeat," Albert says. "Where the hell have you been?"

Eddie reaches into his bag and holds up the photographs he took. "I thought Cookie might like these," he says. "She's always asking for pictures."

Albert swipes them out of Eddie's hand and shuffles through them like cards. "These are shit," he says. "A bunch of boring buildings. What's the point?"

"Those are the places you mentioned earlier," Eddie says. "See?

This is the old Copacabana building, and this one here is Mr Chow, and—"

"I repeat," Albert says, handing them back to Eddie. "These are shit."

"How is she?"

"She's out of the ICU," Albert says. "They've moved her into a regular bed. If she's stable in the morning, we can take her home."

"Already? Shouldn't she stay here for a few days, just in case?"

"Just in case what? If she's better, she's better! And she hates this place just as much as I do."

"I know, but—" Eddie thinks back to Sunset Ridge, about the oldest residents there, about how fragile they are. He can't imagine the medical center ever discharging a patient Cookie's age so quickly. "Does the doctor agree?"

"Look, Eddie. No one can force you to stay in a hospital. It's not a prison. If she wants to leave in the morning, we are signing her out, whatever the doctor's recommendations happen to be. I want her to be at home when—" Albert stops short. He inhales sharply.

"When what?"

It takes a moment for Albert to answer.

"When she gets better," he says.

SEVEN

It's funny how sometimes the most shocking ideas, even the reckless ones, start to seem reasonable the more you think about them. As Eddie putters around Cookie's apartment, he starts to understand Albert's conviction. Of course Cookie should be here, he thinks, surveying the snow globes. Of course this is the place where she'll get better, he thinks, eyeing her record player. She doesn't belong up in that sterile hospital. She should be at home, with all her things. With her books, her bric-a-brac, her portraits, her friends—Dorothy, Tallulah, and the rest. Besides, isn't Cookie the one who warned Eddie about total compliance with authority, even in matters of medicine? In very little time, Eddie's convinced Albert's idea is the right one.

He spends an hour changing the sheets on her bed, just in case. He fluffs the pillows, straightens the shelves, polishes her hand mirror. He dips out for a box of fennel tea from Citarella, and picks up a tub of soup from Grand Sichuan. He'll pick up some alstroemeria tomorrow. Just in case.

Eddie can't remember the last time he had a good shower, and he really needs it. Standing under the stream of warm water, letting it run over his face, chest, waist, he can sense the grit and sweat of the past couple of days (decades, lifetimes) being rinsed away. But not the feelings. Not the crystalline feeling of panic this morning when Cookie wasn't breathing. Not the clouded feeling of anxiety at the hospital while watching her in her oxygen tent. Not the fleeting feeling of tenderness for Albert as he steadied him in the waiting room. And most of all, not the feeling of Francis.

Feelings of Francis, he means. Multiples. Francis was so beautiful there on the floor of the boat, and so protective, and it made Eddie feel beautiful, too, and brave. It was the first time he understood what all the fuss was about, the fuss about the first time. He felt like his body was breathing with more than one set of lungs. He'd never felt stronger. But all that's been eclipsed now, by today. And he's back to one set of lungs, and here, under the shower, after all the waiting and wondering and worry, they feel inadequate. If only he had another set of lungs to help him breathe through the night tonight. How will he ever sleep?

He pulls on a fresh T-shirt, downs a glass of water, and climbs onto the fainting couch, his wet hair still matted to his head. He should be hungry, he thinks, but he can't think of anything he wants to eat. Not noodles, not pizza, not even roasted chestnuts. And so he just lies on his side, staring at the photograph of Francis. Oh, this ache.

Where are you? he thinks. Why aren't you here? What happened to forever?

A thought sweeps through him, leaving a pit in his stomach. What if Francis doesn't want to see Eddie again? What if Francis has another Eddie somewhere else, or sometime else?

He turns away from the photograph and stares up at the slowly spinning disco ball, and tries hard to think of something else, or of nothing at all. He tries to gin up a fantasy, an imagination to distract him. He chooses a photograph on the wall, a grizzled man with a bushy beard. He looks like an old-time sea captain, just back from piloting his trade ship along the coast from New Orleans to Nova Scotia, stopping at ports along the way to trade sugar for seafood, gunpowder for grain. But the fantasy doesn't take, and soon Eddie's staring at Francis again, wondering.

He knows he should sleep. He knows there's no reason not to sleep. He is exhausted. But it doesn't come. It won't come. Now that he knows how it feels to fall asleep next to Francis, it's like he's forgotten how to fall asleep alone.

Eddie gives up, then gets up. He pulls on his jeans, ties up his sneakers, slips his phone into his pocket, and slings the tote bag and camera over his shoulder. He grabs his windbreaker, just in case, and steps out into the hallway, locking the door behind him.

EIGHT

It's after eleven, and Eddie is here in Central Park, standing in the same spot where Francis first introduced himself. He sits on a graffiti-covered bench just a few feet from where they met, and waits.

And waits.

Francis doesn't come, of course, and as the clock ticks past midnight, he is feeling foolish. What did he think was going to happen? None of his encounters with Francis have been predictable yet, so why should he expect Francis to show up now?

You're here now, so that must mean you're supposed to be.

Eddie scoffs at the memory of those words. But when he closes his eyes to clear it, the image of Francis in the water takes shape. When he pinches his finger, the image begins to move. When he whispers to himself to cut it out, he feels Francis's breath on his neck, his lips on his ears.

He sets the camera on the bench beside him and rummages through the tote bag, happy to find a pen in the bottom of it. A black Sharpie, one of those indelible markers that seem to show up whenever you need one. (He also finds a half-full package of chewing gum, a crumpled-up receipt from the Second Avenue Deli, a ticket stub from the Film Forum, a tube of clear mascara, and a little plastic container of dental floss.) The pen is sticky, for some reason that Eddie might not want to understand, but he doesn't care. He uncaps it and scrawls on the bench: *FIND ME.*

It's silly, he thinks. It won't work. Even if it does, he's not sure Francis would come anyway. He hasn't showed up all day and evening. You'd think, after last night, that a gentleman would at least make contact. You'd maybe even think, that Francis, being a ghost, or a time traveler, or an immortal, or whatever he is, might be smart enough to know that Eddie had a really hard day. You'd think that Francis, good Francis, would heed the message.

Eddie writes it again. *FIND ME.* And again. *FIND ME.* And again, and again, and again. *FIND ME. FIND ME. FIND ME.* His words barely stand out against all the other graffiti already on the bench, so he keeps writing.

And waiting. And writing. And waiting.

The hours pass, one o'clock, two o'clock, three. Still he waits.

NINE

And then, suddenly, he's standing right there in front of Eddie, wearing his newsboy cap and his scuffed boots. He smiles. Eddie sees that it is a different smile tonight, weary and worn. But those eyes shine.

"Hello, Eddie," Francis says.

Without thinking, without asking, without looking around or wondering or hesitating, Eddie gets to his feet and walks straight over to Francis. For an instant he fears that it's just an apparition, a hazy dream in Eddie's relentless sleeplessness, but then he feels Francis's arms fold around him, one around his back, the other around his head, pulling it into the recess at the base of his neck. Eddie closes his eyes and leans into Francis's body. He relaxes, goes limp, allows Francis to support him.

"I'm sorry," Francis is saying, though Eddie's barely listening to the words, just feeling the vibrations from his voice box against his forehead. "I've been trying to find you, wandering, wondering, wishing. And then I heard you. *Find me*, you said, and then you said it again, and again, and I followed the trail of *Find me*s and—"

"And here you are," Eddie says.

"What are you doing here?" Francis asks.

"Just had to get out."

"Are you all right?"

Eddie scans Francis's eyes, then closes his own, picturing Cookie in the oxygen tent. He doesn't answer. He just presses his nose onto Francis's neck and inhales. Oh, this scent, like a scent he's known forever. It fills his lungs, chest, heart. He takes two shallow breaths, and then a third, and then, with conscious effort, a long, patient, deep one all the way into his belly. They stand together, breathing.

After a minute (lifetime, forever), Francis speaks.

"Come on," he says. "I want to show you something."

TEN

The first pulse of dawn is just oozing into the sky as they round the corner onto Cornelia Street, and Eddie slows his pace. He's picturing Theo, of course, because Cornelia Street is Theo's street, and suddenly Eddie is seized with anxiety. What would happen if Theo saw him with Francis? Would Theo be jealous? Judgmental? Would he be angry? But then again, Eddie isn't doing anything wrong. There's nothing between him and Theo. It's not like they've ever gone out or anything. Why would Theo care at all? Maybe he wouldn't. But still. Eddie's mind whirls.

"Where are we going?" Eddie asks, his voice quiet in deference to the silence around them.

"Right up here," Francis says.

Cornelia is a short street, just a single block long, and there's no one else out here, so it's easy to see Patisserie Gaston from the corner, the only storefront on the block with the lights on inside. Eddie's happy to see the lights, because it means that anyone inside wouldn't be able to see very clearly outside, so unless Theo comes out, he'll have no idea that Eddie's even here. Keep walking, Francis, he thinks. Lead us up and around the corner, onto Bleecker Street, and away from here.

But Francis steps off the curb and into the street, stopping right in the middle of the asphalt, just a few yards from the front door of Patisserie Gaston. He points to the bakery.

Eddie follows Francis's finger as if he hasn't stood here before himself, looking at the bakery, looking for Theo. And just like the times before, this time he can see straight through the shop and into the back kitchen, a clear line of sight to the countertop where Theo kneads and rolls and cuts and shapes his dough. And yes, Theo is there, doing just that. Eddie can even see the songbird tattoos, dancing on Theo's forearms as he rolls and turns and punches the dough.

"See that place?" Francis says.

Eddie swallows. "The bakery?"

"Yes," Francis says. "You should take a picture of it."

Eddie turns to Francis, slowly, pretending not to understand, hoping that Francis will lose interest, and they'll walk on to wherever Francis was going to take him in the first place. "What?"

"A picture. Don't you have your camera?"

"Yes, I . . . I do," Eddie says, stumbling on his words. "But—why? It's just a bakery."

"It's a special place," Francis says. "Trust me."

Eddie does trust Francis. So he opens the camera.

"Just the front door?" he asks.

"Yes," Francis says.

Eddie raises the camera. Through it, he can see Theo even more clearly somehow, his body exactly in the middle of the frame. His mouth is moving, like he's singing along to something on the radio, or maybe just talking to himself, narrating the process of whatever dough he's working on.

"Wait," Francis says before Eddie releases the shutter. "Can I try?"

"Um, okay," Eddie says, eager to get this done and get off

Cornelia Street. He hands the camera to Francis. "You just push this little button here."

But Eddie's forgotten that he left the flash function on, and when Francis pushes the button the flash fires, sending a burst of light straight at the glass front door of the bakery. Theo's head shoots up. Even from here Eddie can see him squinting at the front door. Theo's shoulders square and the muscles in his neck tense. He grabs his rolling pin and starts walking toward the front door, taking slow steps, tentative, and Eddie, not frightened of Theo but frightened of the impending tornado of humiliation that is about to suck him up, panics.

He takes a flustered step back, and then another, then turns and sprints four more steps to a parked van across the street, an electric delivery van with the Amazon logo. He ducks down to hide. He whisper-shouts to Francis, "Come here!" and beckons him over to hide.

But Francis is not here. All he sees is the camera, lying on its side on the asphalt, a little plastic card protruding from its slot.

Francis is gone.

ELEVEN

Eddie is standing up now, peering out from behind the van across from the bakery to see if Theo is still looking out at the street. But it's not an Amazon van anymore, it's a vegetable delivery truck. And it's not a bakery anymore, it's a bookshop, an unruly-looking bookshop with volumes piled high in the window. And it's not Theo brandishing a rolling pin, it's a young woman in a pink-and-purple dress brandishing a dictionary. She opens the door and steps out.

"Who's there?" she calls.

Eddie doesn't answer. He quickly ducks back behind the truck, tripping over the curb as he does, landing with a scuff on the pair of chinos he's now wearing.

"You!" she shouts. "Behind the truck! Was that you?"

Eddie, embarrassed but not afraid, steps out into the street. He raises his hands in a shrug. "I'm sorry. My friend wanted to take a picture of the bookshop and—" He crouches down to pick up his camera. He holds it up, as if it's proof. The plastic card, the photograph, slips out and falls to the street.

"What friend?" she demands. She looks up the street, and down the street. "There's no one else here."

Eddie looks up and down the street, too, pretending to search for someone he knows isn't there. It's still Cornelia Street—he can tell by the carriage house with the large arched doorway—but it's definitely not 2023 here. The cars are curved sedans with whitewall tires and sharp fins. The taxicabs are checkered. James Dean and Sal Mineo stare out from a movie poster advertising *Rebel Without a Cause*. Marilyn Monroe is across the street from them on another poster, her halter dress blowing in the subway breeze for *The Seven Year Itch. Don't miss the Cinemascope sensation of 1955!*

"What do you want?" she says.

What do you want? The unanswerable question. He looks back at her, not answering.

"You scared the hell out of me, you know," she says, setting the dictionary down in the doorway. "The one day I come in early to get my ledgers in order, and what do I get for it? A scruffy teenager with a camera and an imaginary friend."

"I'm sorry I bothered you," Eddie says. And he is. He'd be startled, too, if he was her. So he'll just get out of here and figure out what to do next. He turns to go.

"Wait," she says. "Are you lost or something?"

Her tone is soft, friendly, concerned, and so he slows his pace. "No," he says. "I was just on my way to Bedford Street. On my way home."

She folds her arms across her chest and takes a few steps toward him. "Do I know you?"

"I don't think so."

"Hmm." She tilts her head, inspecting him. "Are you sure?"

Feeling scrutinized, Eddie turns away again and starts walking toward Sixth Avenue.

She calls after him. "Bedford Street is that way." He turns to see her pointing in the opposite direction. "I live there, too."

He feigns a shallow laugh. "Right. I'm just—I haven't slept much. It's so late. Or, early."

"Same thing, really," she says. She fiddles with a curl at her forehead, still looking intently at him. She points at the camera. "You say that's a camera?"

"Yes."

"Doesn't look like any camera I've ever seen," she says. She takes a few steps closer.

"It's a Polaroid," he says. "An instant camera."

"Instant camera? What does that mean?"

"It means, you take a picture, and you can see it right away. Like—" He pulls the little plastic square, still stuck in the camera's slot, and holds it out to her. "Like this one."

She squints at it, raising an eyebrow. "Not much of a picture," she says.

He turns it back to himself to see. She's right. There's no image at all. Just a black square.

"Must have been a dud," he says. "Here." He raises the camera and aims it down the street, toward Sixth Avenue, and snaps. But it's another dud.

"Some camera," she says, a bemused expression on her face. "You sure you know how this thing works?"

"It does work," Eddie says defensively. "It must have broken when he dropped it."

"He? He who? Your imaginary friend?"

Eddie slumps his shoulders, embarrassed anew. "I should go."

"Take it easy," she says. "Lemme see that thing. Maybe I'll have the magic touch."

He tilts his head, uncertain. "I'm not sure I should—"

"Oh, come on. It's the least you can do, after scaring the wits out of me."

"Are you sure?"

"Trust me," she says, and he believes her.

"Okay, this is the button here. Please be caref—"

"I won't break it," she says, taking it from him. "And I won't drop it. Go stand over there by the truck."

He looks up the street, and then down again, then reluctantly walks over to the truck. He stands stiffly, arms rigid at his side.

She positions herself a few feet from him and raises the camera. "This button here?" she says.

"Yep."

"Say cheese!"

He smiles, or tries to, and she presses the button. She flinches, startled, when the camera starts to whir.

"It's alive!" she says, laughing. "Now what?"

"Now we wait."

But the picture is another dud. Just a black square.

"I don't know what's wrong," he says. "I swear it works. I guess I need to get it fixed."

"I guess you do," she says, handing it back to him.

"Well, I better get going."

She tilts her head, inspecting him again. "What's your name, anyway?"

"Eddie." He doesn't think to ask hers.

"Eddie," she repeats. "You know, Allen Ginsberg is going to be reading some of his poems here later today. Do you know his work?"

"No," he answers honestly.

She smiles, a confident smile. "Well, you should come. I think you might like it."

"Okay," he says. "Maybe."

He turns toward Bedford Street and starts to walk.

"Hey, Eddie!" she yells after him. "One more shot!" She is standing in the doorway of the bookshop now, her pink-and-purple dress rippling in the early morning breeze. She's got the dictionary tucked under one arm, and a broad smile on her face. She waves. "How do I look?"

Eddie smiles back and nods.

"Well?"

"You look great," he says.

"Great? That's it? Hang on." She darts into the shop and quickly returns, cocking a beret onto her head, tugging the curl at her forehead into a perfect curlicue.

"How about now?"

Extraordinary. Fabulous. Devastating. "Beautiful," he says.

Eddie raises the camera, and, through its viewfinder, he finally sees it. He finally sees why Francis brought him to Cornelia Street. He finally understands what the rest of us already knew. This is Cookie's bookshop. This is the Contrarian. This is Cookie. Of course it is. What took him so long? He knows her so well, but as the calendar goes, this is the first time they've ever met. She's right there. His Cookie. He can't believe it. The pieces of this strange, confusing, bizarre, upending, mysterious, magical summer begin to fuse into something like clarity. His mind fires, electric. He can ask her. She can explain this. Now he will know. Now he will see. Now he will finally, truly understand.

"Say cheese, Cookie!" he shouts.

"Cheese, Lollipop!" she shouts back, and joy swells inside him. She sees him, too.

He presses the button.

And just then, just as the shutter fires and the camera snaps and the machine inside starts to whir, the first arc of sunrise crests over the building behind him. That very first beam, sharp and clear like a spotlight from 93 million miles away, glints off the glass of the bookshop, reflecting directly into Eddie's eyes. He squeezes them shut, throws up a hand to protect them, and everything goes dark.

TWELVE

Eddie is back in his jeans. He's on Cornelia Street (still? again?), just across from Patisserie Gaston.

He knows he has to go inside. He promised himself he'd bring opera cakes for Cookie, in case she's woken up.

And he will go inside. He will.

But he's stalling. Not just because he's still a little dazed from what just happened, from what he just saw, from Cookie, but because he's also remembering the last time he saw Theo. Eddie was cruel then, remember? He pushed Theo away and insulted him, when Theo was only trying to be kind. He spat something resentful about Theo's perfect little world and perfect little cakes, a curt and cruel and ugly thing to say. Oh, how can he face Theo now? How can he find the words to apologize? Would Theo even hear them? Would he even accept them?

Eddie finds his answer when he steps through the doorway. Theo looks straight through him, to the little clutch of customers who stumble in behind Eddie, a group of three young women in yoga pants, one of them pronouncing loudly that she is certain this patisserie has the best croissants in the whole Village, because she saw it on the internet.

"Bonjour," Theo says over Eddie's head to the yoga pants. He smiles broadly at them, but Eddie knows enough about Theo's smile to know it's a practiced, artificial version. He steps aside to let the women approach the counter first.

While they contemplate the pastries, pointing at the tarts and brioches and seeking approval from one another about which they'll request, Eddie spies four slices of opera cake in the case. He keeps his eyes fixed on them, hoping they won't choose them, and they don't. Theo wraps up their pastries, taking his time and adding three extra chocolate cookies to their orders with a wink. Soon they're on their way, little white bags and paper cups clasped in their hands, whispering about how cute the guy behind the counter is. How handsome and friendly and sweet. The little bell over the entrance jingles as they leave, and they singsong in unison, "Merci!"

Theo turns to Eddie. His smile recesses to a more neutral expression.

There is no *bonjour* for Eddie, just a flat "How can I help you?" Theo's voice is cool, formal, the kind of voice that anyone who's worked in coffee shops hides behind when they feel like it. Eddie wonders if Theo's truly angry, or maybe hurt, or whether he's simply uninterested in Eddie's presence now, as if he doesn't care about Eddie at all anymore, as if he were just another task to take care of.

"I, um," Eddie stumbles.

"We have croissants, brioche, almond twists," Theo says with a faint sigh, speaking to Eddie as if he's just any old customer. "Cheese puffs, eclairs, chocolate torte. What do you want today?"

What do you want?

Eddie's mind tumbles. *I want to apologize to you, Theo. I want to tell you everything. I want you to forgive me. I want to feel you standing behind me again, to lean into your body, to follow your hands and voice as you show me what to do. I want to taste every pastry you offer me, to tell you how much I love it. I want to be your friend. I want to grasp your hand when you rescue me from the curb and be grateful for you. I want to be surrounded by your warmth, by your world, your real world, where you wake up, and you go to work, and you go home, and listen to music and fall into sleep on the little bed by the window that I can see so clearly. I want to watch you smile, and hear you laugh, and know, like you know, when it's morning, and when it's night and where we are and where we're going. Just to look at you, beautiful Theo. That's what I want. Just to look at you.*

But Eddie doesn't say any of those things. He just clears his throat and says quietly, "I'd like some opera cakes please."

Theo crouches down to slide the tray of opera cakes out of the case. "Two?" he asks.

"Yes please," Eddie says. Then he remembers Albert. "Three, I mean."

"Three?"

"Yes," Eddie says, and then before he can stop himself, "Albert's at the hospital, too."

Theo stops for a moment, catching Eddie's eyes with his own. He squints, and an expression of concern comes over his face. "Cookie?" he asks.

"Yes," Eddie says, or tries to say, but the word catches in his throat. He looks up at the ceiling, blinking quickly to stem the tears that are gathering in his ducts. Please, drain back in, he thinks. Don't cry. Not right now. He clears his throat again. "Yes."

After a moment Theo starts to move again, carefully removing each opera cake from the tray and into a box. "I see," he says.

"She's going to be all right," Eddie says, and then he says it again. "She's going to be all right." He's trying to convince himself as well as Theo.

Theo pauses again, then adds a fourth opera cake to the box.

"I only need—"

"For luck," Theo says, closing the box. He pulls kitchen twine from the spool and ties it around the box very carefully, then loops it up and through itself twice, creating a small handle. "We're out of bags today, but this will make it easier to carry, so you can keep it level as you walk to the train."

Eddie swallows, absorbing the thoughtfulness. Perfect Theo. "Thank you," he says. He reaches into his pocket for money.

"No," Theo says, holding up a hand. "Just give a good wish to Cookie for me."

They look at each other for another moment (day, year, eternity), before Eddie turns to leave.

He stops at the door. The apology, the one he owes Theo, is just sitting there on his tongue. He's afraid to utter it, because he doesn't know if he'll get it out coherently. He doesn't know if Theo will accept it. But if he doesn't get it out now, he never will. It will just sit there in his throat, turning bitter.

He turns back to face Theo. "I'm sorry," he says. "I'm sorry, Theo."

Theo shrugs. "For what?"

No, Eddie thinks. Not that, Theo. Don't pretend that nothing happened. Don't say it didn't matter. Yell at me. Cuss at me. Tell me off. Tell me I am an asshole. Let me know that I hurt you. Make me feel bad. Let me know I matter enough for that, at least.

"I just really want to—" Eddie starts.

But Theo has already ducked down behind the display case to straighten the remaining pastries, leaving Eddie stranded. Theo has moved on. And so should Eddie.

"Thank you," Eddie manages. He turns to go.

When he reaches the door, Theo's voice comes—quiet but clear—from down behind the counter: "See you around?"

The question floods Eddie with warmth.

Eddie looks back to answer, but Theo is still crouched out of sight.

"Yes," Eddie says, just loud enough for Theo to hear. He believes it when he says it, and he wants it to be so, but as the bakery bell jingles on his way out, he wonders if it is the truth.

THIRTEEN

When Eddie gets to the hospital, he learns the good news: Cookie's condition was even better this morning, and Albert took her home first thing. When Eddie finally makes it there, too, Albert goes on and on about how hard it was to get her back up to the apartment, and how Eddie should have been there to help, and where the hell has Eddie been anyway?

"Where is she?" Eddie asks.

"Out at the disco, obviously," Albert hisses. He grabs his bag and leaves.

Eddie steps quietly into Cookie's room.

"Hi, Cookie," he whispers. She answers with a snore. He won't wake her.

He tucks aside a pile of bad get-well cards on her dresser—*Heard you're sick / Get well quick!*—and sets the box of opera cakes there. He reaches into his tote bag for the Polaroids he took yesterday when he was out—Stephen Sondheim's apartment, the old Loew's theater, Mr Chow's—and leans them against her record player, one by one. They really are boring, just pictures of stone, steel, and glass buildings with almost no evidence of life. None of the magic that Cookie talks about. He sets the camera next to them.

He pulls the chair closer to her bed. She seems so small today, her polka-dot dressing gown bunched around her tiny shoulders. He reaches over to straighten it, and she stirs. Her eyes open slowly, like it's an effort.

"Lollipop," she says in a scratchy voice.

"How are you feeling?" he asks gently.

"Happy to get out of that—" She starts, and then stops, like she's straining to speak. She swallows.

Eddie can't tell if Cookie's having trouble finding the word she wants, or having trouble forming it with the muscles of her mouth. Two different things, as he learned back at Sunset Ridge, neither of them uncommon in a ninety-nine-year-old. He waits a beat, then offers, "Out of that hospital?"

"Out of that hellhole," she says, with surprising force. She draws a hand up over her mouth and raises her eyebrows in mock shock. Eddie does, too, and they laugh. She starts to sing, softly. *"Give me land, lots of land, under starry skies above . . ."*

Eddie joins in. *"Don't fence me in!"* He's proud that he can finish the Cole Porter lyric.

She taps the side of her cheek.

Eddie leans in to kiss it.

"Ah, that was lovely. You know I really am fascinated by aviation." She raises a playful eyebrow.

"Huh?"

"Haven't you ever seen *Auntie Mame*?"

"No, I haven't."

"Oh," she sighs dramatically. "Still so much work to do. Now, where is my beret?"

Eddie opens the dresser drawer and chooses a blue one, bejeweled with magenta rhinestones. He helps her put it on. Her bangles jangle as she adjusts it, cocking it to one side. "How do I look?"

"You look great, Cookie."

"Great?"

"Captivating. Stunning. Fabulous."

She flutters her eyelashes. "Oh, go on."

"Devastating. Glorious. Magnificent. Divine." He spies her hand mirror on the side table and holds it up so she can see herself.

"Thank you," she says, touching her lips, her nose, her curl. "Albert was kind enough to do my makeup earlier."

"Where's he gone?"

"Who cares?" She winks, and Eddie can see the blood coming back into her face. "He's being a real jerk today."

"But he brought you home."

"Yes, cussing a blue streak the whole way. You'd think he'd be a little better behaved considering I almost died."

"Cookie! You just said—"

"Kicked the bucket. Bought the farm. Went belly-up. Tripped the light fantastic and launched like a rocket into the great beyond." She giggles.

"That's not funny," he says.

"Oh, lighten up, Lollipop. You're not dead until you're dead, right? Who was it that said everyone on this side of the grave is the same distance from death? Was that Saul Bellow? William Saroyan? I can never keep all those dead guys straight. Whoever it was, I wasn't ready to join them yet. I still have some things to do."

She nods at the dresser. "What's in the box?"

"You know what's in the box." Eddie unties it and opens it to reveal the opera cakes.

She claps her hands together in delight, then swipes a finger across the top of one cake, harvesting a fingerful of chocolate ganache. She lifts it to her mouth and closes her lips around it, and Eddie swears he sees her skin brighten.

"Oh, that Gaston." She sighs blissfully. "No one makes cake like he does. A genius."

Eddie pictures Theo making the cakes. There is a part of him that would love to tell her about Theo. There is a part of him that would love to tell her about everything. About Francis, about the beach, about the ball and the speakeasy and everything else that he's experienced. But when he asks himself the question every storyteller asks themselves—*where should I start?*—he comes up short. No one would understand. Not even Cookie.

"Gaston didn't make it," he blurts out. "The cake."

Cookie leans back. "Why would you say such a thing? I know this cake. It's from Cornelia Street and nowhere else."

"Yes, but, Gaston doesn't actually make the—" he starts, but then he stops himself. "Forget it. It's not important."

She tilts her head. "I think you've got something to tell me."

"No," he says. "Not really. Just—the person who actually makes the cakes is named Theo."

"Ah, yes, Theo," she says, and a look of recognition fills her eyes. "Gaston's handsome apprentice. He must be a very attentive young man, to have learned Gaston's genius ways."

"I suppose he is," Eddie says.

"You've met him, then?"

"Yes," he says.

"And?" She raises an eyebrow. "Is he a nice boy?"

Oh, Cookie, he thinks. Yes, Theo is a very nice boy. But Eddie doesn't really want to talk about Theo right now, so he doesn't answer the question. Instead, he says, "He sends his best."

"Well, that is very sweet of him, I'm sure. But that's not what you want to talk about, is it?"

"No," he says.

"Well?"

"Oh, Cookie. I want to apologize. I said some terrible things last time we talked. I didn't mean them. I really didn't. I'm sorry."

She tilts her head at him and squints. She puts a hand up to touch his chin. "Apology accepted, of course. I was no angel, either."

Eddie doesn't answer.

"But that's not it. That's not what you really want to talk about, either. Is it?"

Is she reading his mind again? How can she know that he wants to talk about anything? How can she know how eager he is to say so many things out loud, to try to make sense of them with words, to ask if she will help him understand? To have her tell him, once and for all, what is real, and what is not?

"No," he says. "It isn't."

"Then talk," she says. She leans back on her pillow. "I'm listening."

And so, after a breath, Eddie begins to talk. Over the next hour, the stories spill out of him. He tells her about the strange experiences with the camera, about the boy with bright eyes who kept showing up in the pictures, about his visit to the Algonquin, about the waiter who sang "I Happen to Like New York" with his hand on Eddie's shoulder—the boy.

As he speaks, her own eyes brighten. Her posture strengthens, her skin brightens. She listens carefully, rapt, never interrupting.

He tells her about what he saw at the Jefferson Market Library, not just about Mae West but about the boy and how he posed for a picture that didn't develop. He tells her about the subway ride uptown, about the concert at Eve's Hangout. He tells her about Central Park, when he finally learned the boy's name. Francis.

She sits up taller.

He tells her about their walk downtown, the party at the speakeasy, their day at the Rockaways, the drag ball. He tells her about meeting Francis at the dock and their wild ride up to the marina on Seventy-Ninth Street. He tells her about his boat ride around Manhattan, and the way he and Francis had looked up at the sky.

He tells her how Francis makes him feel adventurous, and brave, and how he laughs so easily and swims so effortlessly and dances so smoothly. How everyone he comes across seems to know and respect him—the boys at the beach, the queens at the ball, the doorman at the speakeasy, the chestnut vendor. He tells her how their hands fit so perfectly together, how his breath raises goose bumps on Eddie when he whispers. He tells her that every time they were separated, every time Eddie found himself back in this world, he still felt the invisible string connecting them.

He tells her everything.

Well, almost. There's at least one important thing he doesn't tell her: the story of what happened this morning on Cornelia Street. He starts to tell it, then stops. He starts again, and stops. Because when he imagines asking the question, *was that you?*, it sounds impossible. Yes, he believes it happened. (Doesn't he?) He is sure he was there. (Isn't he?) He is sure *she* was there. (Isn't he?) There can be no other explanation. (Can there?)

No, he can't tell her that story. He can't ask if she remembers. What if she says no? What if she says the story is ridiculous, that her bookshop wasn't even on Cornelia, that she never once in her life went to work so early in the morning, that she certainly would have recalled meeting a strange boy with a camera on the street. What if she says his story is sweet but silly, charming but absurd, just a lovely daydream? What if even the woman who talks to pictures doesn't believe him? What then? Would any of it matter then? Would any of it be real?

"That's all," he says. "Do you believe me?"

She sits silently for a moment, studying his face, then says, "Francis." A wave of color sweeps across her face, a rainbow almost, a prism. "Francis," she says again.

"Yes. Francis."

"Hmm," she says, considering. Her eyes seem to glaze over and she bows her head slightly. A breath, and then another, deeper breath. "Well, I'd say he sounds lovely."

Eddie nods slowly. Does she believe him? Does she understand?

"When will you see him next?" she asks.

The question twists around his chest because he doesn't know the answer. When will he see Francis again? How will he see him again? How can he know? Francis comes when he comes, and not when he doesn't. Will it be today? Tomorrow? Yesterday? Never? What does *when* even mean when time itself is a double knot? He looks at his hands, his shoes, her face, the ceiling.

"I don't know," Eddie says finally.

"If you want to find that boy, then go and find him."

"But how?" he asks, desperation in his voice. He grabs the camera and holds it up. "Is this the way? Will this camera bring him to me?"

She smiles and shakes her head.

"No," she says. "The camera is only a camera, that's all. Just a little machine. It can't perform miracles. It can't create magic. All a camera can do, and only sometimes, is help you see the magic that's already there. Remember?"

"But why can't I see the magic without it?" His frustration is mounting. Impatience, urgency. "Where is it? Where is the magic?"

Cookie raises her arm, bangles hanging heavy on her tiny wrist, and points around the room, at the photos, the bric-a-brac, the clock, the doorway, the window, the floor. The gesture is a labor.

"Where?" he repeats.

"Everywhere," she says, sounding sleepy again. "I see it everywhere. Don't you?"

He turns the camera over in his hands, feeling every surface. "I don't understand," he says. "I don't understand anything. The camera, the visions, the beach, the ball, Francis. I don't understand what's real anymore."

"Does anyone?" she asks.

He slumps back in the chair, confusion and anxiety clashing in his head.

"Look at me," she says, sounding serious again. "Even the longest life is too short. When you see something that you know is true, hold it."

"But that's just it. I don't know if he's real."

"I didn't say real. I said true."

"Aren't those the same thing? Real and true?"

"Are they?"

"Cookie, I—"

"Shh," she says. She reaches for his hand, and they stay quietly like that for a few minutes, just being.

After a while, she speaks. "By the way, didn't you bring me a picture?"

Eddie points at the pictures leaning up against the record player. "You mean those?"

"No, not those. Those are bad pictures. I want the other one. The good one."

He doesn't know what she means. Maybe she's confused.

"In your bag," she says.

Just humor her, Eddie. He fishes into his tote bag and feels a little plastic card inside. Surprised, he pulls it out and hands it to her without looking at it.

Her eyes flash when she sees it, almost like sparks. "Yes. This is the one. Thank you."

"Can I see?" he asks, reaching for it.

She yanks the photo away from him and presses it against her chest. "No," she says. "This one's mine."

Suddenly, Eddie's mind floods with realization. She's talking about the photograph he took this morning, or was it seventy years ago? Back on Cornelia Street, when she stood in the doorway and cocked her beret, and shouted *Cheese, Lollipop!* The same photograph!

So she must remember that morning! She must remember *him*! She must know everything! She must know he was just there. She can confirm that all of it is real! Not just true, but *real*!

"Cookie!" he exclaims. "I have another question!"

"Not now," she says. "I'm too tired."

"Please! Cookie! Do you remember a morning seventy years—"

She turns onto her side, away from him, clutching the photograph.

"Cookie! Please tell me what you—"

"Shh," she says. She pulls the cover up over her shoulders. "You have something more important to do."

FOURTEEN

*I*f you want to find that boy, then go and find him.
  Eddie is wandering, searching, unsure what is real and what is true whether true is real and oh, it just feels like he's spinning, tilting, losing whatever belief he thought he had in himself, whatever trust, whatever faith. He walks without thinking, faster than ever before, and yet every step is heavy. When did every step become heavy?

Things were so much easier before. He managed his fantasies just fine back in Mesa Springs. He took them where he wanted them to go, stopped them when he was finished. He had the mountains to the west to let him know where he was. He had his job, his home, his bedroom, Donna. How eagerly he left it all behind.

But an easy life isn't much of a life at all, is it, Eddie? You didn't know who you were there. You didn't have to, because it was decided for you. Work, eat, sleep, repeat. Easy. But empty. Why else would you fill your days with fantasies? Why else would you seek escape every time you closed your eyes? Why were you only yourself when you were pretending to be somewhere else?

Mesa Springs will never have the answers you need. You've always known that. But maybe Francis does. Even if he doesn't stay, can't stay, won't stay, maybe he will know what to do, what to touch, what to say.

Eddie goes first to the familiar spots—Jefferson Market, the Hangout Shoe Repair, the Algonquin, even that same bench back up in Central Park, the one with all his Sharpie marks. But he can't find Francis anywhere.

FIFTEEN

The dim light from the hallway barely illuminates Cookie's chipped fingernail as she draws it slowly across the photograph in her lap—across the pavement, across the bookshop window, across the impossibly young woman in the pink-and-purple dress, standing in the doorway on that morning she's never forgotten. Just look at her smile, her broad, carefree smile, bathed in the soft light of dawn.

"There she is," Cookie whispers as she marvels at the memory. "There she is."

SIXTEEN

Eddie, restless Eddie. He keeps going, searching for the explanation, the evidence, the reasons why. Real, true? True, real? If only he can find Francis, maybe he'll understand. He'll search all day (year, century) if he has to. He'll run the length of Manhattan and back again if he has to. If he can't find the answers, if he can't understand truth, nothing will ever make sense again.

Look, here he is on Christopher Street, taking a photograph at the intersection of Bleecker Street, aiming down toward the blue sky over the Hudson. A car backfires at the corner, and suddenly the tall buildings along river fade into air and Eddie is in 1971, in the thick of the Gay Liberation March, snaking between men and women in faded jeans and leather vests. Is that Francis, there, chanting in the crowd? Eddie shouts his name, but Francis doesn't hear, and though Eddie shouts again, and again, and again, the crowd's chants are too loud. They close around Francis, swallowing him away.

"No!" Eddie shouts, but his voice is drowned out.

Here he is on Waverly Street, outside a stucco building on the corner with a rainbow flag flying over a door that says *Julius'*. He takes a picture, and when the flash reflects in the building's dusty window and straight back into his eyes, the rainbow flag has disappeared, and the electric cars on the street are old Volkswagens now. It's 1966, and three men in dark suits and skinny ties enter the building. Eddie watches them through the window as they order drinks from the bar—until the bartender stops abruptly. He puts his hand over the glass and suddenly everyone inside is standing up, shouting, defiant, and an old-fashioned police sedan comes racing around the corner. They enter the building and the patrons come pouring out—all men. In the middle of the crowd is Francis, unmistakably Francis, but when Eddie shouts his name, the cops shout louder, and Francis runs.

"Wait!" Eddie shouts, but no one hears.

Here he is over by Washington Square, taking a photograph of a newsstand, when a storefront grate comes crashing down behind him and everything around him changes again. The newspaper says 1982 now, and the headline reads "A Disease's Spread Provokes Anxiety." Eddie looks up. Is that Francis across the street, reading the same newspaper? Eddie sprints through traffic to reach him, but before he gets there, a garbage truck rolls past, kicking up dust, and cutting him off. Francis is gone.

"Come back!" Eddie shouts, but Francis has vanished.

Here he is downtown on Park Row, taking a picture of City Hall, when a sharp siren cuts through the air, transforming the street into a 1990 ACT UP rally, a sea of people in white T-shirts shouting "How many more! How many more!" as they lie down on the asphalt, blocking traffic. Policemen in riot gear march in step through the crowd, shields held in front, batons swinging. Is that Francis being dragged across the pavement by a pair of cops to a police bus? Eddie rushes toward him.

"Stop!" Eddie shouts, but a policewoman blocks his way.

Eddie runs from neighborhood to neighborhood, up and down and across the Manhattan grid, through the tangled streets of the Village, across the Brooklyn Bridge and back. He sees Francis everywhere he goes. In Tompkins Square Park in 1988, where Lady Bunny is emceeing the Wigstock stage. Entering Webster Hall in 1913, holding the door for the drag queens as they arrive at another ball. Pressed up against the velvet rope at Paradise Garage in 1980, pushing through the leathermen to the front of the scrum. In the window of a downtown bookshop in 1887, examining a copy of Whitman's *Leaves of Grass*. On Broadway in 1934, waiting at the backstage door for an autograph from Noël Coward. Here he is in 1999, 2012, 1926, 1979. Eddie races, reaches, shouts, dives, more desperate by the minute to connect again with Francis. To grab him, grasp him, hold him, feel him, prove him.

But at every place, in every time, Francis is only a fleeting vision, a vapor, always a beat ahead or behind, never quite there, too impermanent to capture. Too slippery to be real.

SEVENTEEN

It's dark, now, nighttime on Bedford Street, and Eddie is finally home.

He covered every inch of the city, but never found his quarry. After he missed the curb and tumbled onto Seventh Avenue and had to pull himself up by grasping a No Parking sign because his legs were so spent, he finally shuffled home, the wobbling walk of a man who's gone too fast, done too much, fallen too far. He was barely able to stand by the time he got back to Cookie's building. The stairs to the second floor felt like Everest. When he collapsed onto the fainting couch, it felt like he might never move again.

If only he could sleep. But how? Even sleep feels like more effort than he can bear.

The city outside his open window is uncommonly subdued, unusually still even for this midnight hour, so quiet he can hear the linden leaves rustle across the street. He blinks at Francis's portrait, waiting. For what?

A little time passes. Maybe a few minutes, maybe an hour, maybe a lifetime before he hears the voices in Cookie's room. Not just hers this time; there's another voice, too. Is it Albert? No, Albert would never speak so softly. Eddie turns over, certain he's imagining them.

But they come again. Eddie tiptoes into the hallway and listens at the door. The voices stop for a moment. Do they perceive him out here? He freezes.

After a moment they start again, and a rush of recognition cascades down his spine. That's Francis's voice. He's come.

Eddie thrusts his hand out to the knob, but something grasps his hand, pushes it away, keeps him from turning it. Something whispers to him: No, don't interrupt. Let them talk. He complies.

They know each other, of course, Cookie and Francis. Eddie had suspected so after Francis brought him to Cornelia Street this morning. Or was it seventy years ago? It's hard to know anymore.

Eddie should go back to the couch. He knows this. But curiosity is a powerful impulse, so he presses his ear to the door.

Their words are muffled. He can't discern what they're saying, just a word here, a word there. *Yesterday. Depression. Contrarian. Spanish dancer. Theo. Forever.*

Don't you already know what they're saying, Eddie? They're talking about the present. About the past. About yesterday and tomorrow, there and here, then and now. They're telling your story. They're talking about you.

Eddie leans closer to the door. He holds his breath and their words become clearer.

"Does he understand now?" she is saying. "Where he belongs? Who he is? What he wants?"

Francis answers. "Only he can know."

She sighs. "Well. We've done our best, haven't we?"

"Yes," he says. "He's all right now."

"And you? Do you know where you belong? Who you are? What you want?"

There's a long pause. Eddie can almost hear him thinking.

"Yes," Francis says. "Yes."

Yes.

The voices start to quiet again, fading. Eddie can no longer make out their words. But Francis is here. He is here, in the apartment, just on the other side of the door. This knowledge settles Eddie, centers him, anchors him.

He pads back into the den and curls onto the fainting couch under the lazy disco ball. He'll close his eyes, just for a few minutes, to wait.

He won't see Francis come in.

He won't feel Francis kiss his forehead.

He won't hear Francis whisper goodbye.

EIGHTEEN

Cookie's room is quiet again. She is looking at the young woman in the bookshop doorway again, but her eyes are heavy now. She tucks the photograph into the pocket of her polka-dot dressing gown, adjusts her beret, and fiddles with her spit curl, getting it just so. She looks around the room, taking in the gathering: Dottie, Tallulah, Rudy, Ramón, Elsie, Monty, and Mae. So many others. They sip sherry, trade lipsticks, chatter, gossip, spat, mingle, joke. The room pulses with the patter of her old friends, and their laughter warms her.

She puts on a Cole Porter record, "Ev'ry Time We Say Goodbye," and her friends all pair up to dance. She conducts from her bed, her back scratcher her baton, marking the key change from major to minor, savoring the melody to the very last note. When the music ends, and the only sound left is the needle scratching across the final vinyl groove, she sits up, straightens her dressing gown, tilts her head, coquettish. They turn to face her. Everyone smiles.

Cookie looks at each of them, lingering on their lovely faces, before she speaks. Her voice is strong now, rich with satisfaction and gratitude and clarity.

"I'm ready for my close-up."

PART FIVE

ONE

Albert took care of most of the arrangements this morning. He contacted the funeral home, signed the paperwork, sent messages to begin the spread of news. He greeted the undertakers, helped them collect what they needed to collect, chose an outfit (a sequined beret and a green-and-black dressing gown with gold stitching). He'd done this before, of course, with Lyle, with so many others. And when it was finished, when her bed was empty, he said goodbye to Eddie and went home to rest.

And now Eddie is here alone, if you can be alone among the thousand faces on Cookie's walls, the trinkets and knickknacks and books and records, the artifacts of Cookie's exuberant life. He walks slowly through the apartment, touching everything in it, from the bits and pieces on the coffee table to the knickknacks on the bookshelves. He smiles to think that maybe he met her before she had some of these things. Would she have remembered him, if she had? He opens cupboards, opens drawers. The contents just expand, multiply—the more he finds, the more there is. It's endless, an accordion world, unreal in its realness.

What will happen to it all, he wonders? Will anyone want it? Will it even matter? Will it all just turn to vapor in a flash of light, the way everything seems to do these days?

Eddie is still so tired. He should call Donna, and he will, but first he lies down on the fainting couch and stares up at the disco ball for a little while.

Its light—borrowed light, not its own—jitterbugs across the walls, bringing to life the faces that hang there. Greta Garbo, Billy Haines, Sal Mineo. And especially the bright-eyed boy, the one called Francis. Eddie watches the glinting of light, the sparkling miracle of it, in wonder. Is it real? he asks himself. Is it true?

Who can know? You've been trying to understand, Eddie, to put reason to the visions, to understand the folding of time, to make sense of yourself. Call it all fantasy if you want to. Call it dreaming, call it magic, call it real. These are only words, invented by people to fool you into thinking you can understand. But we know better, Eddie. We know.

And then, for reasons no one will ever understand, least of all himself, Eddie begins to laugh. A quiet giggle at first, but it grows, bigger and bigger, expanding in his lungs until it is loud and joyful and open, filling the room, releasing his anxieties, his puzzlements, his fears. They lift up and away in a kaleidoscope swirl, beautiful under the disco ball. He laughs until his belly hurts, until his eyes fill with tears, until all he can do is breathe.

And it's enough to breathe. One breath, then the next, and again, a steady rhythm, still sleeping.

TWO

"It's four o'clock," Albert says, startling Eddie awake. "Sherry hour."

Eddie looks at him, not understanding. "Sherry hour?"

"You think sherry hour is canceled just because Cookie isn't here? It's four o'clock, you've been asleep all afternoon, and it's sherry hour." Albert unwraps the giraffe-print silk scarf from around his neck and stuffs it in his shoulder bag. He smooths his tunic over his belly and turns back into the hallway. "Up!"

Eddie rubs his eyes. He could sleep for another eight hours, maybe sixteen, all the way through till morning. But Albert has a point. Sherry hour should go on. So he swings his feet off the edge of the bed, pulls on a sweatshirt, and shuffles out to Cookie's bedroom.

"Out here!" Albert calls from the living room.

He's right about that, too, Eddie thinks. It feels too raw in Cookie's room today. Eddie sits on the marigold settee, next to the headless mannequin draped in the beaded cape. The coffee table is overloaded with snow globes, leaving barely enough room for Eddie's tiny sherry glass.

"Sorry," Albert says, leaning against one of the barstools. "I took all the snow globes out of the hutch. I was looking for the one with the von Trapps inside, but she must have tucked it somewhere else. You can put them back later."

Eddie has a sip of his sherry. It's sharp, acidic, smoky, bitter, a complex flavor more amplified than he remembers from before. He's not sure he wants it. But he won't say so. He'll just sip.

"I haven't sat out here in this room for ten years," Albert says, scanning the portraits that crowd the walls. "Maybe longer. Cookie and I used to have cocktail parties out here. We had the wedding out here, too."

"I thought you said you and Cookie got married at City Hall."

"Oh, not my wedding to Cookie. My wedding to Lyle. Of course, it wasn't officially a wedding. Not as far as the government was concerned. Even if it had been legal for two men to marry back then, which it wasn't, I already had a wife, Mrs. Gagné, so it would have been bigamy. Lyle thought the whole idea was absurd, but Cookie insisted. And what was he going to do? He was in no position to argue by then. He could barely dress himself, let alone lodge a protest."

Eddie notices Albert's shoes, brocaded yellow slippers with blue tassels. Albert notices him noticing.

"Oh! There's a coincidence. These are the same shoes I wore that day. Cookie picked them out. Lyle thought they were absurd, too, and he was right." Albert's breath catches, and his eyes well with tears. Sorrow. "I loved her so much, you know?"

"Yeah," Eddie says, hearing the fatigue in his own voice. "I know."

Albert straightens his back and cracks his knuckles. "Enough with this melancholy!" he barks. "Don't get old, Eddie. Old men are weepy, weepy things."

"You're not old."

"Says the child." Albert smiles.

(Yes, you heard that correctly: Albert smiles.)

"Anyway," Albert continues. "I don't know what you're going to do with all this crap in here, though, now that it's all yours."

"Mine? What are you talking about?"

Albert pulls a piece of paper from the sleeve of his tunic and hands it to Eddie.

"I stopped by the landlord's office this morning and put you on the lease," he says.

"Me?"

"Who the hell else? Of course, you. This is your apartment now. The apartment, and everything in it."

Eddie tries to read the document, but the print is so small and dense, he's not sure what any of it means. "I don't understand."

Albert taps his finger on the paper. "See here? Where it says *lessee*. Cookie's name has been blacked out with a Sharpie, but yours is right there. It doesn't look official, but it is. As her widower, I have that power. The landlord had no choice but to approve. He initialed it here. He'll slip a fresh copy under the door whenever he gets around to it. But the apartment is yours now. Your place, and your responsibility."

"But I'm only—"

"You're eighteen, aren't you? An adult?"

"But I can't afford—"

"Eddie, don't you know anything about New York City? It's called rent control. This is one of the last units in this neighborhood with that designation. Incredibly rare, a double unicorn. Your neighbors all pay ten times this much, maybe more. But not you. You just need to come up with two hundred and ten dollars a month. I've already paid for July and August, so you don't need to worry until September. That'll give you time to find a job."

Eddie stares at the lease. It's just a piece of paper in his hands, but it feels like so much more. Eddie expected just to come here for a couple of months, wasn't even sure he'd like it, and now here he is holding the lease on a unicorn, a golden ticket, the kind of prize that even he, who hasn't yet begun to understand the extraordinary complexities of what it means to live and rent in New York City, knows is impossibly rare, and impossibly valuable. Does this piece of paper mean he'll . . . live here? Does it mean he'll never go back to Mesa Springs? Does this mean—

He looks at the paper again.

"I don't know," Eddie starts. "I don't know if I—"

Albert cuts him off. "You don't have a choice. You have to take the apartment. It has to stay in the family."

"But what if Donna doesn't want—"

"Donna is not the family I'm talking about, Eddie," Albert says. "I'm sure she's very nice, but I'm not talking about Donna. I'm talking about us."

"Us?"

"Are we a parrot? Yes, us. You and me. The queers. We are a family. For better or worse, whether you like it or not."

Eddie looks again at the paper. "I'm confused."

"Listen, Eddie. I know I'm a cranky old bitch, but I know a few things. It took me way too long to understand our worth, to understand that being gay is not a curse, but a blessing. I don't know what they teach you out in Mesa Ranch—"

"Mesa Springs."

Albert waves the words away. "Whatever. Just don't take as long as I did to catch the train. Don't let anyone tell you that this is all something new, that we just invented it, that someone just had this idea and decided to design a flag and throw a parade. We are not a piece of arts and crafts. We are a culture, and not only that, a multiculture, a history, a past and a present and a future. We are everywhere. That is the reality. That is the truth."

Real, Eddie thinks. *True.*

Albert is still talking. "What you need to do now is live here. In this apartment, in New York City. Don't you see? You can be yourself here. You have examples here. Ideas. Shoulders to lean on. Elders to talk to. Maybe one day you'll go back to Mesa Falls and—"

"Mesa Springs."

"Jesus, Eddie, let this old queen finish, would you? Maybe one day you'll go back there and show them something real, but right now you need to be here, in New York. You need to live here. To embrace this city and embrace yourself. Don't you see? There are a million others like you here, like us. Every age. And you have this goddamned gift of an apartment in the center of it all. Step in, step up, be who you're meant to be. Not just for you. For us. It's up to you to take us further."

Eddie doesn't understand what Albert's talking about, not exactly. He will, one day, but for now he nods as if he does.

"Speech over," Albert says, dabbing his upper lip with the sleeve of his tunic. He holds up his glass, with just a drop of sherry left. "To Cookie."

And with a great, emphatic, almost aggressive sigh, the kind only Albert can emit, he gets up, slides his bag over his shoulder, and sweeps the giraffe-print scarf around his neck with a dramatic flourish. The gust from his gesture causes the pink crystal chandelier above them to tinkle. Albert and Eddie look up at it, just as a single crystal dislodges and falls into one of the Dutch wooden shoes with a loud crack.

"I swear this place is haunted," Albert says. He puts his hand on the front door handle. "But don't burn it down, okay? And don't expect me to come by and vacuum anymore. I'm retired."

"But what about—" Eddie's voice is anxious, tinny, very small.

"What about what?"

"I don't know how I'm going to—"

"To what?"

Eddie looks up. "What if I need you?"

"Don't you have my number?" Albert's eyes soften, just slightly, just for an instant, but in that instant Eddie can see that Albert will be there, if he needs him.

"Thank you," Eddie says finally. "Thank you, Albert."

"Oh, shut up."

THREE

Everyone knows that Cookie wanted a party, and they came for one. Dozens of people have already shown up in the gardens at St. Luke's, and it's just getting started. Eddie's not sure who they all are, but how would he? Whenever he spent time with Cookie, it was just the two of them. With an occasional cameo from Albert. These must be all the friends she mentioned, the ones she couldn't wait to see again once she got out of that bed, the ones who'd sent all those get-well cards. They stream in, one after the other, filling the courtyard and spilling onto the manicured lawns. The melancholy of Cookie's death is eclipsed by the joy of remembering her life. It makes sense for a centenarian. Her death is not a tragedy. But it bears observing. It requires a gathering. It calls for a party. A big one.

And they come. Waves and waves of them. Musicians, actors, writers, dancers, cabaret performers, poets, all the neighborhood artists and eccentrics. The guy from the deli downstairs, the couple from the Chinese restaurant on Seventh Avenue, the house-call doctor who allowed a half glass, the daisy-jumpsuit florist from Val's, even comb-over Paulie from Hangout Shoe Repair.

They come in feathers, leather, sequins, fringe. They wear pony prints and cheetah prints and paisley prints and stripes. Every color of the rainbow, and a thousand more besides. No one comes in black. There's nothing mournful or gloomy here today, just glitter, glam, disco gear and drag. Even Eddie, inconspicuous Eddie, brings the color—Cookie's glitziest beret, bedazzled in blue and purple rhinestones, set jauntily on his head. Donna helped him pin it into place.

Albert, after shouting at everyone to shut the hell up, sings "I Happen to Like New York," entirely off-key. Two guys who used to dance with the David Parsons company perform a modern number in which they unwrap several yards of rainbow gauze from each other, leaving them in nothing but a Speedo and ballet shoes. Donna, wearing one of Cookie's tiaras and two of her boas—pale blue and fuchsia—chats with an old flame from high school, who she doesn't actually recognize until several minutes into their conversation. When she turns and makes a gag-me gesture to Eddie over her shoulder, he comes to her rescue.

"May I?" he asks, holding out his hand.

"Thank you," she says, draping her arm over his shoulder as they move closer to the pianist. "That guy needs a dentist. Don't they have toothpaste in New York?"

The pianist, wearing a purple faux-mink stole, is only playing Cole Porter songs today. But she's played too many of the tame ones ("Night and Day," "Begin the Beguine"), and it's time for something a little more upbeat. Cookie wouldn't just want people to sway politely, she'd want people to *dance*, so Eddie asks for the first song he ever heard her play on her bedside turntable: "Anything Goes."

"Gladly!" the pianist says. "Let's add some octane to this shindig."

As she strikes the first bouncy notes and launches into the tune, Eddie grabs Donna's hand and puts his arm around her waist, spinning her clumsily but confidently, doing his best to approximate the few steps he can remember from the speakeasy with Francis.

In olden days a glimpse of stocking | Was looked on as something shocking!

She trips along with him as the song's pace increases, doing her best to keep up with his haphazard hops and kicks. "Where did you pick this up?" she asks.

"Everyone knows the Turkey Trot!" he shouts, leading her through another twirl. She laughs, and the woman swaying by the piano laughs, and the laughter catches on, as laughter does, and the dance catches on, as dances do, and by the second verse the whole party is dancing, in ones and twos and circles of six, twisting and shimmying and whooping and waving hands over their heads. The pianist shakes her shoulders and hits the keys even harder, faster, and Eddie and Donna twirl and shake right up to the final crescendo, the big-finish note, which Eddie marks by throwing his beret into the air in triumph. *Anything gooooes!* he sings, belting as loud as he can, every cell in his body feeling carefree and conspicuous. Everyone claps and cheers and asks for more.

The pianist moves on to "Blow, Gabriel, Blow" and "Give Him the Ooh-La-La," and Eddie and Donna dance some more. At the first notes of "You Do Something to Me," Eddie, sweating now, leads Donna over to the makeshift bar to catch their breath. The bar—really just a couple of picnic tables covered in Cookie-style zebra-print fabric—is filled with bunches of alstroemeria from Val's and bottles of sherry. They take cans of soda from the ice bucket at one end and guzzle them too fast. Donna burps, Eddie laughs, and they drink some more.

"I'm proud of you, you know," she says, popping a pignoli cookie into her mouth.

"What for?"

"I just am," she says. "I could give you a bunch of reasons but really, I just am."

"Thanks," he says. "I'm proud of you, too, Donna."

She ruffles his hair, like he's four years old again. "You're nuts, Eddie."

"You always say that," he says.

"And I'm always right."

Theo comes, too. He carries a stack of large, flat bakery boxes, so many he has to peek around from behind them to stay on the walk. Gaston doesn't help at all. He just pulls over, drops him off, looks at the gathering of people, and drives away, mumbling in French.

"For him, that counts as paying respects," Theo says when they finally get to talk.

Eddie smiles, knowing Cookie would have approved, and appreciated.

"Wanna see?" Theo asks when he sets the boxes down at the bar table. "I made these special for today."

He tugs at the twine on the top box, setting the songbird tattoos in motion. Inside the box are twelve perfect opera cakes, each decorated with a little red curlicue.

"Her spit curl," Eddie whispers.

"I made ninety-six of them. Do you think that'll be enough?"

"That must have taken forever!"

"What is sleep?" Theo says.

Later, after Donna gets into an Uber with a tipsy Albert to see him home, and the other guests trickle out, Theo stays behind to help Eddie gather the fallen napkins and sweep up the glitter from the walkway. Eddie gives up after a few passes with the push broom, but Theo is determined to gather it all. He sweeps for nearly an hour before the property manager lets them off the hook.

"Leave it," she says, taking the broom back from Theo. "Knowing her, it'll probably sprout into a field of tutti-frutti wildflowers. And we should be so lucky."

The sun is just starting to fade as Theo offers to walk Eddie back to Bedford Street, but that's only a couple of blocks, not far enough. Eddie wants to keep walking. And so they keep walking, winding their way through the Village, across Washington Square, all the way over to the subway station on Twenty-Third Street, where Theo will catch his train uptown.

"That was great," Theo says at the top of the steps. "She would have loved that."

"I think you're right," Eddie says.

An ancient woman pushing a little grocery cart nearly runs into Eddie's feet. She looks up, squinting at his beret. "Hmph," she growls, and pushes on. Eddie smiles, and Theo, too.

"So will you stay in New York?" Theo asks.

Eddie looks up at the last of the sunset reflecting off the art deco buildings above them, illuminating Madison Square with a rich orange glow. Theo looks up, too.

"What do you want?" Theo asks.

That question again. Only this time—thanks to Cookie, Francis, Albert, New York—Eddie has an answer. Many answers. *I want to see more. I want to do more. I want to prove I can walk through this city with confidence. I want to believe that I know where I'm going. I want to know more about me, about New York, about photography. I want to know what's real and what's not, what's true and what's not. I want to know you. Theo.*

He swallows. "I want to stay here," Eddie says. He likes the way it sounds—confident and clear—so he says it again. "Yeah. I want to stay here."

"Me too," Theo says. "I mean, I want you to stay here, too.

Seems like you belong here. Seems, you know, like you're part of this now."

"Part of what?"

Theo gestures around the square at the shoppers, sidewalk vendors, skateboarders, dogwalkers. "This, I guess."

"I used to dream about it, you know," Eddie says.

"And now it's reality," Theo says.

Reality. The word winds through Eddie's ears and snakes through his brain. It tickles in there, and Eddie laughs a little bit.

"What's so funny?"

"Oh, I don't know. There's something about New York that makes me wonder whether any of it is real."

"I know what you mean," Theo says. "This place keeps you guessing."

And then Theo opens his arms and wraps them around Eddie. They stand just like that, breathing together, and Eddie remembers how nice it felt to have Theo's arms around him, like that night in the kitchen. Pedestrians squeeze past them to get to the subway stairs, so Eddie presses even closer. Theo feels so solid against him, so grounded. So real.

"So real," Eddie whispers, not sure if Theo can hear him or not.

After a minute or two, or five, Theo kisses the top of Eddie's head. It's a tender kiss, warm and rich, right on the crown. And then on the forehead, where he holds his lips in contact with Eddie's skin, stopping time. New York rushes around them. Eddie tightens his grip.

A siren fires just a few feet away, one of those sharp, high-pitched beeps that startles everyone on the sidewalk. Both boys jump, falling away from each other, then laugh.

"I better go," Theo says. "I should get home and force a few hours of sleep on myself before work."

"What time is your shift?" Eddie asks, a wave of anxiety low in his stomach. He wants to stand here a little bit longer with Theo, to stop time again. He takes hold of Theo's forearm and turns it over to trace a songbird with his finger.

"Two," Theo says, watching Eddie draw. "I'll be there at two." It almost sounds like an invitation, and it settles Eddie, grounds him. He has somewhere to go, if he wants to. Someone to see. Someone to be with.

After a minute, Eddie inhales deeply and releases Theo's wrist. "Okay," he says.

"Okay."

"Thank you, Theo. Thank you for a whole bunch of things."

Theo squeezes Eddie's shoulder. His curls blow softly across his forehead and his eyes crinkle into a smile. "See you around?"

Eddie looks up at the broad, lovely boy, and smiles back.

"Yeah," Eddie says, suddenly so sleepy. "Soon."

FOUR

It's late. Donna left for the airport a few hours ago, and Eddie's alone again. He crawls into Cookie's bed. This would seem creepy, he thinks, if he saw this in a movie. A dead woman's bed, still perfumed with her lavender spray. But it doesn't feel creepy. It feels true. He pulls her paisley blanket up to his chin and closes his eyes.

Later, when the city outside is as close to sleep as it ever gets, he awakens and, for the first time, notices a photograph on her nightstand, right there next to the record player. An old one, it seems, not a Polaroid, but one that was processed in a darkroom, stained sepia and fuzzy at the edges. One corner is missing, a clean tear, as if it was folded by accident, perhaps when put into an album or taken back out, and after some years, the weakened seam came apart. As seams do.

He carefully gathers it in two hands. How had he not seen this photograph before? Has it been here all this time?

It's a photograph taken on the beach, with a boardwalk on one side, low grassy dunes on the other, and a white-capped sea in the distance. In the center, two people stand in the sand, hand in hand. On the left, a little girl, maybe six years old, in a striped swimsuit and a poof of curly hair, holding one hand up to shade herself from the sun. On the right, a young man, about Eddie's age, with dark hair and luminous eyes and a wide smile.

He turns the photograph over. On the back, scrawled in faded pencil by a shaky hand, is this: "Princess Lenore and her faithful, forever protector, Sir Francis."

Eddie flips the photograph back over. Yes, that is Francis. Maybe that should surprise him, but it doesn't. It's the girl's face that draws him. It comes alive in the image, her eyes shining like Francis's.

His breath stalls as a swell of recognition rises in his chest, a wave carrying a thousand emotions at once: feelings of warmth, of coolness, of celebration, of regret, of sorrow, joy, hope, invincibility, strength, wonder, apprehension, humanity, confidence. Of belonging.

Eddie knows this girl. Just like he knew the girl outside the Jefferson Market, the one who lost her hat. Just like he knew the girl in the shantytown, the one who accepted his coin. Yes, he knows this girl. He'd know Cookie anywhere.

In a cupboard over the kitchen counter, Eddie finds a picture frame, just the right size. He slides the photograph into it and sets it on the table next to the fainting couch. He looks at them, Francis and Cookie, beautiful then and beautiful now. And then he lies down under the disco ball, finally, to sleep.

FIVE

In the days and weeks and months that come, Eddie will take more photographs. The camera will function just fine, aside from the occasional dud, capturing images and sometimes, *sometimes*, even surprising him with something like magic. In those moments he'll wonder if maybe the camera really is more than just a camera, if maybe the camera will bring me back to him, or him to me.

But as the calendar ticks on—predictable now, through autumn and winter and into a new year—Eddie's attention will travel. He'll settle into the apartment, meet a few of his neighbors, make some friends. He'll take down some of Cookie's pictures to make room for some of his own. He'll buy alstroemeria every now and then at Val's, wave to comb-over Paulie when he walks past the Hangout. He'll take a job working for the mustache man at the bookshop on Carmine Street, apply to photography programs at the New School and Pratt. He'll take the bus back to Mesa Springs for Thanksgiving, and Donna will save up to come to New York for her birthday. He'll start to feel at home in the city. He'll get to know Theo better, visit him in the wee hours, help him with the croissants, watch the songbirds while he makes that opera cake.

Maybe he'll even fall in love at the patisserie. I hope so. It's his time.

And every now and then he'll lie on the fainting couch under the disco ball, watching my portrait, waiting for my eyes to quicken in the lazy, glinting light. They won't really come alive, of course. It's only a trick of the light.

ACKNOWLEDGMENTS

Endless thanks to my dedicated partner in this project, editor Mark Podesta. Thank you to my friend and agent, Dan Mandel. Thank you to designer Julia Bianchi and cover artist Nathan Devlin. Thank you to Hayley Jozwiak, Alexei Esikoff, Samira Iravani, Carlee Maurier, Chantal Gersch, Jie Yang, and the entire crew at Henry Holt Books for Young Readers. Gracias a Leo Teti y Ediciones Urano. Thank you to Susan Ottaviano, Doc Willoughby, Buzz Kelly, Jorge Ramón, and Gabriel Duckels. Thank you to Cole Porter, Gladys Bentley, Tallulah Bankhead, Libby Holman, and Gene Malin. Thank you to the eternal Mae West.

Most of all, thank you to Barbara Shaw (1917–2016), who taught me that yesterday and tomorrow are only ideas, that real and true are not the same thing, and that sunlight, moonlight, and spotlights are nothing more or less than magic.